PET TRAINING IN THE PRIVATE HOUSE

Jessica snuggled against Mel, and Mel unfastened the bag. She pulled from it a satin-covered vanity-case. 'No peeking,' she said as she turned back the lid. 'You mustn't see what's inside. Not yet.'

More secrets. Jessica's insides were fluttering with excitement. Mel took from the case a small draw-string purse of black velvet, and from that she extracted a tiny silver key on a long chain.

'Well, Jess,' Mel said. 'Would you like to try on my collar?'

Jessica was aware that something important was going on – something the significance of which she could not grasp. But the idea of wearing the leather collar was too thrilling to resist. She wanted to feel it around her neck, no matter what the consequences. She took a deep breath, and nodded. 'Yes, please, Mel,' she said.

Mel held up the key. 'Undo the lock, then,' she said. 'Unbuckle the collar, and try it on.'

By the same author:

ONE WEEK IN THE PRIVATE HOUSE
AMANDA IN THE PRIVATE HOUSE
DISCIPLINE OF THE PRIVATE HOUSE
AN EDUCATION IN THE PRIVATE HOUSE
CAPTIVES OF THE PRIVATE HOUSE

You can write to Esme Ombreux at:
esmeo@postmaster.co.uk

PET TRAINING IN THE PRIVATE HOUSE

Esme Ombreux

Nexus

This book is a work of fiction.
In real life, make sure you practise safe sex.

First published in 2001 by
Nexus
Thames Wharf Studios
Rainville Road
London W6 9HA

Copyright © Esme Ombreux 2001

The right of Esme Ombreux to be identified as the Author of this Work has been asserted by her in accordance with the Copyright, Designs and Patents Act 1988.

www.nexus-books.co.uk

Typeset by TW Typesetting, Plymouth, Devon

Printed and bound by Clays Ltd, St Ives PLC

ISBN 0 352 33655 2

All characters in this publication are fictitious and any resemblance to real persons, living or dead, is purely coincidental.

This book is sold subject to the condition that it shall not, by way of trade or otherwise, be lent, resold, hired out or otherwise circulated without the publisher's prior written consent in any form of binding or cover other than that in which it is published and without a similar condition including this condition being imposed on the subsequent purchaser.

With thanks to
'Rebecca'
(no, not you, Bex, don't be daft)
the artist whose works, posted on internet web sites
(no doubt in defiance of copyright law), inspired the story.
The author knows nothing about 'Rebecca' except that she
(he?) seems to have provided the illustrations for a
comic-book story entitled *Housewives At Play*. Which is
what *Pet Training in the Private House* is all about.

Prologue

Field agent's report to the Private House
From: Detective Chief Inspector Lucy Larson
For the attention of: The Supreme Mistress

. . . One final thing. Might be of interest. I found a report filed by a constable in Buckinghamshire. His patch includes Hillingbury: a swanky suburb in the commuter belt. Apparently there had been complaints about public indecency: women glimpsed behind their net curtains, stark-naked, in their living rooms. The constable's report was squeamishly vague as to details of what the women were seen doing.

His report suggests that the complaints were accurate and justified, so I can assume only that a group of Hillingbury residents was seen doing something fairly depraved.

But no action was taken. The report was filed and forgotten. And that in itself is odd. It suggests to me that pressure was brought to bear.

I thought you might like to send someone out to investigate. There could be recruitment opportunities. Or, if this group really does have some political clout, it would probably be wise to nip it in the bud, or take it over. I'm sure you'll do whatever is necessary.

One

Field agent's report to the Private House
From: Matt
For the attention of: Mistress Julia
  Hello, Mistress.
Before I start my preliminary report I'd like to thank you again for sending me on this mission. I know my mentoring work has been lacklustre recently, and I'm grateful for the chance to make a fresh start and to show you and the Supreme Mistress what I can do. I think that it will be good for me to be away from the House for a while: while I was there I couldn't stop thinking about Anne. I realise now that it's unwise for a Mentor to become too attached to one of his trainees. I am determined to be a success as a field agent (and I know that I'll feel the wrong end of your whip if I'm not!).

I'm writing this while at my post on the reception desk. Don't worry: the place is closed for the night, and I'm alone. The Hillingbury Health and Exercise Club is pretty much as I expected it to be. It's housed in what used to be the stable-block of the old farmhouse on the edge of the Hillingbury estate. It's now separate, in its own grounds, and some distance from the farmhouse – which is no longer a working farm, as most of the fields have been built on, it's just a big house surrounded by paddocks. So the site would be suitable as a Private

House offshoot – although I suppose it's premature to speculate about that.

The conversion was done about five years ago, to a high standard, so the club is well appointed and in good repair. There's a swimming-pool, a gym, Turkish baths, changing-rooms, a sauna, massage rooms and a coffee bar, as well as offices, storerooms, a boiler room and even a staffroom. It's spacious and airy. The walls and floors are entirely tiled in white, with very little decoration. The furniture, including the desk on which I'm writing this, is all made of pine.

None of the staff, let alone any of the members, is aware that Hillingbury Health and Exercise is now owned by the Private House.

The club isn't busy, so I'm afraid the House won't turn much of a profit from membership fees. The records show that all of the members live on the Hillingbury estate. The few men who swim and exercise here turn up early in the morning or late in the evening – before and after work, I assume. During the day their wives come and go, but the place is never crowded.

The other staff are part-timers, who come in on the train from the city, and they're happy to work fewer hours and let me look after the club most of the time. And, as I'm living in the flat above the club, it's easy for me to do so.

I've had few opportunities to roam outside the club, but as far as I can see there aren't any other places where the locals can socialise. Hillingbury consists of almost nothing but houses. There's the railway station, a small shop, and this club. So I should be well placed to meet the residents of the estate and to find out what they're up to, if anything.

The trouble is, though, that I'm not making much progress yet. Nearly all the female members are young – I mean they're mainly about my age, in their mid-twenties, or a little older – and so I had thought that it would be easy for me to get into conversation with them. But they arrive in tight little groups of two or three or four, and they seem too busy talking among themselves even to notice me. Sometimes I catch sight of them looking at me – particularly when I'm wearing shorts or swimming trunks – but that's all. I suppose they think of me as just a member of the staff. Some of the older women are rather snobbish, I think, and the younger ones follow their example.

Therefore I've delayed writing this until I had something interesting to report. And, while I'm no closer to getting to know anyone from the estate, I'm now sure that some of the young women, at least, have secrets.

A group of three arrived this afternoon: one of the haughty older women, a tall blonde in her mid-thirties, with two younger friends. After they'd signed in I checked their membership files. All three live on the Hillingbury estate. The tall blonde is Olivia Reynolds; she's been a member of the club almost since it opened. Karen Beavis is younger, but almost as snooty. She's stunningly attractive, though, and she knows it. She has short, dark hair and a permanent pout. The youngest of the three is Jennifer Adams: another blonde, but with short, curly hair – very pretty, and not as reserved as the other two.

Jennifer was the only one who spoke to me, and that was only to say hello. They emerged from the changing-room wearing swimming-costumes and carrying towels and little vanity-cases. They swept past me without a word, even though it must have been obvious that I was looking at them: the costumes that Jennifer and Karen were wearing didn't leave much to my imagination.

They splashed about in the pool for a while and then, carrying their towels and bags, they disappeared into the Turkish bath.

'Turn the temperature and the steam down a bit,' Olivia Reynolds shouted to me from the door. 'We're going to be some time in here.'

I did as she asked, even though I didn't like being addressed as if I was a servant. And they did spend a long time in the Turkish bath. I began to wonder whether they were all right in there. I couldn't go in: during the day the Turkish baths are for ladies only. But I listened at the door.

It was clear that they hadn't been overwhelmed by the heat and steam. I could hear female voices, talking and whispering and giggling. I recognised Olivia Reynolds' abrupt tone.

As you know, Mistress Julia, when one has been in the Private House, even for a short time, one rapidly becomes familiar with the sounds of sexual activity. I am sure that the three women in the Turkish bath were enjoying each other. I heard gasps and sighs, and stifled cries. And I heard the unmistakable sound of a hand smacking against flesh – not once, but many times, in a steady rhythm.

When they finally emerged, all three of them – even Olivia Reynolds – were flushed and glowing and damp. But then, they had been in a Turkish bath. The heat and the steam couldn't account for the brightness of their eyes, though, nor for the fact that Jennifer was quite obviously wearing only a towel, and was being supported and cuddled by the other two as they made their way to the changing-room.

Once they had left the club, and I had the place to myself, I propped open the door to the Turkish baths, put up a sign saying that cleaning was in progress, and went in to explore. There's a whole suite of rooms: an anteroom with doors leading to a steam room, a hot pool, a cold pool, and a warm room.

I found nothing until I left open the door of the steam room, and the clouds of vapour dissipated. Then I could see it, on the tiled floor: a slim cylinder, made of dark wood, shaped to resemble a phallus, and polished. I picked it up: it was still warm. It was sticky to the touch, and the clear, viscous liquid smelled of female arousal.

I've washed it and put it in the lost-property cupboard, although I doubt that Olivia Reynolds will ever claim it.

I am now convinced that at least some of the women of Hillingbury are secretly pursuing interests that their husbands know nothing about. There is something going on here: something that might well be of interest to the House.

Now all I have to do is to find some way of finding out what it is.

The decorators had finished the previous day, and the smell of paint and wallpaper paste was fading. The furniture had been delivered and positioned throughout the house. All of the boxes had been emptied and stacked in the garage, and their contents had been placed neatly in cupboards and on shelves.

For the last two hours Jessica had had nothing to do but to wander from room to room. After the months of planning and saving and waiting, everything had happened so quickly. She could hardly believe that she was here, in Hillingbury. She had done it; she and Brian had done it. They had moved from their city apartment to this big house, set in its own big garden, in this most respectable of neighbourhoods, almost in the countryside. Their old furniture looked pitifully small in these spacious rooms, each chair and table a tiny island in a sea of brand new carpet.

She found herself touching the doors and walls of each room, as if to reassure herself that it wasn't a dream. For three years she had yearned for a house like this. She had persuaded Brian to complete his management course; she had socialised with his colleagues and prepared dinner parties for his bosses; she had urged him to take on more responsibilities and to ask for promotions. And now, with Brian a junior partner in the firm, they could afford to live in Hillingbury – just.

She stopped at every window, as if she needed to check that the house was still surrounded on all sides by suburban tranquillity. Looking from the back of the house, through the French windows or standing in one of the guest bedrooms, Jessica could almost believe that she was in the countryside. The garden wasn't just one of a row of thin strips of grass or paving, like the back gardens in the city; irregularly shaped, and bounded by tall, dense hedges, it stretched away from the house in a series of terraces that ended, far away, at a brick wall in which was a gate that led to the woodland beyond. It contained curvaceous flower beds, and masses of shrubs, and mature trees, and still there were expanses of lush grass.

I'll have to buy a lawnmower, Jessica thought. The exercise will be good for Brian.

The view from the front windows was hardly less rural. All of the houses had big, square, front gardens, and the road was lined with tall trees. No matter how long she stood and watched, not a single vehicle swept along the grey ribbon of tarmac. There were only a few pedestrians: a woman, walking her dog; two women, striding along purposefully. Jessica, who was used to being surrounded by the bustle and noise of the city streets, began to find the silence almost eerie.

It's as quiet as the grave, she thought, and she felt her stomach clench as she realised that for the first time she was allowing herself to doubt whether she was going to like living in Hillingbury.

She gazed across the road at the empty windows of the house opposite hers, and then at the rooftops beyond. In every house she imagined a woman, like herself, alone, bored, restless, with nothing to do but wait until her husband came home from the city.

She shook her head and told herself not to be silly. It might take some time to become used to living in such a grand suburb, but she was confident that she would do so. There was no reason to suppose that Hillingbury didn't have a vibrant social scene.

And I won't find out about it by staring out of the windows, she said to herself. It's a sunny afternoon: I'll go out for a walk and inspect the entire estate.

Jessica checked her hair and make-up, and straightened the seams of her stockings, before putting on her best coat and setting out on her expedition. She intended to impress any of her new neighbours that she might chance to meet.

As she closed the front gate behind her she stopped and looked back at her new home. She could still hardly believe that the whole house, and its vast gardens, were hers. It had four bedrooms. A bathroom with a bath and a sink and a bidet and a shower. And another shower in the downstairs cloakroom, and yet another in the little bathroom attached to the main bedroom. The kitchen had a breakfast bar, and was big enough to accommodate a dining-table as well, but there was also a dining-room. She was almost offended by the profligate waste of space.

As she walked along the road she was soon reminded that her house was by no means the grandest. The larger properties were L-shaped or E-shaped, with imposing porticoes at their centres. One had a conservatory that covered half of the front lawn; another had a landscaped front garden with a pond; and she glimpsed through an archway the shimmering blue water of a swimming-pool.

She found herself wondering when Brian would be able to put himself forward for another promotion. It had taken a disappointingly short time for her to arrange the decoration of the new house: planning the construction of a conservatory or a swimming-pool would be a more challenging project.

Having dispelled her slight sense of disappointment, Jessica began to enjoy inspecting each garden and house-front for the improvements and enlargements its inhabitants had made. There were, in any case, no people to speak to. But she was happy to stroll along the tree-lined lanes of Hillingbury. It had been a cloudy morning, but the spring sun was out now, and birds were chattering in the trees and hedges.

It's even better than the countryside, she said to herself. The roads are hedged and empty – but they're well paved and not at all muddy; with their exposed beams, and diamond-paned windows, and wooden gable-ends, the houses look like antique cottages – but they're as big as mansions, and recently built to modern standards. It's a sort of paradise.

She noticed that despite the length of the front gardens all of the houses, like hers, had translucent curtains at the windows to prevent passers-by looking in. But many of them had intricate designs, and looked like lace, and some had frilled edges. Hers were made of plain net.

There were so many things that she was going to have to attend to.

She had been walking aimlessly along the curving avenues, and now she found that she had reached the edge of the estate. In front of her the railway embankment, covered in wild shrubs, obstructed her view of the countryside beyond, except for the glimpse of empty fields framed by the semicircle of the arched bridge through which the road escaped from the confines of Hillingbury. The station, perched on the embankment, looked empty and forlorn: there were trains in the morning and in the evening, to and from the city, but there were none during the afternoon, and the platforms were deserted.

For a moment Jessica felt isolated and very alone, and again she realised that she missed the rush and noise of the city, and the friends and the job she had left behind there.

But it was not in Jessica's nature to brood or fret for long. She decided to visit Hillingbury's one and only shop. There, she thought, she might find company, and perhaps some information about Hillingbury's social scene.

Between the last house of the estate and the railway embankment there was a high brick wall surrounding an old house and, as far as Jessica could tell from the assortment of rooftops she could see, a number of other buildings. Jessica had noticed the house the previous morning, when she had gone with Brian to wave him off at the station, because it fronted on to the road and one of its large bays contained the shop.

Through the little leaded panes of the window Jessica could see shelves piled high with groceries and household goods. There were advertisements for ice cream and confectionery taped to the inside of the glass, and a handwritten note listing the shop's hours of opening – which were, Jessica noted, very limited. There were no notices about social events, however.

A bell jingled above her head as she pushed open the door. The interior of the shop was gloomy, compared with the sunshine outside, and it smelled of polish and soap. Once the bell fell silent there was no noise at all. There were no other customers in the room, and no one behind the counter. Jessica began to feel that she was intruding: perhaps the shop wasn't open for business.

There was a sound: a cry, like a breathless gasp, from somewhere else in the house. Then silence again.

'Hello?' Jessica called out. 'Is there anyone here?'

She remembered why the smell of the shop was familiar: it reminded her of her schooldays. The classrooms had smelled of nothing but children and chalk, but the offices – the head teacher's study and the matron's room, for instance – had always had that scent of polish and carbolic soap. Jessica had been a studious and well-behaved scholar, and on the few occasions she had been summoned to see the headmistress or the matron it had always been simply to deliver a message. But each time she had found herself imagining the fear and anticipation of the pupils who were summoned to the offices because they had misbehaved or needed to be examined for an embarrassing ailment. The clean odour of the shop brought the memories into her mind for the first time in years.

She suddenly felt rather warm, and uncomfortably encumbered by her coat. She struggled out of it, and folded it over her arm. When she looked up there was a woman standing behind the counter. She realised that the woman must have come through the open doorway at the back of the shop that appeared to lead into the wood-panelled depths of the house.

'Good afternoon,' Jessica said.

The woman nodded.

'I'm just looking around,' Jessica said, and began to study the goods arranged on the floor-to-ceiling shelves. Whenever she glanced towards the counter she found that the woman was still looking at her.

The woman was tall and slim, with a round face that would have been pretty if her expression had not been so stern. Her light-brown hair was short, but fashionably cut, so that she looked young, although Jessica thought she was in fact almost middle-aged. She was wearing a white overall, like a doctor's, that was tailored to fit tightly.

Jessica became very aware of her own clothing. Now that she had removed her coat she was wearing only the light clothes she had pulled on that morning in anticipation of staying indoors: a short tartan skirt and a thin blouse. She realised that, despite her stockings and high-heeled shoes, she must look very young.

Why is she watching me like a hawk? Jessica wondered. Does she think I'm a thief? She's still staring at me. Perhaps I should put my coat back on. But it's so warm and close in here. This is ridiculous. I refuse to be made to feel uncomfortable.

Jessica strode to the counter. 'My name's Jessica,' she said. 'I'm new to Hillingbury.'

The woman nodded again, as if she already knew who Jessica was. 'Elfrida Morgan,' she said. 'Mrs Elfrida Morgan.'

'Pleased to meet you, Mrs Morgan,' Jessica said. 'I was wondering – do you have a noticeboard in the shop, about events in Hillingbury?'

Mrs Morgan smiled, very briefly, as if at a private joke, and pointed to the wall next to the counter.

'Oh,' Jessica said. 'How silly of me not to have seen it.' Jessica stared at the expanse of green baize. There were only two papers pinned to it. One was an advertisement for the Hillingbury Health and Exercise Club: Jessica memorised the information. The other was a typed notice that said only:

HYWAPOC
NEXT MEETING – COMMITTEE ONLY
THURSDAY 11AM AT NUMBER 4

'What's this?' Jessica asked.

'HYWAPOC?' Mrs Morgan said. She pronounced it 'highway-pock'. 'It's just a local committee.' The half-smile had returned to her lips.

'Like a residents' association?' Jessica asked. 'I might be interested in joining.'

'A bit like that,' Mrs Morgan said. 'The question is, will they be interested in you?' Her light-blue eyes scanned Jessica from her head to her toes, until Jessica felt herself blushing. 'And I expect they will be.'

'Are you a member?' Jessica asked, hoping to divert Mrs Morgan from her intensive study of Jessica's appearance.

'No,' Mrs Morgan said. 'It's only for those living on the estate. But I'm always here to help out. They rely on my services.' She leaned forwards a little, opened her eyes wide, and gave Jessica a dazzling smile.

Jessica was so pleased to find that the stern woman was suddenly friendly that she hardly noticed that Mrs Morgan had given her no information at all about the mysterious committee. She smiled back, and chided herself for judging a person on first appearances.

'It's a lovely day,' Jessica said. 'I don't really need this coat. But I thought I couldn't go out with these old things on.'

'You look lovely, my dear,' Mrs Morgan said. 'It is warm, isn't it?' she added, and she undid the top two buttons of her overalls.

As Mrs Morgan leaned her elbows on the counter and folded back her lapels Jessica found her gaze drawn to the V of exposed flesh. She could see the deep cleavage between the woman's heavy breasts, which were pressed tightly together under the close-fitting garment. If she undoes one more button, Jessica thought, her breasts will pop out. And I can't see any underwear. The material of that overall coat is quite thin, but I can't see any straps.

She looked up to see that Mrs Morgan was looking at her with a quizzical expression. She blushed again, and turned away.

'Oh,' she said, desperate to make light conversation. 'It's a bit of a surprise to find this sort of thing in here.'

She was looking at a display of goods that covered almost half of one wall. It contained an odd mixture of things for horses and dogs: collars, leads, reins, riding crops, and even a small saddle.

'That's my other business,' Mrs Morgan said. 'But I do it for pleasure, too. I train pets. Obedience, deportment, and so on. I have several clients on the estate. In fact I do all of my work for members of the committee.'

'Pet training,' Jessica said. 'How interesting.' Jessica didn't have a cat or a dog or even a goldfish, and so she didn't want to become involved in a long conversation about pets. But she felt she ought to be polite, so she asked, 'Do you do the training here? I noticed from the road that you have a walled garden and several outhouses.'

Mrs Morgan smiled again, and this time Jessica thought she looked both pretty and a little sinister. 'I have all the equipment and space you could wish for,' she said. 'Although I'm often asked to do sessions at my clients' homes. But I hope you'll find out for yourself.'

Jessica didn't know whether she should explain that, as she didn't have any pets, it was unlikely that she would need Mrs Morgan's services. 'I don't think I've ever seen such beautifully made collars and leads,' she said, hoping to change the subject. 'It seems almost a waste to use them for cats and dogs.'

Mrs Morgan laughed: a light, tinkling laugh that sounded entirely natural but which nonetheless made Jessica shiver inexplicably. 'My clients like their pets to look always at their best,' she said. 'A well-groomed, obedient pet reflects well on her owner. Don't you agree?'

'I suppose so,' Jessica said. She was beginning to suspect that Mrs Morgan's words had hidden meanings. 'I'd better be getting on. I thought I'd go and take a look at the Health and Exercise Club.' She made for the door.

'All right, my dear,' Mrs Morgan said. 'I expect I'll be seeing a lot of you in the near future.'

Two

Field agent's report to the Private House
From: Matt
For the attention of: Mistress Julia

Another report, coming hard on the heels of the last one. But I thought I should tell you straight away – and in detail – about a new member who joined the club yesterday afternoon. Her name is Jessica, and she's very promising.

She came through the door late in the afternoon. I was alone in the club: the women who had been there during the day had all left, but the men, who come in on their way back home after working in the city, had not started to arrive. I don't yet know all the members by sight, but I could tell she wasn't one: she wasn't carrying a bag, and she was clearly unfamiliar with the layout of the premises.

I could see at once that she was young and attractive. (I know now, having taken her particulars for the membership form, that she's twenty-five years old.) She has long, straight, dark hair, which she was wearing in a loose ponytail; a wide face with prominent cheekbones; huge, slightly slanting eyes with dark-brown irises; a wide mouth; and light-brown skin, which I think is her natural colouring rather than the result of tanning. Although she's obviously not foreign herself, I suspect that a little of her ancestry is Eastern. As you can probably tell, I was attracted to her immediately.

She was wearing a long and fashionable overcoat, which must have been rather too warm even outside, let alone in the humid atmosphere of the club. I felt warm and I was dressed in only swimming trunks, as I was in the middle of cleaning the tiles around the pool. My first hint that she might be useful to us was that her gaze lingered on me as I came to the reception desk to attend to her.

'I've recently moved into the area,' she said. 'I'd like to have a look around the club.'

The fact that she is new to Hillingbury was encouraging: as I've said before, the female club members who have lived here for some time seem to be in self-absorbed cliques. On the other hand, her tone was confident and almost brusque: I thought (wrongly, as it turned out) that she would prove to be as haughty and uncommunicative as all the others.

I decided to try a small test at once. Instead of going behind the desk, I stood in front of her and put my fists on my hips. She was less tall than I had thought at first: even though she was wearing high heels her eyes were no higher than my shoulders. She had either to look up at my face, or let her gaze rest on my chest – which, as you know, is impressively muscular and was at the time glistening with chlorinated water from the pool.

'It's hot in here,' I said. 'You should take off your coat.'

She looked as though she was going to demur. Then I saw her cheeks colour slightly, she shrugged, and she began to undo the buttons. As she pulled the coat from her shoulders she gave me an up-and-under look and a little smile. It was difficult not to smile back at her, as she looked inordinately pretty, but I kept a straight face.

Inside, I felt elated. I have found, in my short experience of mentoring trainees at the House, that a woman who obeys a direct instruction to take off a layer of clothing is likely to have submissive tendencies. And Jessica's smile told me that – unlike all the other women in Hillingbury, it seems – she was prepared to flirt with me.

I understood why she had blushed. Underneath the expensive coat she was wearing very ordinary and rather skimpy clothes: a little skirt and a plain, thin blouse. I made it clear that I was studying her long, slender limbs, and she moved to hold her coat in front of her, as a shield.

Studiously unsmiling, I held out my hand, and reluctantly she surrendered the coat to me. I placed it carefully on the desk and resumed my inspection. Jessica has a body like a ballet dancer's: her long legs, willowy slimness and straight-backed carriage make her appear taller than she is.

'You look reasonably fit,' I acknowledged grudgingly. 'I'll show you the facilities.'

As we toured the rooms of the club I tried to answer each of her questions with one of my own, so that I could gain information about her. She has lived all of her life, until moving to Hillingbury, in the city, and I formed the impression that she is already beginning to feel isolated and bored. Her husband takes the train to work early each morning, and doesn't return until well into the evening. As yet she knows none of her neighbours, but she seems determined to discover whatever social life there is in Hillingbury, and to join in with it.

She is, therefore, in all respects suitable for our purposes. As we talked I made up my mind that I would have to form a relationship with her as quickly as possible, so that through her I can discover what, if anything, of a perverse nature is going on behind the prim façades of these expensive houses. I knew I had to gain her trust and friendship before she was recruited into the close-lipped ranks of the Hillingbury women. The fact that she is pretty and lithe certainly added to my enthusiasm for the project.

I kept up my formal, stiff demeanour, as it didn't appear to put her off talking to me, and I began to insert into my conversation a few of those words and phrases that sound innocuous but which, as we know, have peculiar resonance for those of our sexual persuasion. I told her that in order to get the most from a course of exercise she would have to be disciplined; I said that while she was in the club she would have to consider herself under my control.

She didn't make any obvious response, but I caught her glancing at me. By the time we finished the tour, at the door to the interview room, her cheeks were flushed and she seemed flustered. She seemed to want to stand close to me, but I maintained a professional distance.

She recovered her poise as she sat opposite me in the interview room; she answered my questions as I filled in her application form. I reached the end of the questionnaire. I looked at the clock on the wall: I could expect the first of the male members to arrive soon. Jessica was in no hurry to leave, but I knew that I would have to act decisively or risk losing her. I weighed up the scant evidence I had collected. I was almost sure that she was attracted to me and, despite my manner, she probably realised, I thought, that I was attracted to her. It was worth taking the risk of finding out for certain. If she was inclined to be submissive, so much the better.

'I have to weigh you,' I said, indicating the tall machine next to the desk. 'You haven't brought any gym clothes, have you? Never mind, just strip down to your underwear.' I did my best to make it sound as though this was perfectly normal practice.

She could have pointed out that the few clothes she was wearing would have made a negligible difference to her weight; she could have insisted on being weighed by a female member of the staff, or on weighing herself in private; she could have simply walked out of the room. Instead she stared at me, her eyes even larger than usual and her high cheeks blazing, and I stared back at her with the sternest expression I could muster. And then she started to unbutton her blouse.

When all the buttons were undone she stood up and turned away from me before starting on the buttons down the side of her short skirt. When the skirt fell to the floor around her high-heeled shoes the tail of her blouse remained to conceal her body from my gaze.

She looked over her shoulder. 'Should I take off my shoes and stockings?' she asked.

'That won't be necessary,' I replied, with what I hope was a knowing smile that let her know that she was undressing entirely for my benefit.

She shrugged off the blouse and turned quickly to face me, with her arms folded over her chest.

'Put your arms at your sides, please,' I said. When she obeyed I stood up. 'I have to include on the form an assessment of your level of fitness. Keep still, please.'

She stared straight ahead as I walked around her. I admit I was impressed. I can report that her light-brown skin is flawless, her stomach is as flat as mine, and her body is as slender as a boy's – except that she has a high, round bosom and a well-rounded and prominent bottom, both of which were straining against the black cotton fabric of her underclothes. Her stockings were of the sort that support themselves, and they were long, so that the elasticated bands were right at the tops of her thighs. The slight bulging of the flesh above her stockings showed that although her long, slim legs were very slender they were not formed entirely of bone and sinew. She was standing with her legs pressed together, but even so there was an inviting gap between the tops of her thighs, an inverted triangle below the plump gusset of her knickers.

And I'm sure that she found the situation exciting. Her face was flushed, her dark eyes, when she glanced up at me, were shining, and her nipples were so hard that I could easily discern them through the black material.

'You look fit enough,' I said, trying to sound grudging. 'I'll set a training programme for you when you next come in. You'll need shorts, a vest, and plimsolls. But I can take you through the warm-up exercises now. Just a bit of stretching and bending. All right?'

Once again I stood in front of her, so that she had to choose between looking at my naked torso or up into my face. She kept her eyes downcast, and I wondered whether she could see that inside my trunks my penis was straining to become erect. This was another crucial moment: she must have realised that there was nothing normal about being asked to perform exercises, in front of a man she didn't know, in a private office, while dressed only in her underwear. She must have known that she should refuse to comply. Instead she breathed deeply, licked her lips, looked up at me, and whispered, 'All right.'

I took her wrists in my hands. 'First, stretch up towards the ceiling,' I said, and lifted her arms above her head. I watched her breasts, under the taut black cloth, rise up her ribcage. I moved my hands to her arms, holding her in position until I was sure that she had noticed where my gaze was directed. I lowered my hands to her waist. 'Very good,' I said. 'Very firm stomach muscles. Stay like that a little longer.' Her waist was so thin that my hands almost met around it. Her skin was soft. I wondered whether she had noticed the tremor in my voice. She was – she is – supremely desirable, and I was having difficulty remaining aloof.

'Now lower your arms to your sides,' I said, 'and then hold them straight out behind you. Push back as hard as you can.'

She leaned forwards as she lifted her arms, trembling with the tension of stretched muscles, in a straight diagonal line behind her back. Her face was almost touching my chest. I could feel her breath on my skin.

'No,' I said. 'Try to keep your arms level. Head up, shoulders back.'

As she arched her back inwards her head rose and she looked up at me. Her breasts were pushed forwards. I had only to sway forwards a little and her hard nipples would be pressed against my chest. Somehow I resisted the temptation. 'That's better,' I said. 'Now relax again. Arms at your sides.'

I stepped back. 'When doing stretches,' I said, 'you should stand with your feet apart. You'll find it easier to keep your balance.'

She looked at me. Her eyes were wide with disbelief, but there was a half-smile on her wide lips. She gave a little shrug of her shoulders, and slowly and deliberately lifted her right foot and set its high heel down again a few inches from the left one.

I waited until she looked at me again. 'More,' I said.

She watched me looking at her as she moved her feet further apart.

'Next,' I announced, 'stretches of the leg muscles. Bend forwards and touch your toes.'

She performed the movement easily. I had intended to let her remain in the bent-over position for a little while, but in any case I was for a moment unable to speak. She kept completely still, except for her hair which, as I watched her, slipped from the band that had been holding it and cascaded about her lowered head and hung like a curtain to the floor. Still she didn't move.

I stepped behind her and admired the slim length of her stocking-clad legs. 'Good definition,' I managed to mutter. 'The muscles of your calves and thighs. But don't bend your knees.' She started when she felt my hands touch the backs of her legs, and for a moment she began to draw herself up, but then, as she realised that I was tracing the curves of her taut muscles, she resumed her position with her fingertips touching her toes.

'Very good,' I said, trying to keep my voice businesslike. 'Do you run, or cycle?'

'I used to cycle,' she said. Her voice was a little unsteady. 'And I like to take long walks.'

My hands reached the tops of her thighs, and I let them rest on the elasticated bands at the top of her stockings. With my thumbs I massaged the silky, bare flesh above them: between the tops of her stockings and the tight black cotton of her knickers the lower slopes of her buttocks were temptingly revealed. I confess that for a moment I wished that it was Anne bent over before me: she would have wriggled her bottom, and giggled, and asked me for her daily spanking, and she would have become more and more aroused as I whipped her until she was ready to take me inside her in whatever manner I chose.

I was sure that Jessica found the situation stimulating. Bent over, and with her legs parted, she had only the black cotton of her knickers to protect her most intimate parts from my gaze. The material was pulled tight between her legs, and I could see the contours of her sex. The cloth appeared to be damp in the furrow between her rounded labia.

'Stand up straight,' I said. When she did so, and turned her head to look at me, I told her that her knickers were preventing me from inspecting her gluteal muscles. 'Gather the material into the centre,' I said, 'and pull your knickers up as tightly as you can. Then bend over again. Don't touch your toes this time. Just lean forwards and rest your arms on the table.'

She stared at me for a moment, and then reached behind her back to pull the material of her knickers into the valley between her buttocks. 'Like that?' she asked softly, blushing.

Now that it was completely exposed, and divided by the thin black line of her bunched knickers, I could confirm that her bottom was not large, but it was well rounded and jutted prominently from her slender frame. 'The muscles look good and firm,' I said, 'but there's only one way to test them. Bend over, please, as I told you to.'

I'm sure she knew that I was going to smack her. As she rested her elbows on the table her bottom was lifted up and back. The flawless globes rounded and swelled and separated.

I didn't allow her any time to have second thoughts. I brought the palm of my hand down, firmly but not too hard, on the right buttock and then on the left.

'Very good,' I said. 'Your gluteals are in good shape. Very resilient. It's almost like being spanked, isn't it?' I added, and gave her another two smacks, a little lower than the previous ones.

'Ow!' she cried out, but she didn't move. In fact I'm pretty sure she arched her back inwards a little and pushed her bottom back, as if anticipating more smacks.

'Just a few more,' I said. 'It's best to test these muscles thoroughly.' I gave her another six smacks, a little harder now, in quick succession. The rounded peaks of her buttocks were blushing as pink as her face.

The urge to tear aside her knickers, release my aching cock and plunge it into her was difficult to master. Instead I merely patted her warm backside. 'Very good,' I said briskly. 'That's all for today. I'll need to see you again, in the gym, so that I can give you an exercise programme. Shall we say the same time tomorrow? I'll leave you to get dressed.'

And with that I left the office before Jessica had had time to gather her thoughts, still less her clothes.

It had excited her, I'm sure, to be told to undress. And she had let me spank her a little. Now, as I write this in the chill of the deserted club, silent but for the lapping of the pool and the roaring of the boilers as they heat the water and prepare the steam for another day, I find myself beginning to wonder whether she'll return this afternoon. I hope very much that she will.

Jessica was so angry that she had not yet dressed. She strode from room to room in her silk dressing gown. She tried to compose herself by making a mental list of the curtains and cushions she intended to order for each room, but her thoughts kept returning to the events of the previous afternoon in the Hillingbury Health and Exercise Club.

How dare he? The young man had abused his position. He had taken advantage of her. And how could she have been so naïve as to let him?

As she had walked back home the previous evening she had felt merely confused and surprised. And then the grocery van had been waiting for her in the drive, and she had had to concentrate on choosing provisions, and then Brian had come home, and they had made dinner, and she had listened while he had described the difficulties of his day at work.

It wasn't until she had awoken in the morning, and had remembered with sudden clarity what had happened at the club, that she had realised that she should feel outraged. Over breakfast she had said hardly a word to Brian, and he had left for the station without even a peck on the cheek.

Her first thought, once she was alone, had been to write a letter of complaint to the owners of the club. But she didn't know who they were; nor did she know the name of the young man. All she could do was to fume, and to remember over and over again, in painful and humiliating detail, the things he had made her do.

It was all such a cruel disappointment. When she had arrived at the club she had been impressed by its modernity and cleanliness and by the quality of its fixtures and equipment. And her first sight of the young man – wearing only brief swimming trunks, and energetically swabbing the floor next to the pool – had quite taken her breath away. With his rippling muscles, blond hair, and pale skin glistening with water, he had seemed like a statue of a god from antiquity that had come to life.

If only his behaviour had been as pleasing as his appearance. But he had proved to be humourless and strictly businesslike. It was because he was so formal, she thought, that she had continued to obey his increasingly outrageous instructions. And, she had to admit, because she had hoped to provoke some sign that he was interested in her.

Having marched through every room in the house, Jessica had returned to the master bedroom. She stood in front of the wardrobe and considered her reflection in the mirror. The dressing gown had been a wedding present, and it was one of her favourite garments. Now that she was no longer working, and with the new house to pay for and furnish, she wouldn't be able to allow herself many such personal luxuries until Brian gained another promotion. She pulled the sleek, soft material tightly about her slender body, so that the round shapes of her bottom and her breasts, and even the points of her nipples, were visible through the fabric.

She knew that no one could call her unattractive. She supposed that some men might prefer women with plumper bodies, and she recognised that she had unusually wide cheekbones and large eyes. But ever since she was a teenager she had had men pursuing her: she had married Brian partly to escape unwanted attentions. She had been described, by friends and lovers, as exotic, feline, and even beautiful. And her breasts and bottom were high, round and firm.

She threw off the dressing gown so that she could see herself naked. She turned from side to side; she cupped her breasts in her hands, and then caressed her ribs, stomach and hips.

Was it possible that the young man in the club could have been unaware of her body? The idea was almost insulting. She had thought that she had seen an erection pushing out the front of his trunks, but she concluded that she must have been mistaken: he had remained cold and distant, even when she was standing before him in just her underclothes. He'd seen her as nothing more than a potential customer: a collection of muscles to be tested and toned.

The arrogance of the man confounded her. Didn't he appreciate how vulnerable he had made her feel? When he had told her to undress, and then to stand with her feet apart, and then to bend over, she had done everything she could to let him know that she understood that his instructions and her compliance could be seen as sexual. And he had ignored all of her looks and significant hesitations. He was utterly horrible.

And so she had ended up bent over, with her legs parted and her knickers pulled uncomfortably between her buttocks, while he felt her legs and slapped her bottom.

It had been mortifying. And, what was worse, at the time she had enjoyed it. In fact, she realised, as her hands brushed against the thicket of her pubic hair, remembering the incident was making her excited again.

There could be no mistaking the symptoms. Her skin felt warm, and she felt warm inside, too. And, as there had been while she was obeying the stern young man's commands, there was a delicious tingly tickling growing within her loins. She could see, in the mirror, that her nipples were stiff, and that her cheeks and neck were blushing.

She watched herself move her feet apart: a little, and then more, as the young man had instructed her. She caught her breath as she felt the lips of her sex part, and again when her fingertips touched the delicate folds of skin. There could be no doubt: she was wet, and ready for sex.

What with all the packing, and moving house, and Brian now leaving so early in the morning and arriving home, tired, so late, it had been weeks since they had made love. Jessica tore her gaze away from her reflection – her hand moving slowly, the tips of her breasts swaying, her lips slightly parted – and looked towards the candle on her bedside table. She liked to feel it inside her when she masturbated and, she remembered, she had been thinking about using it while she had been on the way home the previous afternoon. The sight of the grocer's van in the driveway had driven the idea from her mind.

'Not yet,' she whispered to her reflection. She took her hand from between her thighs, stretched her arms above her head, and shook her hair loose. She would save the candle for later. First she would brush her hair, and put on make-up and perfume, and then, before she dressed for the day, she would lie on the bed, with the wardrobe door open so that she could see herself in the mirror, and she would use the candle.

As she sat, naked, at her dressing table, and performed her cosmetic rituals, she began to think about all the things that made her feel sexually excited. It was strange, she thought, that she had become aroused while the obnoxious young man had been ordering her about. But then, as images and emotions from dimly remembered events floated into her mind, it began to seem not so strange after all.

Even when she had been a little child, she had felt thrills of excitement – thrills that she had been too young to recognise as sexual – when reading stories about captured princesses, and pretty maidens held captive by pirates. She had had a favourite doll, and she had played over and over again games of make-believe in which the doll was held prisoner, or punished for being naughty. And, although she had never told anyone, she had known that in all these games the doll represented Jessica herself.

In the playground at school she had liked best those games of chase in which the boys ran after the girls. She had always tried to let herself be caught, so that she could enjoy the delicious moment of capture, of feeling helpless in a boy's arms. And when she and her friends had played doctors and nurses, or teachers, she had always volunteered to be the patient who needed to be examined or the naughty schoolgirl who deserved to be punished.

Suddenly, she remembered that once she had actually been spanked. Her best friend, Hilary, had been playing the part of the teacher. She had insisted that Jessica needed a spanking, and she had pulled down Jessica's knickers and had slapped her little bottom.

And Jessica remembered that instead of protesting, she had asked for more smacks because, she had claimed, Hilary hadn't done it properly.

Then, much later, while she had been at college, she had met Jonathan. She had almost forgotten him, but now the memories returned. He had been older than her: two years ahead. She remembered him as tall and dark. They hadn't met in class, or at a party, or in any conventional way: he had simply stopped her in a corridor, asked her name, taken her hand, and pulled her into a cupboard where he had held her tightly and kissed her. She remembered that he had held her wrists together behind her back. His kisses had been warm, sometimes slow, sometimes fierce. She had felt herself drowning in his embrace, in the tightness of his grip, with his fingers stroking and pinching the tips of her breasts, in the dark, dusty, secret cabinet.

He had written down the address of his room, and had told her to be there that night at seven-thirty. 'I'll take you out for dinner,' he had said, 'and then we'll go back to my place. I'm going to tie you up and hurt you. I promise you'll enjoy it.'

Jessica had taken the piece of paper, but she hadn't kept the appointment. And all that night, and for many subsequent evenings, she wondered what she had missed. The idea of being at Jonathan's mercy had fuelled her fantasies for that whole college year.

Jessica felt her heart beating quickly. She squeezed together her thighs: goodness, but she was suddenly very excited again. With her hand, holding her hairbrush, frozen in mid-air, she remembered the sensation of the young man's hand landing, with a stinging report, over and over again on her naked buttocks.

She knew at once that, despite her previous vow never again to step over the threshold of the club, she would keep her appointment with the young man that afternoon. She had been young and innocent when she had met Jonathan; she was a little older now, and afraid of nothing, and she wouldn't be a coward this time. The young man was, after all, remarkably good-looking. And perhaps he would want to test the resilience of her gluteal muscles again. Even his arrogant aloofness could be turned to Jessica's advantage: she could pretend that she was his prisoner, and that he was a guard or, better still, an interrogator.

She stroked the bristles of the brush lightly against her nipples, and shivered. Now the young man would fill her fantasies while she played with herself and the candle on the bed.

The ring of the doorbell was so loud and unexpected that Jessica dropped the hairbrush.

Damn! she thought. Who could that be at the door? She pulled on her dressing gown and, tying the belt around her waist, she skipped down the stairs and into the hall.

She opened the front door to find in the porch a young woman with long blonde hair and blue eyes.

'Hello,' the woman said. 'I'm Melanie Overton, from number fifty-seven. But please call me Mel.'

The young woman seemed rather agitated, almost nervous, and she didn't volunteer any more information.

'I'm Jessica,' Jessica said. 'Jess for short, if you like.' She paused. Mel said nothing, but looked at her expectantly. Jessica stood back and pulled the door further open. 'Would you like to come in?'

Mel nodded, smiled, and stepped into the hall, looking all around her. Jessica pointed towards the sitting room. 'That way,' she said. 'Would you like a cup of coffee?'

'Oh, yes. Black, no sugar, please. We have to keep ourselves trim, don't we? And you obviously succeed,' she added, glancing down from Jessica's face to her body.

Jessica was suddenly reminded that her dressing gown was very thin, and that she was naked under it. She pulled the front more tightly together, and went into the kitchen.

She served the coffee in cups, rather than in the mugs that she and Brian usually used. When she carried the drinks into the sitting room she found that Mel had taken off her coat and was sitting on the sofa. She admired the simple elegance of Mel's button-through dress, set off by a boldly coloured neck-scarf. She hesitated, wondering where to set down the cups and where to sit.

'Sit next to me,' Mel said, holding out a hand to take one of the cups, and she gave Jessica a friendly smile.

'I'm afraid the furniture is a bit dowdy,' Jessica said as she settled on to the sofa, trying to keep her cup steady and prevent her dressing gown from falling open. 'It's from our old place. We've only just moved in.'

'I know,' Mel said. 'Lovely coffee, thank you. That's why I'm here. To welcome you to Hillingbury. I've been, well, delegated, I suppose you might say, to greet you.'

Jessica was delighted to have a visitor, and she felt very pleased that she had had time to put on her make-up before Mel had arrived. But there was something odd about Mel's manner: she was doing her best to appear relaxed, but her fingers were tight around her coffee cup and she was looking at Jessica intently.

'You must be from the H, Y, W, A, P, O, C,' Jessica said, trying to remember the exact letters she had seen.

Mel's blue eyes widened in alarm. 'What do you know about the committee?' she said.

Curiouser and curiouser, Jessica thought. She was now thoroughly intrigued by the mysterious organisation. She shrugged. 'It's some sort of residents' association,' she said. 'I saw a notice in the shop. Mrs Morgan wasn't very informative.'

'Oh. I see.' Mel seemed relieved. 'Yes, she's rather stern, isn't she?' She looked away from Jessica, and seemed for a moment to be lost in her thoughts. 'She trains all the pets for the committee members,' she said, as if divulging a secret. 'You'll see.'

'I doubt it,' Jessica said. 'I don't have any animals.'

For some reason this remark made Mel giggle. It crossed Jessica's mind to be offended, but Mel's laugh was so infectious, and she looked so pretty, that Jessica found herself laughing too, without really knowing why. It felt as though the ice had been broken.

'I'm lucky it was my turn to welcome a newcomer,' Mel said. 'You're nice. I hope we can be friends. And I'm so glad you're young and attractive.'

Jessica didn't know which part of Mel's speech to regard as the most remarkable. What did she mean by saying that it was her turn? And the compliment was rather personal, considering they had only just met. Jessica felt herself blushing. 'It's silk,' she said, stroking the sleeve of her dressing gown and hoping to indicate that she took Mel's compliment as a reference to her attire. 'A wedding present.'

'It's wonderful,' Mel said. 'Have you been married long?'

Mel was so eager and chatty that Jessica forgot her reservations. 'Two and a half years,' she said. She paused. 'It seems longer than that, somehow.'

'I know what you mean,' Mel said. She put down her cup beside the sofa and moved nearer to Jessica so that she could rest a sympathetic hand on Jessica's arm. 'Wedded bliss doesn't live up to one's expectations, does it?'

Jessica found herself pouring out her most private worries to her new friend. She had had no one she could confide in: her family thought that Brian was the perfect husband, and her friends in the city had become Brian's friends too. But she felt she could talk to this friendly stranger whose situation must be similar to her own.

'Oh, you know what it's like when you're getting married. Everything's exciting and new: living with the man you've chosen, and setting up home together, and all your friends happy for you and a little bit envious. It's almost as if you've temporarily lost your senses.'

Mel smiled ruefully. 'And then you come back down to earth.'

'Exactly.' Jessica sighed. 'I suppose I expected the wedding to be the start of something. My adult life. A big adventure. But I think Brian saw it as an ending. He was so dashing, and enthusiastic about everything, when we were courting. Once we were married he seemed to slow down. He even once said, "Only another thirty-five years, and then I can retire." I don't think he was joking.'

'He'd got you,' Mel said. 'He didn't need to impress you any more. I expect he wanted you to give up your job and have babies.'

Jessica grimaced. 'Brian never liked the fact that I earned more than him,' she said. 'And yes, he did drop hints about continuing his family line. I soon put him right about that. But I did stop work. It wasn't just for Brian. I'd never seen myself working in an office for the rest of my life, and anyway to start with it was fun to have the time to throw myself into furnishing the flat and making myself and my home look lovely for Brian.'

'And you do look lovely,' Mel said.

'Thank you,' Jessica murmured. She found herself blushing, and to avoid Mel's searching gaze she turned to place her cup on the floor. 'Brian stopped noticing,' she added quietly. She took a deep breath. 'That was partly my fault, I suppose. Having abandoned my own career, I sort of sublimated my ambitions into pushing him forward. I knew he could do well in his firm, and I encouraged him to work hard. We both enjoyed the money that he earned. And I wanted all of this.' She spread her arms in a gesture that encompassed the house and the whole of Hillingbury. 'Or I thought I did.'

Mel squeezed Jessica's hand. 'The suburbs can seem very quiet,' she said. 'But I'm sure you'll come to like living in Hillingbury. The houses and gardens are so much bigger here than in the city. And much more private. I suppose you're worried about being bored and lonely all day. I was, too, to start with.'

Mel's voice had dropped almost to a conspiratorial whisper, and Jessica felt that she was on the verge of discovering a wonderful secret. 'What can we do?' Jessica said, her voice as soft as Mel's.

Mel squeezed Jessica's hand again, and pulled Jessica towards her, so that she could whisper into Jessica's ear. 'While the husband's away,' she said, 'the wife can play.' Her fingers were gently caressing the sleeve of Jessica's dressing gown.

'What do you mean?' Jessica asked. Her senses were suddenly very acute. The touch of Mel's fingers was making her tremble. She could smell the musky undertones of Mel's floral perfume. She realised that Mel's words could be interpreted as having sexual connotations, and that somehow she wasn't shocked or repelled.

'This silk feels so soft,' Mel said. 'It must feel marvellous against your skin.' Her caressing hand crept further along Jessica's arm.

Jessica had wondered, from time to time, what it would be like to make love to a woman. She took a deep breath, and licked her lips because they suddenly felt dry. How could she be thinking of kissing and cuddling this pretty young woman whom she had first met only minutes ago? It was something to do with the pervasive quiet of the Hillingbury estate: it was a place where anything could happen behind the high hedges and the net curtains. And it was something to do with the young man at the club: she was still feeling aroused by the memories that he had awoken. What would Mel think, she wondered, if I asked her to test the resilience of my gluteal muscles? She couldn't suppress a laugh at the thought.

Mel's hand flew from Jessica's sleeve as if it had been stung.

'It's all right,' Jessica said, reaching for Mel's hand and moving to sit close to her. 'I just had a silly thought. You can carry on stroking me if you like. It feels nice. You know,' she added, turning her head so that her nose was almost touching Mel's, 'I'm not wearing anything but this dressing gown. You rang the doorbell when I was about to get dressed.'

The pupils of Mel's eyes were so large that they almost filled the blue irises. Her pink lips smiled mischievously. 'How do you know I'm wearing anything underneath this dress?' she whispered. 'It's another very warm day.'

So Mel had set out with the intention of seducing her. Jessica knew that she should be surprised, at the very least. But she found that she didn't care. She wanted to feel Mel's lips and fingers on her body. It had been such a long time since she had felt anyone's fingers but her own arousing her. 'I've always wondered,' she said, enclosing Mel's hand in her own, 'what it would be like to kiss a woman.'

Mel pushed her face forwards, and Jessica trembled again at the touch of Mel's cheek against hers. 'Then it's time you found out,' Mel breathed, and she placed her lips on the corner of Jessica's mouth.

Jessica gasped, and held herself still as Mel planted little kisses along her lower lip. And then Jessica could hold herself back no longer, and she opened her mouth and pressed it against Mel's.

Jessica had expected to find the kiss pleasant. It was like kissing a man, really, but without the prickly stubble and the jutting jawbone. Mel's mouth was soft, and tasted of lipstick and mint, and her skin was scented. But she hadn't been prepared for the stab of desire she felt in her loins as her lips and Mel's seemed to melt together, and again when their tongues tentatively met.

Mel ended the first kiss by pulling away slightly. Her face was flushed and she was breathing deeply. 'All right?' she asked softly. 'Again?'

Jessica nodded and pushed her face forwards eagerly. While their mouths were locked together and their tongues were twisting against each other, Mel pulled her legs on to the sofa and turned so that she was kneeling beside Jessica. Now she was able to press her mouth down on Jessica's, and had both hands free to stroke Jessica's hair and face. Jessica reached up to curl her arm around the back of Mel's neck.

Mel's fingers caressed Jessica's earlobes, making her whimper with arousal, and then stroked down her throat and came to rest on her chest. Mel ended their second long kiss. 'May I?' she said, stroking the lapels of the dressing gown.

Jessica was so overwhelmed with sensations and excitement that she would have let Mel do anything. 'Please,' she breathed, and leaned back with her arms extended along the back of the sofa. Mel kneeled beside her, her blue eyes bright with anticipation. 'I can't move,' Jessica said, remembering the fantasies that had excited her. 'It's as if my wrists are tied. I'm at your mercy.' It was surprisingly easy to say the words. She would never have said anything like that to Brian, for instance. But Mel was a stranger. And anyway, they were just playing. It was a game.

Mel stared into Jessica's eyes as she pulled undone the bow that secured the belt of the dressing gown. 'I want to look at your tits,' she said. Her hands caressed Jessica's breasts through the silk, making Jessica gasp and squirm. Then the material was pulled aside. 'Oh, Jess, they're lovely,' Mel whispered. 'Keep still. I'm going to stroke them while I kiss you.'

But Jessica couldn't keep still. With Mel's lips pressing down on her mouth and Mel's hands caressing and squeezing her breasts, Jessica was frantic with desire. She was sure that she was about to come. She wrapped her arms about Mel's neck, and then suddenly thrust her away.

'Let me see yours,' she said, and reached to undo the clasp holding the scarf at Mel's throat.

Mel's hand stopped her. 'No,' she said. 'Just undo the buttons of my dress.'

Jessica wondered, briefly, whether Mel had a scar or a birthmark on her neck, but she was too excited to worry about it. With shaking fingers she undid the buttons, starting at the top, folding aside the cotton after undoing each button, and stopping, with a giggle of delight, when Mel's small, conical, pink-tipped breasts spilled out.

She didn't know what to do next. She had never touched another woman's breasts. 'What pretty little nipples,' she said, and giggled again.

'I like yours,' Mel said. 'Big and dark, with wide haloes around them.' She leaned forwards, so that her breasts were hanging just in front of Jessica's face. 'But if you like mine, I think you'd better kiss them.'

Jessica gasped. This was getting serious. Kissing and cuddling was one thing, but now both she and Mel were half-naked. Where was it going to end?

'Come on,' Mel said. 'Kiss them, then lick them, with the tip of your tongue, and then suck them. If you're good at it I'll play with yours again.'

Dimly, in the back of her mind, Jessica knew that she would usually baulk at doing as she was told, particularly by someone she hardly knew. But the brusque tone of Mel's voice seemed only to increase her arousal. Mel was the pirate captain; Jessica was the captured maiden. Her lips touched, and held, the nut of crinkled skin at the tip of Mel's left breast, and both women shivered with pleasure.

Jessica lost herself in making love to Mel's breasts. She was aware that Mel's hands were clutching the sides of her head; she heard the gasps and moans issuing from Mel's lips. But these were distant sensations compared with the smell of Mel's soft skin against her face, the yielding firmness of the curves of Mel's flesh under her fingers, the corrugated texture of Mel's nipples against the silk of her lips, the sandpaper of her tongue.

When she sucked, she found that she could draw from Mel little cries and quivers of ecstasy. She held a nipple between her lips, and drew it in slowly, sucking and releasing, but pulling it further in each time, until the whole of the point of the breast was inside her wide mouth. Then she simultaneously sucked, and licked with her tongue, until Mel cried out. And then she released the nipple, and transferred her attention to the other.

At last, breathing heavily, Mel pulled her breasts out of reach of Jessica's searching lips. 'Good girl,' she gasped. 'Very good. But now it's your turn. Put your hands behind your head.'

Jessica knew it was silly, but it gave her a thrill of pleasure to be told that she was a good girl. And with her hands clasped together at the nape of her neck she could easily continue to pretend that she was Mel's prisoner.

Mel's lips were on hers again, placing little kisses on her mouth and face, and Mel's hands were once again caressing her breasts. 'That feels so good,' Jessica whispered. 'Let's do this all day.'

'I'm afraid we can't,' Mel said between kisses. 'I have to go soon. But before I do I'm going to do this.'

Jessica gasped as a jolt of sensation travelled from the tip of her left breast into the centre of her being. Mel's finger and thumb had closed on the nipple, and pinched it, and had not let go.

Jessica didn't know whether she was experiencing pain or pleasure. With wide eyes she gazed at Mel, who was regarding her steadily.

'Tell me when it hurts too much,' Mel said. She smiled, and gently increased the pressure of her grip.

'It hurts,' Jessica gasped. But did it hurt too much? No, not yet: it was bearable. It was better than bearable: it was exciting. Each incremental tightening of Mel's finger and thumb sent a thrill of pleasurable pain through Jessica, and drew an anguished cry from her throat. Each time she thought, at first, that she couldn't stand it; but each time the ripples of pain faded into a deepening pool of pleasure. Swimming in the pool were memories of the things that Jonathan had done to her in the dark, secret cupboard.

'I don't think I can squeeze any tighter,' Mel said. 'You're a very good girl, Jessica. Keep still while I kiss you again.'

It was another long, deep kiss. The throbbing pain in Jessica's breast urged her to respond fiercely to the pressure of Mel's lips and tongue. 'It's time to stop,' Mel whispered at last, and as she applied her mouth to

Jessica's for a final kiss she twisted the nipple she was holding. Jessica lost control of her reactions: she gasped, over and over again, to the rhythm of the pulsing pain, but her lips continued to mould themselves to Mel's. It was almost as good as an orgasm.

When Jessica had recovered her breath, she opened her eyes to find Mel looking down at her as she stood buttoning her dress.

'I've got to go, Jess,' she said. 'I'm sorry. I would love to stay. But I'll visit you again tomorrow morning.'

Jessica grinned. 'Please do,' she said.

'You've been very good,' Mel said. 'In fact, I'm delighted with you. I think we're going to have lots of fun. Now then: after I've gone, are you going to play with yourself?'

Jessica was shocked. It was a very personal question. And Mel looked so serious and businesslike, now that she was dressed again. 'I expect so,' she said, blushing.

'Good,' Mel said with a laugh. 'I want you to do it here, on the sofa. And think of me while you're touching yourself. Will you do that for me? I'll be sure to ask you about it tomorrow.'

Jessica nodded. She stood up, and the dressing gown slipped to the floor around her feet.

Mel's blue eyes scanned her from head to toes. 'Oh, Jess,' she said, 'I'm so glad you're young and so gorgeous. It's going to make things so much more enjoyable. Come here and give me a goodbye kiss.'

Jessica was still trembling so much with suppressed desire that her knees felt weak as she stepped into Mel's embrace. Their kiss, relatively chaste compared with the passionate kisses they had shared on the sofa, seemed more indecent because Mel was clothed and Jessica was completely naked.

Arm in arm they went to the front door. Jessica opened it a little, standing back so that no one outside could see her. 'Until tomorrow,' she said. 'And, before you go, let's see if you're really wearing no knickers!' Playfully she plucked up the hem of Mel's dress.

'Stop it!' Mel said firmly, but with a laugh. She twisted away from Jessica, and smoothed down her dress as she escaped through the doorway. 'I'll be back tomorrow,' she promised.

Jessica closed the door and rested her back against it. She wanted more than anything to return to the couch, wrap herself in the silk of her dressing gown, and touch herself on the nipples and between her legs until she reached a climax – one that she was sure would be spectacular. But Mel's visit had given her so much to think about: not least the glimpse she had had of Mel's bottom, knickerless above the stocking-tops, which was no surprise, and clearly marked with several bright-red, horizontal stripes – and that was so much more than merely unexpected that Jessica decided, with a shake of her head, that she must have imagined it.

This, Jessica told herself as she looked in the changing-room's mirror, is where reckless overconfidence gets you.

In the privacy of her house, where she had spent the last few hours naked and in a euphoria of sensuality, forever finding her fingers wandering to her breasts and her permanently damp sex, it had seemed like a good idea to pack for her session at the Hillingbury Health and Exercise Club the skimpiest sports clothes she could find. She would show the arrogant young man what he was missing, she had thought: let's see if he can ignore me while I'm wearing next to nothing.

Now, in the impersonal, white-tiled surroundings of the club itself, she was having second thoughts. But there was nothing she could do: these were the only clothes she had brought to change into. She had ransacked her wardrobe for old clothes: things she had worn during the summer holidays as a teenager. She had tried everything on, struggling into garments that were threadbare and much too small for her as she searched for the most revealing. It had seemed an exciting game.

Now she heaved a sigh, and then grimaced as she saw her breasts become even more prominent. The T-shirt was made of thin white cotton, and it was a very tight fit. It didn't reach her waist, so her navel was exposed. The material was tight under her arms. Worst of all, her dark nipples and only slightly lighter areolae were clearly visible, pressing so hard against the cloth that they looked as though they were seeking a way through it.

The shorts, also of white cotton, were if anything even more disgraceful. In her bedroom, with her fingers trembling with excitement at her own daring, Jessica had used scissors, cutting away strips of cloth to make the shorts even more revealing. They didn't look too bad from the front, but when she turned her back on the mirror and looked over her shoulder, she gave another sigh. Her bottom was almost completely uncovered. She had been wearing the shorts for only a few minutes, and already the material had disappeared between her buttocks. She leaned forwards, and realised that if she wasn't very careful the thin band of white cotton between her legs would work its way into the divide between her outer labia. If only she wasn't so sexually aroused today! She was grateful that she had at least had the sense to trim her dark pubic curls into a short, neat mat.

Apart from the plimsolls on her feet, and a band to hold back her long dark hair, she had nothing else to wear. She had, of course, intended to wear the T-shirt and shorts without any underclothes and, inspired by Mel's example and her own sense of dangerous fun, she had worn nothing under the blouse and skirt she had worn on her way to the club. There was nothing she could do but go home, or go through with her appointment with the stern young man.

Jessica emerged cautiously from the changing-room. She half-hoped, but also half-feared, that by now there would be some other members in the club. But her footsteps on the tiles echoed emptily. There was no one swimming in the pool; no sounds from the door that led to the Turkish baths. And in the gym, when she slowly pushed open the door, she found only the arrogant young man, waiting for her with his gaze fixed on the watch around his wrist.

He looked up. 'Jessica,' he said. 'Good afternoon. You're rather late.'

He looked her up and down, making her blush, but his face showed no surprise at her skimpy attire. All thoughts of impressing him, of making him notice her, had long since fled from Jessica's mind. He was tall, strong, confident in immaculate black shirt and shorts, and unsmiling. She was so embarrassed that she wanted the ground to open and swallow her.

'Come here,' he said, beckoning to her and then pointing at the centre of a green mat that was in front of a vast mirror. 'Stand here. Arms behind your back to start with. Shoulders back. Feet apart.'

Jessica hurried into the required position.

'You have to warm up your muscles, and get your circulation going, before you exercise. Perform the stretches that I showed you yesterday.'

Jessica felt his eyes on her as she stretched her arms up, and then to the front, and then behind her back. Her face went crimson with mortification as she felt her breasts surge forwards against the constriction of her T-shirt, and again when she bent over to touch her toes and could feel the material riding up into her sex and her bottom. The young man's silence was worse than if he had made lewd comments.

When she straightened her body and rested with her arms at her sides, the silence continued. The young man was simply staring at her – at her breasts, in particular.

She couldn't stand the silence a moment longer. 'Perhaps I shouldn't do the exercises today,' she said. 'I mean, it's just that I don't think these clothes are very suitable. And I forgot to bring any support.'

'Support?'

'Yes.' Jessica hated him. He was going to make her explain. She lifted her hands to her chest. 'You know, for my breasts.'

'That won't be necessary. The clothes you have on are perfectly adequate. You're young, and I can clearly see that your breasts are very firm. You don't need any support. I'll make sure that your programme of exercises doesn't include any jumping up and down.' He smiled briefly.

'I think I should –' Jessica began.

'No,' the young man stated. 'You will perform your exercises dressed as you are. Now and every day. Is that understood?'

Oh, goodness. He was giving her orders again. It was horribly demeaning, but it was also so exciting. Jessica felt her nipples hardening, and a warm glow began where the shorts were pressing into her. 'Yes,' she said, and lowered her head.

'My name is Matt,' the young man said. 'But while you're undergoing instruction here you will address me as Mentor. I find that it helps to maintain a clear hierarchy of authority. Is that also understood?'

'Yes, Mentor,' Jessica said, and felt a thrill of excitement.

'Very good. Now I'll take you through the programme of exercises.'

Matt – her mentor – remained at her side throughout the next hour. His eyes were always on her; his humourless voice gave her concise but exact instructions; his strong hands adjusted her position as she panted and perspired through the exercises he taught her. As she ran on the treadmill she was acutely conscious of the bouncing of her breasts, and even more aware of the attention Matt paid to them. Perched on the saddle of the rowing machine, pulling on the oars with all her strength but never enough to satisfy Matt's urgings, she felt the hard leather pressing again and again against the taut cloth that was barely covering her sex. She did press-ups, with Matt's hand on her bottom to keep her back straight; she did sit-ups. The most humiliating exercise was the last: she lay on her back, lifted her legs into the air, and was then obliged to spread them apart, bring them together, spread them apart – over and over again, with Matt standing directly in front of her and making no attempt to move his gaze from the junction of her thighs.

By the end of the session Jessica was limp, breathless and aching. Her thin clothes were damp with sweat, and she was as aroused as she had been when at the mercy of Mel's lips and fingers. But she also felt a small glow of triumph: she could clearly see that the front of her mentor's shorts was bulging. He had also found the lesson stimulating. He wasn't entirely impervious to her charms.

'Well,' he said, 'I suppose that will have to do to start with. Your performance will improve with regular practice. Ideally I want to see you in here daily. I'll supervise you. Now you should shower and change. If you've brought a swimming-costume you could relax in the pool or the Turkish bath before you go. That is, unless you have any questions. In which case you should come to the office.'

Jessica had thought that he was dismissing her, but his final words sounded like an invitation. To what, she wondered.

'Yes, Mentor,' she said. 'In fact, I do have some questions.' She was sure that she would be able to think of something to ask him.

'Come along, then. We'd better talk before you change.'

In the office, standing before his desk, Jessica was lost for words. She wanted to find a way to make him touch her, or at least to make him acknowledge that he found her desirable.

'Well?' he said.

She had to say something. 'Yesterday,' she said abruptly and bitterly, 'you spanked me. You had no right to do that. You were taking advantage of your position.'

Matt's face showed no expression. 'I was conducting an assessment of your physical fitness,' he said. 'I find it odd that you perceived it as a punishment. You didn't object at the time. But if you think I was punishing you, then perhaps that's because you thought you deserved to be punished. Perhaps you find physical exercise something of an imposition; perhaps you need the encouragement of a smack from time to time. In which case, to be frank, I would be remiss if I didn't spank you again, whenever you seem to need it.'

He had stopped speaking. It was her turn to say something. She should protest; she should storm out of the room. But she couldn't deny that she wanted precisely what he had promised. It would be so exciting to offer her bottom to him again, and to feel the sting of his palm. She could feel the warm wetness of her arousal seeping from her sex.

'Well?' he said, his voice surprisingly gentle. 'I begin to suspect that you have been doing something naughty. You'd better tell me about it.'

Oh, yes: she had been very naughty. With Mel, and only that morning. Could she really talk to Matt about something so private, so intimate, so scandalous? It would be terribly embarrassing. And very, very exciting.

'This morning,' Jessica began, 'a neighbour called at my house. A young woman named Mel. I was alone, and I wasn't expecting anybody . . .'

Matt listened intently as Jessica confessed every detail of her passionate meeting with Mel. She even mentioned the red stripes that she had thought she had seen on Mel's bottom and, with her face blushing redder than ever, she went on to describe how, after Mel had left, she had caressed herself until she had a fantastic orgasm.

When she finished her account Matt was silent for a moment. 'Yes,' he said. 'I think that behaviour could well be seen as naughty.' He opened a drawer in the desk and took out a long wooden ruler. 'You might as well remove those shorts,' he said. 'You're going to change out of them anyway.'

He was really going to do it. And with that long, thin, wickedly flexible ruler. It would hurt more than a spanking. It would hurt a lot. But it didn't occur to her to disobey him. Her fingers were already unbuttoning her shorts, and pushing the tight, damp material down over her hips. She had to reach behind her back to prise the bunched material from the cleft of her bottom and her sex. Her fumbling fingers brushed against the curves of her bottom, and she let out a little moan when she imagined how hot and sore the soft skin was about to become. As her fingers pressed into her sex to gather and pull out the material of her shorts, she moaned again, this time with frustrated desire. She glanced at her mentor, and found that his gleaming eyes were fixed on the awkward movements of her hands. He was flexing the ruler between his fists. His biceps bulged. He looked up, met her gaze, and smiled. She was sure that he was aware of her embarrassment; she was sure that he knew she was aroused; she was helpless in the face of his strength and authority.

'Take them off,' he said. 'They weren't covering much of you, anyway.'

The shorts were so tight that Jessica had to push them all the way down her thighs. Only when they were past her knees did they slide down her calves to rest around her plimsolls. She stood straight and covered her pubes with her hands. The fact that she was wearing the little tight, short T-shirt made her feel more ridiculous and vulnerable than if she had been naked.

The shorts weren't covering much of me, she thought, but they were just about hiding my most private parts. He'll make me bend over, I'm sure of it. And then I won't be able to stop him seeing everything: all of my bottom, including the little hole, and he'll see my sex, and I'm sure it's so wet there that he'll notice that too.

'Perhaps we should do this another time,' she said. 'There might be other people in the club by now. And if there's anyone in the ladies' changing-room I won't be able to get showered and changed if I've got a red bottom.'

Matt shook his head. 'There's a bell on the door,' he said. 'It rings in here if anyone comes into the club. We're still alone. Step forwards and bend over. Legs wide apart, please, and keep them straight. Rest your forearms on the desk, as you did yesterday, and arch your back inwards so that your bottom is well presented.'

Jessica uttered a sigh that was almost a sob. She shook her shorts from her feet and took a step forwards. She leaned forwards a little, and then lifted her head and glanced at her mentor in the hope that he might, at the last minute, spare her. He merely stood up and tapped the top of the desk with the end of the ruler.

As Jessica rested her arms on the desk, and shuffled her plimsolls across the floor until her legs were wide apart, she tried to decide why she was going to let Matt punish her. Was it because she had taken such a liking to the handsome blond mentor that she was prepared to do anything to impress him? Or was it that she felt guilty about what she had done with Mel, and therefore deserved to be chastised? Or was it simply that she had been feeling sexually aroused all day, and she suspected that being smacked would add to the sensations?

All she could be sure of was that she wanted to feel the ruler landing on her bottom. She curved her back downwards, so that her bottom was lifted up. Matt had moved out of her sight, and was presumably standing behind her. She knew that he would be able to see her sex. The lips were parted – they had been since almost the start of the exercises – and she could feel wetness gathering between them. She thought that she would inevitably produce more liquid once the punishment was under way. What if it started to drip from her sex on to the floor? It would be unbearably embarrassing. Almost more embarrassing than the fact that Matt could see her little bottom-hole: she was shy of showing that place even to Brian.

'As this is your first time,' Matt said, 'I'll give you just ten strokes. I assume you don't want anyone to know about this. How long will you be able to keep your bottom concealed?'

Jessica glanced over her shoulder. Oh, goodness: the ruler was so whippy in his big, strong hands. 'Until tomorrow morning,' she said. These days, working such long hours at his office, Brian was usually asleep by the time Jessica undressed and slipped into bed beside him. In fact, the next person to see Jessica naked would probably be Mel. It was only after she had answered that she realised the significance of her mentor's question.

'Good,' he said. 'I'll make them quite hard, then, and we'll see if we can get five distinct marks on each side. Keep still.'

Then everything happened very fast. Jessica heard the ruler swish through the air, and then there was a stinging pain across her left buttock, and before it had begun to fade there was another swish, and her right buttock felt a blaze of fire, and then the ruler was swishing again.

He stopped after six, and at last Jessica could catch her breath. Her heart was pounding in her chest, and her bottom seemed to be throbbing with pain to the same rhythm. She wanted to clench her muscles, and to stand up and massage the sore flesh, but she was determined not to show any sign of weakness.

'Six clear stripes,' Matt said, evidently satisfied with his work. 'Not entirely horizontal, but certainly parallel.'

Jessica couldn't feel six differentiated stripes. Her whole bottom was hot. The stinging was fading, and being replaced by a steady, pulsing warmth. She sighed, and rested her cheek on her crossed forearms. She edged herself forwards, and gasped as her tightly confined breasts touched the edge of the desk. Her nipples were as hard as the wooden surface. She felt simultaneously energised and languorous. The sensations were similar to those she experienced when she played with her sex, using her fingers or the candle in her bedroom: similar, but even better.

She was being punished – properly punished, not just spanked – for the first time in her life. And she was loving it. She inched her feet further apart and tried to lift her bottom even higher. She was glad that Matt had paused to allow her time to appreciate the changing sensations, but now she wanted him to continue. Or to pull down his shorts and enter her sopping vagina. Best of all would be if he could somehow put his manhood into her and at the same time carry on smacking her bottom. The thought of being smacked while being fucked gave her such intense pleasure that she shivered and uttered a little moan.

'The last four,' Matt said, 'will go here, here, here and here.'

Jessica felt the tip of the ruler touch her skin four times. Each touch made her shiver.

'Yes, please, Mentor,' she said. And then a thought struck her. Perhaps she hadn't imagined the red lines on her pretty blonde neighbour's bottom. She lifted her head and looked over her shoulder.

Matt stopped, with the ruler raised, and looked at her questioningly.

'You've done this before, haven't you?' Jessica said.

'Of course,' he replied. 'But not for some time. I'm glad to have found someone who might need regular discipline: it will help me to keep in practice.'

So he wasn't responsible for the marks on Mel's bottom. And he saw her only as a means of maintaining his training skills. Before Jessica had time to feel disappointed, the ruler hissed through the air again and drew a line of fire on her left buttock. She gasped. Only three more to go. She wanted more; much more.

After the tenth stroke had been delivered Jessica remained quite still. She thought that if she moved she might break the spell: the wonderful, enchanting feelings that were swimming through her body. She knew that if Matt so much as touched her between her legs she would start to come. And she hoped that, if she remained with her bottom open and pushed out, he might give her a few more smacks. She pressed her breasts against the top of the desk and wondered whether it was possible to have an orgasm just through being smacked on her bottom. How could she persuade Matt to help her to find out?

'Your vulva appears to be very wet,' Matt said, as casually as if he was chatting about the weather. 'Are you feeling sexually stimulated?'

Oh, why couldn't he just smack her again, or put his erection into her? 'Yes,' she groaned, turning her head to look at him. 'Very, very stimulated.'

He was clearly as excited as she was: the front of his shorts seemed ready to burst open. But he had more self-control than she could muster.

'If you need to masturbate,' he said, making the word sound distasteful, 'you'd better do it here. We can't have that sort of thing going on in the changing-rooms. Would you like to?'

He knew exactly how to make her feel naughty and humiliated. And the feelings only stoked the fires of her desire. He wanted her to play with herself while he was watching her. He would watch her until she reached an orgasm. Unsmiling, severe, he would remain expressionless while her face reddened, and her fingers worked furiously, and she started to gasp and then to moan, and finally to lose control of her limbs and thrash about and cry out.

It was such an intimate act. Brian, even in the days when he and she had first become lovers, and had made love quite often, had rarely seen her coming: they usually made love after dark, with the lights off, under the bedcovers. But she always liked to watch herself when she was alone. Ever since she had discovered the pleasure of touching the secret places between her legs she had made sure there was a mirror in which she could watch herself. While she had been living with her parents she had angled the mirror of the dressing table in her bedroom so that she could see her body reflected in it while she was lying on her bed; in her room at college she had had to make do with a small, portable mirror; once she had had a place of her own – the flat in the city she had shared with Brian – she had been able to surround the bed with mirrors; and the new house had huge, full-length mirrors set into the doors of the wardrobe. She knew that it was nothing but vanity, but she couldn't help admiring the slim lines of her limbs, the narrowness of her waist, and the round swellings of her breasts and bottom. Did she have the courage to touch herself in front of her mentor? He couldn't help but enjoy watching her.

'If you like,' Matt said, 'I'll give you a few more smacks while you're masturbating. Not hard enough to leave marks, but just enough to sting a little.'

That clinched it. Jessica was prepared to do almost anything to feel the ruler on her bottom again, and the thought of being smacked while she caressed herself was overwhelmingly exciting.

'All right,' she said, doing her best to sound reluctant. She pushed herself up from the desk and stretched her arms and back. Her legs were trembling.

'Of course,' Matt went on, 'you'll have to clean up the mess you've made on the floor. Kneel in front of the desk.'

Oh, goodness! What had she done? As she stepped back and looked down to the floor she became aware that the insides of her thighs were coated with the wetness that had seeped from her sex while she was being smacked. And some of the wetness had dripped from her, on to the white tiles. Her right hand flew between her legs, and she gasped as she touched the hot flesh. Her labia were widely parted, and her sex was like a lake. She had never known herself to produce this much lubrication. Her hand was as wet as if she had held it under a running tap.

'Come along,' Matt said. 'On your knees. I want you to clean the floor with the front of your T-shirt.'

What did he mean? Did he want to see her naked? She couldn't think clearly about anything. All she wanted was more smacks and an orgasm. She crossed her arms, grasped the hem of her T-shirt, and began to pull the tight material up her torso.

'No, no!' Matt said, impatiently. 'Leave it on. I want you to use the front of your T-shirt to wipe the tiles clean, while you're wearing it.'

Of course. That would be even more humiliating. 'Yes, Mentor,' Jessica said, and kneeled on the hard floor. She pulled her ponytail over one shoulder, and bent forwards to rest her left forearm on the floor. She found herself looking down at the three little pools of clear liquid that had dripped from her.

'Start wiping the floor,' Matt said, 'and lift your bottom up so I can see everything. Don't touch yourself until I give you permission.'

It was demeaning to be ordered about by such a young man. But it was so exciting to obey. Jessica arched her back downwards, pressing her breasts against the hard, cold tiles and lifting her bottom towards her mentor. She swept her breasts from side to side, and each movement sent a thrill from her nipples to her sex. She couldn't help moving her hips as she wiped her breasts against the floor. She imagined the view that she was presenting to her mentor – her parted thighs, her open, dripping sex, her glowing, rounded, red-striped buttocks – and the thrills of pleasure came faster, and began to merge into a pre-orgasmic feeling that made her shudder and gasp with each movement she made.

And then she felt the ruler. Matt used it as a pointer, at first, touching the lips of her sex, and then the sensitive little hole between her buttocks, and then the marks of the smacks he had given her. When he struck her bottom, the blows were almost gentle – to start with. Jessica lowered her forehead to the floor and ground her breasts against the tiles. The smacks continued, at a slow rhythm but a little harder, each one a reminder of how much the ruler could sting and how sore and sensitive it had made her bottom.

'You can start touching yourself now,' Matt said. 'Keep your bottom well up so I can see what you're doing. Don't stop until you come.'

That won't take long, Jessica thought, and then her fingers slid into the wet folds of her sex and she was incapable of further coherent thought. She pressed and rubbed her fingers frantically into her flesh, without any of her usual finesse and delicacy. She had been ready to come for a long time – almost since the first smack of the ruler – and she couldn't wait any longer. She was desperate. Even the steady stinging of the ruler on her bottom, harder and faster now, and the thrilling pleasure-points of her nipples as they caressed the cold tiles, began to fade as her thrusting fingers pressed again and again against the hood of her clitoris and into the soaking-wet interior of her vagina, causing jolts of pleasure that convulsed her entire body. Her gasps became guttural cries.

She heard Matt say, 'Very good,' and then she was coming: her body shook and she uttered a long, loud wail as wave after wave of pleasure rolled over her.

It was the best orgasm she had ever had.

She realised, at last, that the convulsions had ceased. Her body felt heavy and pleasantly tired. She didn't want to move, even though she was still kneeling on the floor with her bottom in the air and her breasts pressed against the tiles. Matt had stopped smacking her.

'I trust you feel better now,' Matt said. 'If you've finished, that is.'

Still there was that hateful, provocative tone of contempt in his voice. How could he not want her, after she had put on such a performance for him? She pulled herself to her feet, and winced when her sore bottom brushed the edge of the table.

He had set aside the ruler and was standing with his arms crossed, watching her. The bulge in his shorts seemed no smaller, but he was more than ever in control of himself. He was only two steps away. Why wouldn't he come to her, and take her in his strong arms, and kiss her? Did he have no feelings for her at all?

'I must look a mess,' she said. She ran her hand through her hair, which had escaped from its band. The front of her T-shirt was crumpled and stained. The wetness between her legs was cold. Her bottom, on the other hand, felt hot and swollen.

'Yes,' Matt said. 'You need to shower and change. And you should do so quickly, before any other members arrive.' He picked up her shorts and held them out for her to take.

'So is that it?' Jessica asked. She did her best to keep her voice steady, but she felt close to tears.

'That's all for today,' Matt said, and at last he gave a smile of genuine warmth. 'But I'll expect to see you here again tomorrow. It seems to me that you need daily exercise and discipline.'

So he did want to see her again, after all. 'Thank you, Mentor,' Jessica said. 'I expect I will have done something naughty again by tomorrow afternoon.' She was already looking forward to seeing Mel again.

'And I'll require you to tell me every detail.'

A little later, as Jessica stood in one of the shower cubicles and let rivulets of steaming water course down her face and body, she tried to organise her thoughts about the day's remarkable events. She now had a new friend, Mel, with whom she expected to have lots of wicked fun and who could tell her all about how to enter Hillingbury society; and she had a mentor who was a gorgeous hunk of a man and who seemed willing to help her explore her newly found delight in being spanked and punished. And she had had two orgasms!

She frowned, as she wondered whether she was being unfaithful to Brian. But Mel was a woman, and so anything Jessica did with her couldn't possibly count as adultery. And Matt was merely her fitness instructor. Anyway, Brian would never find out what she got up to while he was away at the office. He wouldn't even be interested.

And if she did ever feel a little bit guilty, she was sure that she could ask her mentor to be extra strict with her.

Jessica hummed happily as she soaped herself. She was going to enjoy living in the suburbs, after all.

Three

Field agent's report to the Private House
From: Matt
For the attention of: Mistress Julia

. . . In conclusion of this morning's report, I trust that my account of the events of yesterday afternoon convinces you that Jessica will prove to be a considerable asset to our plans. If there is some kind of underground organisation here in Hillingbury, then Jessica's vivacity and striking looks would be enough to recommend her to its leaders; the fact that she has discovered a taste for sexual games with other women makes it a certainty that they will try to recruit her; and her barely repressed sensuality makes it certain that she will want to join.

As long as I can keep her returning to me at the club on a regular basis, I should be able to extract from her everything she learns about the social life of the estate.

I am doing my best not to let my feelings for her cloud my judgement, and looking at her as objectively as I can I remain sure that, even if there proves to be nothing else of interest to us here, Jessica will become a valuable member of the Private House. She is more than sufficiently attractive, and I'm sure her submissiveness and her enthusiasm for punishment and exhibitionism are unfeigned.

Therefore the only problems are to do with my self-discipline. I'm convinced that part of my attraction for her is the remote, aloof and self-controlled persona that I adopt with her, and I'm finding it increasingly difficult to conceal from her how desirable I think she is. I am, I confess, counting the minutes until her next visit. I have little doubt that she will want to be punished again, and no expectation that I will be able to resist her. I will have to take her further, this afternoon, than I did yesterday: she will expect something more, and I'm desperate to do more with her. It will be all right, I think, to have sex with her, as long as I maintain the role of Mentor. It will have to be all right: I mean to have her.

I will report again tomorrow.

Jessica looked over her shoulder at her reflection in one of the long mirrors in her bedroom. The stripes on her bottom had disappeared. She was disappointed: she hadn't yet decided whether to tell Mel about Matt, and she had half-hoped that the marks on her bottom, which, had they lasted, Mel could hardly have failed to see, would oblige her to confess how she had acquired them.

She slapped her bottom, hard, until it was bright pink, but the stripes made by the ruler didn't reappear. And although it felt nice to have a stinging bottom again, because it reminded her of everything she had done the previous day, it wasn't the same as being under her mentor's instruction.

And she couldn't decide what to wear. At first she had kept on her silk dressing gown, as it felt soft next to her skin and because Mel had liked it. But then she thought that it might be a mistake to be discovered *en déshabillé* for the second time: when Mel arrived she might think that Jessica was too eager to resume their previous day's games. She might even think it slovenly.

So Jessica had to dress. But in what? Something smart and fashionable? But that might seem too formal, given that Jessica didn't want to deter Mel. Something comfortable and casual? But Mel might be offended if she thought that Jessica had made no effort about her appearance.

Jessica told herself that it wasn't like her to be indecisive, and she sat down at her dressing table to apply her make-up. She used only a little of her very lightest foundation cream; mascara and a little eyeliner, both of dark brown to match her eyes; the merest hint of highlighter above her wide cheekbones, which really needed no emphasising; and lipstick of a subdued dark red. She brushed out her hair and collected it at the back of her neck in a tortoiseshell clasp. She turned her head from side to side, clipping plain amber earrings to her lobes as she admired her reflection.

If I were Mel or Matt, she whispered to herself, opening wide her large eyes, I'd fall in love with me.

She had decided what to wear. No underclothes: if she and Mel were going to continue to explore each other, they would only get in the way. And she didn't expect Mel to be wearing any. Matt was right: her breasts were very high and firm, and didn't need any support.

However, she would wear a suspender belt and stockings. She didn't know whether Mel would find them attractive, but Jessica liked to wear them. As she tightened the suspenders, and checked the straightness of her seams in the mirror, she found once again that wearing stockings was more exciting than being completely naked. The tightness of the belt, and the touch of the suspenders against her thighs, and the coolness of the skin above the stocking-tops, reminded her constantly that her bottom and sex were exposed. Since her training session with Matt the previous day she had a much better understanding of the desires and fantasies that had lain unacknowledged within her and that explained why she found it so exciting to know that her private parts and her bottom were accessible and ready to be revealed.

Next she pulled on a short skirt and a plain cotton blouse. She left undone the lower buttons of the blouse, and tied the front tails together above her navel. Her idea was to look as though she was about to undertake some light housework – although she desperately hoped that Mel would keep her fully occupied with much more interesting activities. She let her fingers roam across her breasts as she remembered how she had enjoyed kissing and sucking the tips of Mel's sharp little cones, and the sweet agony of Mel's fingers squeezing her nipples.

She looked down. Her nipples were hard, and clearly visible through the thin cotton of the blouse. Mel would notice that she was wearing nothing but the blouse over her breasts. Would that matter? Would Mel consider it charming, or forward? I'll wear a pinafore apron, she decided; I've got a short one with a lacy front. It will keep me a bit covered, and it'll help to make it look as though I'm doing something useful, rather than just waiting for Mel to arrive.

But Jessica had to admit that she was doing nothing but listening for Mel's footsteps on the gravel drive. She wandered from room to room with a feather duster in her hand, but didn't stray far from the front door. And the feathers remained pristine, as she did no dusting; the tip of the long, thin, wooden handle, however, frequently found its way under her skirt, and it became wetter and wetter as her anticipation of Mel's arrival grew.

When the doorbell rang it awoke Jessica from a reverie. She pulled the handle of the duster slowly, and with a sigh, from the crevice of flesh in which it had been lodged, wiped it on her apron, and on slightly trembling legs she went to the door.

Today Mel had no coat. She was wearing another simple, button-through dress, of cotton lawn with a delicate floral design, cinched at the waist with a wide belt. She had a shoulder bag, and a scarf tied round her neck.

'Hello,' they both said at once. Jessica held open the door, and then followed Mel into the sitting room. They sat, as they had the previous day, side by side on the sofa, with a gap between them.

'I've got such a lot to tell you,' Mel said, but then she seemed not to know where to begin.

Jessica was aware that once again Mel was studying her intently, and Jessica was also stealing glances at Mel. Was it possible, really, that she was attracted to a woman? But there could be no doubt that Mel was pretty: from her oval face, with blue eyes and pink lips, to her trim ankles, she was more than merely pretty, she was desirable. And Jessica had enjoyed kissing her, and being kissed. But it was still a very awkward situation. Jessica knew almost nothing about Mel, except that she lived in Hillingbury and had pink-tipped breasts that Jessica liked to lick and suck. It wasn't the usual basis for a friendship.

'This is silly,' Jessica announced. 'Why don't we just kiss each other again and, if we still like it, then it will be easier to talk.'

Mel smiled gratefully. 'Good idea,' she said, and spread her arms so that Jessica could cuddle against her. 'I'm afraid I'm not used to taking the lead.'

'That's better already,' Jessica whispered as she settled into Mel's lap and burrowed her face into Mel's neck. Her lips found Mel's, and soon the two women were kissing as avidly as teenage lovers.

When they paused to gather their breath, Mel said, 'You're wearing too many clothes. If you were my maid, I wouldn't let you wear anything under your pinafore.'

One of the things that had made Jessica wear the apron was the thought that it made her look a bit like a servant. It felt naughty and exciting to wear a costume, and Jessica was glad that Mel had noticed. 'Would you like me to take off my skirt?' she asked.

'Of course,' Mel said. 'And that blouse. Stand up and let me see what else you're wearing.'

Jessica felt a familiar thrill inside her sex. Only a few days ago she would have fiercely rejected the suggestion that she enjoyed being given orders. She had Matt to thank for showing her how much fun it could be to submit to someone else's commands. She stood up and untied the knot at her midriff, and then started to undo the buttons of her blouse. Every time she looked up she found Mel gazing at her. It was terribly embarrassing, but even more exciting.

'If I take off my blouse and skirt,' she said, feeling very daring, 'will you let me see what you're hiding under your scarf? You were wearing one yesterday, too.'

'All right,' Mel said. 'If you hurry up and get those things off. That's right. Oh, Jess, you darling! You're wearing nothing underneath but stockings. How thoughtful. You're a good girl. And you look adorable in that little frilly apron. Now come and sit here again, and you can take off my scarf – to start with.'

Standing in her own sitting room, wearing nothing but stockings and a little apron, Jessica felt ridiculous and embarrassed – and very aroused. The top of the apron wasn't large enough to cover both of her breasts, so that whichever way she turned one or the other was exposed. And the frilly border tickled her nipples. The lower part of the apron extended only as far as her stocking-tops, and it had no back, so her bottom was completely bare. It was impossible to be dignified, and Jessica was glad to take refuge in Mel's arms. She giggled like a schoolgirl while Mel cuddled her, and kissed her, and tickled and stroked and pinched her breasts and thighs. It was heavenly.

It was obvious that Mel was enjoying the embrace as much as Jessica was, and soon the women's kisses became more and more prolonged, and their breathing deeper. Mel wasn't sitting upright any more, but was reclining against the cushions piled at the end of the sofa. Jessica was curled on her lap. Mel's right arm was supporting Jessica's shoulders, so she could kiss Jessica's face, and her hand was underneath Jessica's bottom, the fingers moving gently in the wet cleft of Jessica's sex. Mel's other hand was under the front of the apron, teasing the hard, brown tips of Jessica's breasts.

Jessica, adrift on a balmy sea of sensations, was happy to let Mel touch her. She uttered only a muted moan of objection even when she felt one of Mel's fingers press against the delicate wrinkled skin of her little back hole, and she didn't object for long because she found that she enjoyed the feeling. Inasmuch as she could think coherently about anything she concentrated on undoing the buttons of Mel's dress, and when she had opened the garment she grasped Mel's breasts. She found that whenever she squeezed them, or rotated her palms over the nipples, she could make Mel groan, and Mel's kisses became fiercer.

At some point she remembered that she was supposed to remove Mel's neck-scarf. She drew back from Mel's kisses, and did her best to focus her attention on undoing the brooch that secured the scarf. Mel's wicked fingers did their best to distract her from her task, but at last, after much wriggling and giggling, the catch was undone, and Mel finally gave Jessica some respite as she slowly drew the scarf away.

Jessica had concocted all sorts of theories about what Mel's neck-scarf might conceal. A scar; a tattoo; a birthmark; a priceless, jewelled necklace. None of her guesses was correct. Under the scarf, Mel was wearing around her neck a collar of blue leather.

Jessica didn't know what it signified, or how she should respond to seeing it revealed. It reminded her of something she had seen, quite recently, but she couldn't remember where or when. And it excited her: it looked out of place around the neck of a young woman, and seemed redolent of danger and secrets. 'It's pretty,' she said, and reached to touch it.

The leather was soft, and of a very high quality. It fitted snugly against the pale skin of Mel's neck, but there was no sign of chafing. The circumference was decorated with bright metal rings that were set into the leather and, when Jessica's fingers reached the nape of Mel's neck, they discovered that as well as being fastened with a buckle the collar was secured with a small padlock.

'Mel, it's locked,' Jessica breathed. She was mystified, and couldn't analyse why the sight and feel of the collar made her insides feel so quivery.

'Yes, my darling Jessica,' Mel said. 'But today's a special day. I have the key. Be a good girl and pick up my bag.'

Mel's shoulder bag was on the floor next to the sofa. Eagerly, and making sure that Mel had a good view of her bottom, Jessica leaned over the arm of the sofa and retrieved the bag. It was surprisingly heavy.

Mel patted her thighs. 'Sit here again,' she said. 'And I'll find the key.'

Jessica snuggled against Mel, and Mel unfastened the bag. She pulled from it a satin-covered vanity-case. 'No peeking,' she said as she turned back the lid. 'You mustn't see what's inside. Not yet.'

More secrets. Jessica's insides were fluttering with excitement. Mel took from the case a small draw-string purse of black velvet, and from that she extracted a tiny silver key on a long chain. She stared at it for a few moments with an expression that Jessica found impossible to read.

'Well, Jess,' Mel said. 'Would you like to try on my collar?'

Jessica was aware that something important was going on – something the significance of which she could not grasp. But the idea of wearing the leather collar was too thrilling to resist. She wanted to feel it around her neck, no matter what the consequences. She took a deep breath, and nodded. 'Yes, please, Mel,' she said.

Mel held up the key. 'Undo the lock, then,' she said. 'Unbuckle the collar, and try it on.'

Jessica took the key and reached her hands behind Mel's neck. She rested her chin on Mel's shoulder, and absent-mindedly kissed her throat as she concentrated on unfastening the collar. As she pulled the collar loose she felt Mel exhale a sigh.

The two women, nose to nose, looked into each other's eyes. 'This is important, isn't it?' Jessica whispered.

'Yes, my darling,' Mel replied. 'I'll explain everything in just a moment.' She watched intently as Jessica placed the collar against her throat, bowed her head, and fiddled with the buckle until the collar was fitted and fastened.

The leather was warm from being against Mel's neck. The collar felt like nothing Jessica had ever worn: it wasn't tight, or at least not tight enough to be uncomfortable, but she knew that however long she wore it she would always be conscious of it. She wanted to jump up immediately and look at herself in a mirror, but she could imagine how she looked. Who wore collars? Slaves; captives. The little band of leather seemed to summon into Jessica's mind all of her old fantasies.

Jessica held out the key so that Mel could secure the padlock. Mel took it, but replaced it in its velvet purse. 'Don't worry,' she said. 'I won't lock it.'

'I don't mind,' Jessica started to say. She liked the idea of being unable to remove the collar.

But Mel had put away the purse, and dropped it, and the satin case, and the shoulder bag, on the floor. With gentle, trembling fingers she touched the collar, and made sure that it wasn't too tight, and stroked Jessica's neck, and brushed her long hair off her shoulders. 'It suits you,' she said. 'I knew it would. You look wonderful. Delicious. Blue isn't perfect for your colouring, of course. It was chosen for me.'

There were so many questions that Jessica wanted to ask. What did the collar signify? And who had chosen it for Mel? And why was it locked, and why did Mel have the key to it only on special days? What did Mel keep in the vanity-case? But wearing the collar seemed to make Jessica more than ever aware that she was wearing nothing but stockings and a little frilly apron, and that between her naked thighs her sex was warm and pulsating and moist, and that her nipples were yearning to feel Mel's cruel fingers again. Although Mel was no taller than she was, curled in Mel's lap she felt like a doll. 'Tell me,' was all that she managed to say.

'All right,' Mel said. 'Are you sitting comfortably? Then I'll begin.' Jessica rested her head against Mel's shoulder, and Mel stroked Jessica's hair as she explained everything. 'I suppose I should start with the committee. It's a group of ladies – there are eight at the moment – who are, well, I suppose they're in charge of everything in Hillingbury. Everything that matters, anyway: who gets invited to dinner parties, which residents are allowed to plant new hedges, that sort of thing. They set the fashions for interior décor, for instance – and woe betide any of us who put up new curtains without checking first with the committee.'

'Oh,' Jessica said. She was disappointed. She had expected Mel's revelations to be more interesting than an account of the pecking order on the estate. 'And who elects the committee?' she asked. 'The Hillingbury residents?'

Mel giggled. 'They're not elected,' she said, as if the very idea was absurd. She stroked Jessica's breasts and stared into the distance. 'Once you're on the committee, you're there until you move away from Hillingbury.'

'Oh,' Jessica said again. Now she was even more downhearted. 'Then the committee isn't of much interest to a newcomer like me.'

Mel leaned forwards and kissed Jessica's lips. 'Oh, yes, it is,' she whispered, and she pinched Jessica's nipples. 'And you're certainly of interest to them.'

A thought occurred to Jessica. 'Stop that for a moment,' she begged. 'It's lovely, but I'm trying to think. Is this committee the one I saw the notice about? The H, Y, W, A, P, O, C?'

'Of course it is,' Mel said. 'It's the only one there is. The Hillingbury Young Wives' Association Pet Owners' Committee.'

'Pet owners?' Jessica was appalled. She imagined a gathering of staid, middle-aged ladies exchanging dull pleasantries while surrounded by their dogs, cats and budgerigars. 'But I don't have a pet. I don't particularly like animals.'

Mel giggled again. 'You still haven't guessed, have you? Oh, I do hope this isn't going to shock you. The owners are the members of the committee. But lots of the young wives on the estate are, um, involved. The committee is restricted to owners, you see. But the rest of us – well, we're the pets.' She touched the collar at Jessica's neck and gazed earnestly down into Jessica's eyes.

Jessica couldn't comprehend Mel's meaning. It made no sense. 'Are you on the committee?' she asked, trying to gather more information and to give herself time to understand what she was being told.

'Not yet,' Mel said. She stroked Jessica's face. 'But I might be soon, with your help. At the moment I'm still a pet. That's why I wear my collar. My owner is Lydia Henshaw, at number eighteen. She's very nice.'

Now Jessica was utterly confused. She could imagine only that the women of Hillingbury had organised themselves into some sort of feudal hierarchy in which the newcomers acted as servants for the long-standing residents. 'That sounds awful,' she murmured.

'Not at all,' Mel said. 'You still don't understand, do you? I quite like being Lydia's pet. And anyway, you can't become an owner until you've been a pet. It's the first step towards being on the committee.'

It still seemed to Jessica a strange and unfair system. She assumed that the women who were called pets had to run errands and do skivvying for their owners. 'What do you have to do for her?' she asked. 'Is it hard work?'

Mel laughed. 'You silly thing,' she said. 'It's not work at all. It's more like playing. But I'll give you a demonstration, if you like. We can do the thing that an owner and her pet do most often. After all, you're still pretending to be my maid, aren't you?' She ruffled the lace frill on the front of Jessica's apron, making Jessica gasp as the rough material brushed against her nipples.

This was more interesting than being told about some stuffy committee. 'Yes,' Jessica said, and then felt a thrill as she added, 'Yes, ma'am, I'm still your maid.'

'Then undo the rest of the buttons on my dress,' Mel said. 'And be quick about it, girl.'

Jessica was becoming used to the quivering excitement she felt when Matt or Mel gave her instructions to do something naughty. Eagerly she unfastened the remaining buttons, until the dress was open from neck to hem. Mel was wearing nothing else.

'Get off the sofa,' Mel said. 'A maid shouldn't sit on the best furniture. Kneel on the floor.'

Jessica scrambled off the sofa. Mel moved to the centre seat, lifting the dress from beneath her as she did so. 'Look at me,' she said to Jessica, and she lay back against the cushions, spread wide the opened dress, brought her heels up to rest on the front of the seat, and slowly parted her thighs.

Jessica stared in amazement. She had never seen anyone behave in such a brazen manner – except herself, she thought, when instructed by Matt. Her eyes were level with Mel's sex, and although she knew she should turn away, she was frozen in surprise. And Mel had, in any case, told her to look.

Mel's thighs, pale and flawless, opened to reveal a sex that was completely hairless. The outer labia were plump, and only a little ruddier than Mel's general complexion. As Mel's knees fell towards the seat of the sofa, the outer labia parted to reveal delicate fronds of pale pink, glistening with moisture. The tip of Mel's clitoris gleamed like a pearl from beneath its sheath. Jessica had seen women exposing themselves in this way only in the dog-eared pages of a magazine she had once found.

She tore her gaze from between Mel's thighs, and found Mel looking at her with an amused expression. 'Well?' Mel said.

Jessica didn't know what Mel expected her to say or do. 'You're very pretty down there,' she said. 'And you've got no hair.'

'Lydia likes me to be smooth,' Mel said. She laughed. 'Poor old Keith got a surprise when I first shaved myself. I had to say I'd done it for him, of course. I think he found it rather weird. But Jessica, come a little closer. I want you to touch me.'

Jessica shuffled forwards on her knees. The scent of Mel's perfumed skin mingled with the musky aroma of her sex and made Jessica's senses swim. 'You mean, touch you here,' she said, hesitantly extending a hand.

'Yes, of course,' Mel said. 'Stroke the edges first. I like that. Then you can put your fingers inside. Don't touch my clit, though. Not yet.'

'Mel,' Jessica said, 'I've never –' She shook her head slightly, amazed at finding herself on her knees with her hands and face hovering over another woman's open sex, and equally amazed at her willingness to proceed.

But Mel's plump, pink labia were, indeed, very pretty, and very enticing, and Jessica knew that she was going to do it. She was going to touch Mel's private parts. She had never before touched any vulva other than her own.

Jessica felt Mel shiver when she placed the tips of her fingers against Mel's hairless labia. She stroked downwards, very gently, again and again, and heard Mel sigh. In silent fascination she watched her fingers moving, and Mel's labia swelling, and the little tip of Mel's clitoris nosing its way from beneath its covering. She rested her cheek against the smooth inside of Mel's thigh, and it seemed entirely natural to turn her head a little from time to time and to plant little kisses on the alabaster skin. Mel's scent was intoxicating, and Jessica felt her own sex unfurling and moistening.

'Oh, that is nice, Jess,' Mel breathed. 'Would you like to feel how wet you're making me?'

Jessica could see the clear liquid that was gathering in the folds of skin between Mel's parted sex-lips. She put her fingers there, and Mel shivered again, and once again when Jessica's fingers pressed inwards, opening the entrance of Mel's sopping vagina.

'Now then,' Mel said, 'it's one thing to have my pet scrabbling at me with her paws. But there's something that feels even better. Can you guess what I want you to do next, Jess?'

Jessica understood. Mel wanted her to perform oral sex. And she found that she didn't mind at all. She knew how wonderful it was to be kissed and licked down there. When she and Brian had first become lovers they had done oral sex quite frequently, and she had never understood why that sort of thing had stopped after they were married.

Even so, Jessica had never expected to be required to put her mouth on a woman's private parts. She told herself that it was silly to find the idea strange, and that the important thing was to concentrate on giving pleasure to Mel. She lowered her head towards the warm, moist source of Mel's musky scent.

Her first kiss was tentative: she let her lips touch the bare skin of Mel's pubic mound, above the beginning of the pink-lipped slit. It was rewarding to feel Mel tremble and hear her gasp with each movement of her mouth. She parted her lips and let the tip of her tongue protrude, and lapped with flickering licks down towards Mel's clitoris. She circled her tongue around the pearl, not quite touching it. She kissed, and then gently nibbled, each of Mel's outer labia in turn.

'That's very good,' Mel whispered. 'It's so much better with a woman, Jess. You know just what to do.'

Jessica lifted her head. 'Is this what pets do for their owners, then?' she asked.

Mel smiled mischievously. Jessica saw that she was blushing. 'It's what I do for Lydia,' Mel said. 'She just loves it. And I can certainly understand why. Please carry on.'

Jessica heard Mel gasp, 'Oh, yes!' as she once again pressed her open mouth to Mel's sex. She extended her tongue into Mel's vagina, and was gratified to feel Mel squirm and thrust her hips forwards. Mel's liquid tasted simultaneously bitter and sweet: not unpleasant in the slightest. In fact, Jessica decided that she could easily develop a taste for Mel's delicious juices.

'All pets do this for their owners at some time or other,' Mel said. 'But most of the owners like their pets to do other things as well. I think I'm lucky to have Lydia as my owner. As long as I give her plenty of licking, she's very good to me.'

Jessica, contentedly teasing Mel's wet sex with her lips and tongue, wondered vaguely what other things a pet might be called on to do. She thought it would be interesting to find out.

'Jess, stop a moment,' Mel suddenly said. 'If you're pretending to be my pet, we ought to do this properly. Pass me my bag again.'

Jessica lifted her head. Her lips, her chin and the tip of her nose were wet with Mel's juice. Mel's sex was as open and wet as a blown rose after a rainstorm, its vaginal entrance a gaping sea-cave. Jessica wanted only to plunge her face into it again, but she grabbed Mel's shoulder bag and lifted it up. Once she felt Mel take the weight of the bag from her, Jessica bent once again to her task. She wanted to drown in the warmth and movement of Mel's sex.

Therefore she didn't see what Mel took from the vanity-case that she kept inside her bag. She merely felt Mel's fingers brushing aside her hair, and plucking at the back of the collar. She heard a click.

'This is my lead,' Mel said. 'It matches the collar. Lydia puts it on me sometimes when we go for walks in the countryside, but I don't wear it as often as some of the other pets wear theirs.'

Jessica felt her insides flutter with excitement. There was something delightfully wicked about being on a leash. She really was Mel's pet now, and under Mel's control. Mel tugged experimentally on the lead, and Jessica's face was pulled more tightly against Mel's sex. Mel kept the lead taut, and Jessica couldn't pull back. She licked with renewed enthusiasm, and rubbed her face into Mel's delicate membranes.

Jessica was not surprised to find that she didn't mind performing oral sex on a woman. But she hadn't been prepared to discover that she would enjoy it herself. It was the collar and the lead, she realised: they made her feel that she had no choice but to obey Mel's whims. She was Mel's pet; Mel's slave. And that idea made her head spin, and her nipples stiffen, and her sex pulse with warm, wet excitement.

'Oh, Jess,' Mel cried out. 'I think I'm going to come. Lick round my clit, now, please. Oh, my goodness, that's it. That's fantastic. I'm nearly there. Lydia didn't say I could, but I'm sure she won't mind. She won't have to. It's too late. Here I come.'

Mel pulled on the lead, crushing Jessica's face into her. Jessica could hardly breathe, and couldn't open her mouth to lick. She could only rotate her face, grinding her nose and mouth against Mel's sex. Mel's gasps and cries came louder and faster, and then Jessica felt Mel's body vibrating with a crescendo of spasms that, once they had reached their peak, died away gradually as Mel sighed and released her grip on the lead.

Jessica felt almost as elated and exhausted as if she had had an orgasm herself. She kneeled back on her heels and shook her head. She looked up to find Mel, with her legs still parted, looking down at her.

'That was wonderful, Jess,' she said. 'And now you know a bit of what it's like to be a pet. Come and sit on my lap again.'

Jessica hurried to obey. Her body was still electric with desire, and she wanted to feel Mel's hands and lips touching her again.

'You don't mind wearing the collar and the lead?' Mel asked, stroking Jessica's breasts with the loop of blue leather that made up the handle of the leash.

'No,' Jessica said. 'Not at all.' She wondered whether she ought to admit that wearing the collar and lead excited her.

'That's good,' Mel said. 'Your face is all wet and sticky,' she went on with a giggle. 'I'll have to kiss you until it's clean.' She pressed her open mouth against Jessica's. After a few moments she pulled away to say, 'I taste nice,' with a grin, and then she resumed kissing and licking Jessica's mouth.

After a while her kisses became less intense, and she began to interrupt them in order to talk. 'So, Jess, now that you understand something about the Hillingbury Young Wives' Association Pet Owners' Committee, the question is: do you want to be a part of it? Will you be my pet? Please say yes. I know we'd have lots of fun together, and I promise I won't be an inconsiderate or cruel owner.'

There could be only one answer, Jessica realised, even though she had felt a pang of disappointment when Mel had, no doubt with the best of intentions, promised not to be cruel. To wear a collar, and to be instructed in all sorts of sex games, were exactly the things that Jessica wanted.

'But you're a pet,' she pointed out. 'Not an owner.'

'I'm a pet now,' Mel said. 'But I've reached the top of the list. And that means it's my turn to try to persuade the next newcomer to the estate to become my pet. And you're the newcomer. And I'm so glad it's you, Jess, because you're so slim and lovely. All the other owners will be madly envious of me.'

'What will happen if I refuse?' Jessica said.

Mel looked anguished. 'Oh, don't even talk about it,' she begged. 'If you refuse, I'll stay as Lydia's pet. And I'll go to the bottom of the list. It will be years before I have another opportunity to get on the committee. Please, please, Jess: say yes. I'll be such a kind owner, and we'll both benefit. I'll become an owner, and I'll be on the committee, and you'll have made your first step into Hillingbury society. If you're not an owner or a pet, you're nobody. And you can't become an owner until you've been a pet.'

'And if I say yes,' Jessica said, cuddling against Mel's body, 'what will become of Lydia? I mean, she won't have a pet any more, will she?'

'Oh, you're being beastly,' Mel cried. 'I wish you'd tell me. You're going to be my pet, aren't you, Jess? You absolutely must. Lydia will be all right. It's true that I'm her only pet. Most of the other owners have two or even three. That's why I'm so grateful to her. A different owner in her position would have done everything she could to stop her pet becoming an owner. But Lydia was really sweet about it. I know how much she likes owning me, and I've always done my best to be a good pet, but she realises how long I'll have to wait until I get another chance. So she's been incredibly generous, and given me loads of help and encouragement. It isn't easy, after three years of being a pet, to think and act like an owner. I'll have to be strict with you, you know, Jess, if you misbehave.'

'That's all right,' Jessica murmured. She wanted Mel to be strict.

'Anyway, Lydia's already arranged to borrow Vicki, one of Helen Travers' pets. And of course an owner who loses a pet, for any reason, goes straight to the top of the list. Lydia will be the one to recruit the next newcomer. So you see, everything's organised. There's absolutely no reason not to say yes, and then you'll be my pet and I'll be an owner at last.'

Mel was right. There was no reason at all for Jessica to hesitate. 'All right, then,' she said. 'I agree. I'll be your pet. But you must promise to play lots of games with me, just like we have today.'

Mel's blue eyes were bright with tears of happiness. 'I'll be the best owner a pet could wish for,' she vowed. She rained kisses on Jessica's face. 'We'll play every day. I'll let you lick me and, if you're good, sometimes I'll lick you. I can't wait to show you off to the other owners. But we'd better wait until you've had a bit of training, I suppose.'

Jessica struggled free from Mel's enthusiastic caresses. 'Training?' she said. And then she remembered the enigmatic conversation she had conducted with the worryingly stern shopkeeper. 'Mrs Morgan,' she murmured.

'That's right,' Mel said. 'Jess, you're so clever. I'm going to have to keep my eyes on you. Yes, I'll have to book you some sessions with Mrs Morgan. She's a bit of a tyrant, and at first I'm sure you'll think she's being too strict, but it's worth it in the end. And I'm certainly not going to be seen with a pet who's less well behaved than everyone else's. So I'm afraid you'll have to endure

Mrs Morgan and her lessons.' She looked at Jessica defiantly, as though daring Jessica to object.

But although Jessica was daunted by the idea of being trained by the formidable Mrs Morgan, she couldn't deny that she was excited too. So she merely nodded, and said, 'All right. I don't mind.'

Mel threw her arms around Jessica's neck and hugged her. 'Oh, Jess,' she exclaimed, 'I knew I could count on you. You're going to be the best pet in Hillingbury. We'll look spectacular together. Now, stand up, and help me get dressed.'

Jessica's body was still throbbing with passion, and she was still trying to order her thoughts about suddenly becoming Mel's pet. She would have happily have spent another hour in Mel's arms. But Mel's mind was on other things.

'I've got so many things to do,' Mel said, fretting as Jessica fumbled with the buttons of her dress. 'I'll have to talk to Lydia first, of course. And then I ought to see Mrs Morgan. Will Lydia tell Bella Northrop, or should I? And I'll have to start thinking about the garden.'

'The garden?' Jessica said.

Mel smiled contentedly. 'Members of the committee,' she said, 'are allowed to have summer houses. And swimming-pools, if they want them.'

'I see,' Jessica said. Although she was delighted with the morning's events and decisions, she felt a little put out that Mel was more interested in garden improvements than she was with the prospect of having Jessica as her pet.

'There's one more thing,' Mel said at the front door. 'Now, what was it? Of course! I have to impress on you that the committee, and the whole business of owners and pets, and everything we do, must remain absolutely secret. You mustn't tell anyone – not even your husband.'

'Of course,' Jessica assured her. There was no possibility that she would tell Brian that she was now a pet, and owned by the one of the neighbours. He simply wouldn't understand. 'I won't tell a soul.'

Except, she thought as she closed the door, I suppose there would be no harm in telling Matt. After all, he's not a Hillingbury resident. And if I don't tell him about the naughty things I get up to, he won't have a pretext for punishing me. And I do want him to punish me again. And again and again.

When she touched herself between her thighs she shook so much that she had to lean against the door for support. She could hardly wait until it was time to visit the Hillingbury Health and Exercise Club again.

By the time Jessica was at the club, changing nervously into her ridiculously skimpy shorts and T-shirt, she had decided that it would be wrong to tell Matt about Mel and the committee. It wasn't worth jeopardising her position, even though it was lowly, in Hillingbury society; and her relationship with Mel offered the prospect of months, if not years, of naughty fun, and it would be silly to risk that just in order to get another punishment from her supercilious mentor. In any case, she told herself, she could easily make up a story that would provide Matt with a pretext for disciplining her.

As she bent and stretched, under Matt's watchful gaze; as she ran and rowed and cycled on the machines in the gym; as she panted and perspired and became more and more aroused anticipating the inevitable interview in Matt's office, she felt her resolution weakening. After all, she had already told him about her first morning with Mel. He would expect her to have more news.

Her mentor seemed even more distant than usual. No matter how much she exerted herself in her exercises, and no matter how often she smiled at him, and pushed her breasts and her bottom towards him, he seemed dissatisfied with her performance. His eyes never left her body, and the bulge in the front of his shorts showed that he liked what he saw, but his face remained impassive and his tone was brusque. Apart from the shorts his body was uncovered, and the sight of his strong arms crossed over his muscular torso only added to Jessica's yearning for him. She knew that the only way to please him, and to get what she wanted from him, was to submit to his instructions. And how could she be entirely his slave if she didn't tell him everything that had happened to her?

'That will do for today,' Matt announced at last. 'You've exercised reasonably proficiently. I hope you've brought a swimming-costume today. You should shower and swim, and use the Turkish baths, after strenuous activity.'

Didn't he want to interview her? Jessica could hardly believe her ears. 'Shall I come to the office afterwards?' she asked in a small voice.

He smiled coldly. 'By all means,' he said. 'If you have any misdemeanours to report. There's no hurry, though. Enjoy the club's facilities. When you're ready, you'll find me in the dance exercise room.'

Jessica tried to prolong each stage of her mentor's suggested relaxation programme. She took a shower in the changing-room, pulled on her swimming-costume, and made herself complete five lengths of the pool. She stood under the shower again, then wrapped herself in a towel, and spent some time in the steam room of the Turkish baths. She tried to think of anything but Matt's hard body and handsome features; anything but the thought of kneeling before him and displaying her naked body to him; anything but the smack of his hand and the cruel sting of the wooden ruler on her bottom. It was no good: she could think of nothing else, and she was so desperate for him and his discipline that her sex was throbbing and leaking.

She stood up and gathered the towel around her. There was no point in delaying any longer. She knew what she wanted.

In the changing-room she did her best to dry and brush out her long, dark hair. With trembling hands she applied a little make-up to her lips and eyes. What should she wear? She smiled to herself. She would be standing before him naked soon enough. She wrapped herself once more in the towel, and set out to find the dance exercise room.

As she tiptoed along the bright, tiled corridors she realised that she was no longer the only member in the club. She heard voices from behind the door to the Turkish baths; someone was splashing in the pool. A middle-aged woman, presumably on the staff of the club, was standing behind the desk in Matt's usual place.

Jessica was nervous. What if she were seen? She told herself to be calm. There was nothing remarkable in the sight of a member walking through the club with a towel around her.

She came to a door whose sign said that it led into the dance exercise room. This was a part of the club that Matt had not shown her. She didn't know whether she should knock. She decided she would.

'Just a moment.' It was Matt's voice. Jessica's heart was thumping in her chest while she waited. He seemed to like to make her wait. 'Come in!' he called.

She entered a large, almost empty room. Three of its walls were covered with mirrors, so that it seemed endlessly vast. The only item of furniture was an upholstered, leather-covered armchair, which Matt had placed facing one of the mirrored walls. He was standing beside it. In his right hand he was holding the long, wooden ruler. He was tapping the end of it against the side of the chair.

'You'd better lock the door,' he said. 'And take off that towel.'

Jessica stood indecisively by the door. This was very different from the intimate atmosphere of the office.

Today there would be no pretence that Matt was helping her to exercise. There was just the big, empty room, her naked body, Matt's body almost as unclothed, and the wickedly flexible ruler. She bridled at his presumption that she was there simply to be punished. But the warmth of her sex told her that she wanted just that. If she turned the key in the lock, she would be his prisoner, his plaything.

She locked the door, and let the towel fall to the floor.

'Come here,' Matt said, tapping the end of the ruler on the matting between the chair and the wall. 'Face the mirror. Hands behind your back.'

No matter which way she turned, the mirrored walls showed her, naked, walking towards him. The distance from the door to the opposite side of the room seemed infinite. She liked to look at her own body, but she had never before felt this exposed. Her legs were unsteady by the time she reached his side. She faced the wall, clasped her hands together in the small of her back, and stared at her reflection. Her breasts seemed even more prominent than usual, and her nipples were erect. She moved her legs apart slightly, and felt cool air on the warm, damp membranes of her sex.

'I think it's time we faced a few facts,' Matt announced. 'Your body is in good shape. Your arms, legs and stomach are slim. Your gluteal muscles, as I have established, are particularly firm.' The ruler rested across her bottom, and she shivered. The cold, hard edge moved to lie across her breasts. 'And the muscles of your torso provide excellent support. You don't need daily advice and encouragement in order to keep fit.'

What was he saying? Did he not want her, after all? But she knew that he desired her. And she wanted him. She dragged her gaze away from her reflection and turned to him. 'Mentor?' she said.

'And yet you return, day after day.' He smiled briefly. 'Why, Jessica? What do you want?'

She looked from his face to his hand, gripping the ruler. 'You know,' she whispered.

'I want you to say it,' he said. 'I want to hear you ask for it. If you want me to be your mentor, you must be completely honest with me.'

Was that all he required? She was so relieved that he wasn't dismissing her that she found the words easy to say. 'I want you to punish me, Mentor,' she said, smiling at him. 'Please.' She was his prisoner: she would let him do whatever he desired.

'Very well,' he said. 'But you must be prepared to commit yourself to a regular regime. I will expect to see you here every day. And on each occasion you will, at the very least, provide me with a report of your sexual activities, submit to a chastisement, and masturbate according to my instructions. Is that understood?'

It sounded too good to be true. But Jessica wondered whether her position as Mel's pet would interfere with her daily visits to the club. 'I'll do my very best, Mentor,' she said.

'Then that will have to do,' Matt said. He sat in the chair. 'Turn to face me,' he said, 'and kneel. I want to hear about everything naughty that you've done since your last punishment.'

Jessica kneeled on the mat in front of the chair. Matt was sitting with his knees wide apart: if she had leaned forwards, she would have been able to rest her face on the taut front of his shorts.

'Don't forget,' he said, gesturing towards the mirrored wall behind her, 'I can see the back view as well.' He leaned forwards and took her left nipple between his fingers. 'So move your feet wide apart and push your bottom out. If your report is interesting I'll let you play with yourself while you're talking.'

He released her nipple, sat back in the chair and watched as she displayed herself as he had instructed. Jessica wondered whether Mel would be as domineering as her mentor: probably not, she concluded. Which was a pity, because simply obeying Matt's perverse orders was setting her senses on fire.

'That's good,' Matt said. 'You enjoy showing off, don't you? Now tell me what you've been getting up to.'

Jessica took a deep breath. This was the crucial moment. She could either betray her owner, or disobey her mentor. And if she did the latter, she wouldn't feel the ruler on her backside, which was already tingling in anticipation of the stinging strokes.

The decision was easily made. Jessica prided herself on her pragmatism. She would remain true to Mel, and the rules of the committee – except when she was here, in the club, with Matt. She would have the best of both strange new worlds: she could enjoy being Mel's pet and receive regular discipline from Matt.

She told Matt about Mel's visit to her house that morning. When she reached the point at which she took the scarf from Mel's neck to reveal the blue collar, Matt leaned forwards with particular interest. He was evidently pleased with her report, and he gave her permission to put her hand between her thighs so that she could stroke her sex as she continued to speak. She did so, but only very gently: kneeling naked before her mentor, in the expectation of a punishment, while remembering and describing everything that she and Mel had done that morning, had already aroused her so much that her sex was dripping. It would not take much to bring her to the point of a climax.

Matt made her recount all the details about the organisation of the committee, which she had thought he might find tedious. Instead he listened intently, making her repeat the names of committee members and their pets. While she was gratified that he was interested, she was slightly put out that he wasn't shocked by her story. It was such an unlikely tale that she had thought it possible he wouldn't believe it. But he didn't even seem surprised.

'So that's that,' she said as she finished her account. 'Mel's now my owner, and I'm her pet. But I don't think she's going to be very strict with me,' she added with a smile, 'so I'll definitely still want to see you.' And, she thought, I'm really very, very ready for my spanking now. Do it soon, Mentor, please.

Matt leaned forwards and took her breasts in his hands. She shuddered with desire. Be careful, please, she thought. I'm so close, if you keep touching and squeezing like that I won't be able to hold back.

'That was an excellent report, Jessica,' Matt said. He glanced in the mirror. 'And I can see that you've enjoyed giving it. It certainly merits a smacked bottom. Would you like that?'

She nodded. 'Yes, please, Mentor. Now, please.'

He laughed. 'All right. You've earned it.' He stood up, and stepped aside. His hand took her arm, and made her shiver again. 'Up on the chair, Jessica. Kneel on the seat, and press your breasts against the back. Push your bottom out. That's very good.'

There were no other preliminaries. As soon as she was positioned to his satisfaction, the punishment began.

When the ruler slashed across her buttocks she let out a loud cry – of relief and pleasure, more than of pain. Her cries lessened with each stroke, and when Matt paused after the sixth she lowered her head on to her hands, which were crossed on top of the back of the chair, shifted her knees as far apart as the seat would permit, and thrust her bottom further back.

'Oh, Mentor,' she sighed. 'That's wonderful. It's like coming home to a log fire after you've been out in the cold all day. I can't believe I've lasted twenty-four hours without any spanking at all. I wish my bottom could feel like this all the time.'

For once Matt's voice sounded amused and friendly. 'You'd like more, then?'

'Yes, please, Mentor,' she said dreamily. 'Lots more. But be careful,' she added. She put her right hand behind her back and placed it over her sex. Even this lightest of touches made her tremble. 'If you do it there, I can't guarantee that I won't start to come.'

'All right,' Matt said. 'I'll concentrate entirely on making your bottom red and sore.'

Jessica soon lost count of the strokes. It was strange, she mused, almost miraculous, that this rhythmic, flaming pain on her bottom should cause her such swooning, delirious pleasure – but then Matt began to ply the ruler more vigorously, and the pain and pleasure overwhelmed her so that she could only grip the back of the chair, and utter guttural cries, and enjoy the waves of harsh sensation as she offered her bottom for more – and more – and more.

She gradually became aware that the smacks had stopped. She lifted her head, brushed a hand through her unruly hair, and looked at her mentor. 'More?' she whispered.

'That's enough for today,' he said. 'I have to be careful not to make any marks that will last until you see your new owner. Anyway, it's time for us to have a different sort of fun. You're obviously ready for it.'

Jessica looked over her shoulder. The cheeks of her bottom were scarlet. Strands of clear, viscous liquid were hanging from the open pouch of her sex.

'You should be thoroughly ashamed of yourself,' Matt said. He placed his left hand on the small of her back, and held his right between her parted thighs and coated it with her juice. 'Keep still,' he said, and he began to anoint her sore bottom with the liquid he had collected.

The pleasure was almost too intense to bear. Jessica lowered her head on to her hands again and began to move her hips to match the circular caresses of his hand. She had always known that she had a pert, attractive bottom, but until she had met Matt she hadn't thought of it as an erogenous zone. To arouse herself she had always touched her breasts and her sex, and she had encouraged her lovers to do the same. And now just the thought of being spanked was enough to excite her, while the reality of a thorough punishment at Matt's hands was not merely the most thrilling way to become ready for sex, it was as good as an orgasm in itself.

'I had thought you'd had enough,' Matt said, running his fingers along the sopping slit of her sex and making her shudder, 'but I can see that you're quite incorrigibly naughty.'

He spanked her sore buttocks with his wet hand. Helplessly she moaned and writhed with each smack. It was too much; her bottom was already so sore that even the lightest of caresses stung – and Matt's smacks weren't light; and the splatting noise made by each smack echoed around the room and reminded her that there was an apparently endless flow of liquid seeping and dripping from her private parts. It wasn't too much; it was sublime.

And it became even better when he started to smack her right on her open sex. The smacks sounded even more embarrassingly wet, and they sent jolts of electric pleasure through her body. Her mind was so full of sensory delight that she could hardly think, but she knew that if he continued she would soon reach a climax. And what was he doing now? His left hand had slid into the cool, wet valley between her heated buttocks, and a finger was pressing against her little hole, and then sliding into it. It felt so glorious that she didn't make any protest. As Matt's finger probed into her, and his hand kept up a steady smacking of her sex, she felt herself being lifted towards the brink of a tall cliff. Just a little further – just a few smacks – and she would reach the edge, and fly off into ecstasy.

The spanking stopped.

'Not yet,' Matt said. 'I don't think it's reasonable that you should have all the fun. Take a few deep breaths and then, when you're feeling calm, come down from the chair and kneel in front of it again.'

Jessica could have screamed with frustration. She had been so close. Calm? It would take more than deep breathing exercises to make her calm. She needed to come. But she did as he instructed: even now, high on the cliff, surrounded by clouds of pleasure, it excited her to obey him. On unsteady limbs she descended from the chair to the floor, and she kneeled on the mat.

He stood between her and the chair. She looked up at him, and found him gazing down at her. 'You really are exceptionally gifted, Jessica,' he said. He looked beyond her, in the mirror, and Jessica knew that he was admiring her red, swollen bottom, smeared with the wetness that she could feel still oozing from her sex.

'Unbutton my shorts,' he said.

Her eyes were level with his waist. The front of his shorts was bulging so prominently that she wondered how the seams were staying together. She brought her hands up and began to struggle with the buttons.

She knew what he wanted. He would make her lick and suck his manhood, while he sat back in the chair and took in the view of her face as her lips caressed him and, in the mirror, the view of her glowing bottom.

'Do you know how to perform fellatio?' he said.

He was wearing nothing under the shorts. His erect penis sprang free, long and thick and hard. She held it against her cheek. It was hot, and smelled of maleness. 'Of course,' she said. She knew what to do. Or, at least, she used to know. One of her college boyfriends had expected her to do it, and although she found it very exciting she hadn't always acquiesced because she had thought that it wasn't really respectable. She had done it with Brian, too, as a special treat for him when they had become engaged to be married. But it had been several years since she had last done it. She tried to remember how to hold her mouth open. What should she do with her tongue? And should she start swallowing as soon as Matt started to come?

There was no question of refusing to do it, though. Matt was her mentor, and while she was with him she had to do as he told her. In her fantasies she was his prisoner, and he could make her do anything. That made it particularly exciting.

Matt's shorts fell to his ankles and he stepped out of them. He sat in the armchair with his muscular legs spread apart. She started to move forwards, but he stopped her. 'Stay there,' he said. 'Lean forwards and rest your arms on my thighs. Keep your back arched downwards, your knees as far apart as possible, and your bottom lifted up so that I can see it clearly in the mirror.'

'Yes, Mentor,' she said. How could he remain so emotionless while she was trembling with pent-up desire? His penis stood vertically in front of her face. A drop of clear fluid glistened at the tip of the swollen crown.

'Lick it,' he said. 'I'll tell you when you can take it into your mouth.'

Jessica did her best to ignore the throbbing of her sore bottom and the tingling nerves that seemed to connect her sex and her nipples. She concentrated on Matt's penis.

It jumped when her tongue touched it. She curled the fingers of her left hand around the shaft to keep it steady, and started to lick the shiny head.

The skin was soft and warm against her tongue. The clear fluid tasted of nothing but salt. Matt's erection was already big and hard, but she could feel it stiffening and growing even more as she licked and kissed its bulbous head.

'There's no rush,' Matt told her. 'I'm enjoying watching you.'

Jessica uttered a murmur of protest. She didn't want to wait. She wanted to take him in her mouth. She pulled back a little, and between little kisses on the tip of his penis she said, 'The ruler? Will it reach?'

He laughed, and leaned forwards, pushing the head of his penis into her mouth. 'No more talking from you,' he said. 'Suck my cock and make me come.' He leaned over her bowed head and cupped her breasts in his hands. He gripped, and squeezed, and didn't let go. 'I've done enough for you today,' he whispered. 'If you want more, you'll have to do it yourself. I can support you like this, so your right hand is free if you want to use it.'

It took her some time to understand what he was suggesting. She had so many other sensations to think about. His hot, hard cock was filling her mouth: she could slide her tongue from side to side, and by moving her head back and forth she could press the bell of his glans against the roof of her mouth. The taste and smell of him made her dizzy with lust. His fingers were like bands of steel about her breasts. But still she couldn't ignore the pulsing heat of her bottom and her sex.

What had he said? She could use her right hand? He wanted her to play with herself, then. But that wasn't it. She had been on the point of starting an orgasm, and he had been spanking her sex. That's what she wanted: more spanking. And she was to do it herself.

She couldn't. It would be too humiliating. But he was the pirate captain; she was the captive maiden. She had no choice.

Slowly she moved her right arm from his thigh. He was right: his hands, clenched around her breasts, supported her upper body. In fact she found that he was able to lift and lower her slightly, so that the head of his penis slid back and forth inside her mouth. He was still leaning forwards, so that when he lifted her up the top of her head brushed against his chest. He was all around her, and filling her mouth. She surrendered to the feeling of being confined and controlled.

She reached behind herself. Her hand encountered the curve of her right buttock. She gasped at the cool touch on her inflamed skin. Her hand slid into the valley, and went lower, and found the hot, wet, open membranes of her sex. She caressed herself, and felt her body shivering as tremors of pleasure radiated from her sex. Immediately she was once again almost at the cliff-top. The fingers of her left hand tightened around his shaft, and she began nodding her head and lapping with her tongue against the base of his glans.

She couldn't wait any longer. She lifted her right hand from between her thighs, and slapped it down again. A loud, wet slap. Yes! That was it. Not painful. A jolt of pure sensation. She did it again. This time the tips of her fingers landed around the tip of her clitoris, and the explosion of pleasure made her shudder. If Matt hadn't been holding her she would have curled her body into a ball; if her mouth had not been full of his manhood she would have cried out.

She was spanking herself. She was smacking her own sex, while her mentor used her mouth. In a moment of clarity between the bursts of pleasure she pictured what Matt could see in the mirror. This was more humiliating than letting him punish her; more humiliating than masturbating while he watched. She couldn't imagine anything more degrading. And she loved it. She smacked herself harder and faster. Each smack took her another step higher, closer to the brink. She couldn't concentrate on licking him any longer; there was nothing but the unbearable spasms of delight that made her body shudder, again and again.

She was on the edge. Another smack, and another, and her body was racked with explosive pulses of ecstasy. She was soaring through the clouds. Dimly she heard muffled, guttural noises, and then realised that she was the source. The pulses slowed, and she began floating downwards. It was like being in heaven.

She felt Matt's chest pressing against the top of her head, pushing the velvet hardness of his cock into the back of her mouth. 'Here I come,' he said, and her tongue felt the underside of his erection throb.

She tried to cry out again. She hadn't expected the jet of semen to flood into her throat with such force. She swallowed, and swallowed again, but the salty liquid overwhelmed her. His strong hands lifted her, and the next jet coated her tongue. Then the head of his penis slipped from her mouth, and he held her still as pulses of semen splashed on to her lips and chin. She choked, and swallowed again, and tried to control her breathing. Matt's semen was less viscous than any she remembered: almost as liquid as water, but hot and salty. And there was so much of it! He had filled her mouth and covered the lower half of her face.

'That was very good, Jessica,' he said. 'I suggest you shower again before you go home. I'll expect to see you tomorrow.'

As Jessica strolled back to her house she glanced behind her, partly because she expected to see Brian's train arriving in the station at any moment, and partly to reassure herself that the club was real, and that she hadn't imagined the afternoon she had spent with Matt.

She didn't see the train, but as she reached her front gate she heard the distant clatter of its wheels on the track. She was home well before Brian, then: she would have time to change into sensible clothes – clothes that would conceal from him the redness of her bottom and the marks of Matt's fingers on her breasts. There might even be time, as she changed, for her to lie on the bed, with the wardrobe door open so that she could see herself in its mirror, and touch herself again.

And she didn't need to see the club to know that it, and her mentor, were real. Her buttocks were so sore that she would have to be careful not to wince each time she sat down, and she could still taste Matt on her lips.

She smiled as she closed the front door behind her. She was even more sure, now, that she was going to enjoy living in the suburbs.

Four

When Jessica opened her front door the next morning it was a different Mel who strode proprietorially into the hall. Instead of a simple, button-through frock she was wearing a tailored suit: a skirt and jacket of pale-blue silk. And around her neck, instead of a scarf and a collar, she had a silver chain and pendant. Her blonde hair had been styled into a mass of curls.

'Don't look so surprised,' she told Jessica. 'I've been dying to be allowed to wear some of my smart clothes. And don't you have a kiss for your owner?'

'Oh, yes,' Jessica said eagerly, and she let Mel fold her in an embrace. As they kissed, Jessica began to undo the buttons of Mel's crisp white blouse.

'Stop it, Jess,' Mel said. 'We don't have time for that. I've made an appointment for you to see Mrs Morgan. And she doesn't like to be kept waiting. We'll have to get you dressed.'

Jessica had put on nothing but a shirt, in the expectation that Mel would want to see her naked as quickly as possible, and she felt rejected and disappointed. She couldn't say it to Mel, but she preferred Mel's previous choices of clothes and make-up and hairstyle. And she didn't want to get dressed and go out; she wanted to stay in and play games with her new owner.

'Come along,' Mel said, and she led the way upstairs.

As Mel chose clothes from the wardrobe for Jessica to wear, Jessica began to feel excited again. It was mortifying to have to stand and watch while Mel inspected every garment, and made disparaging remarks about most of them, but it brought home to Jessica her new status as a mere pet. And it soon became clear that Mel didn't intend Jessica to wear very much: she picked out a short, pleated skirt, a jersey top and a pair of wedge-heeled sandals. She watched as Jessica changed into them.

'That's better,' Mel said. 'It's another warm day, so you won't need anything else. Come and stand next to me.'

The two women stood side by side and looked at their reflection in the mirror.

'There,' Mel said. 'Everyone will realise that I'm your owner, and that you're my pretty little pet. Everyone who matters, anyway.'

I'm not that little, Jessica thought. But she had to admit that the clothes she was wearing made her look young and, indeed, even small, compared to the sophisticated lady beside her. She was glad that her skin looked always naturally tanned, as her legs, naked from her ankles to halfway up her thighs, felt very exposed. The top, made of soft, stretchy fabric, moulded itself to her breasts so that it was obvious she was wearing nothing under it.

'Should I have a collar?' she asked. It would be the finishing touch to her costume. It would make her look and feel utterly subservient.

'Not yet,' Mel said. 'I'll choose one for you once you've had your basic training. I'll present you to the committee and, if they approve – and I'm sure they will – you'll be awarded your collar. Now we must be on our way.'

Both Mel and Jessica were disappointed that they met no one as they walked from Jessica's house to the shop.

Mel admitted that she wanted to be seen as an owner with a pet, while Jessica knew that the embarrassment of being noticed would arouse her.

With the bell above the door still tinkling behind them, Mel and Jessica waited in the shop for Mrs Morgan to appear.

'I have to confess,' Mel whispered, 'that I still find this place rather daunting. I must remember that, now I'm an owner, Mrs Morgan is my employee and not my trainer. You will be good, won't you, Jess? The others are dying to see you, but first you must learn at least a little about how to behave as a pet. Mrs Morgan is a bit of a disciplinarian, but it's all for your own good. Even so, I don't like to think of leaving you with her.'

A disciplinarian! Jessica's heart beat faster, and she felt a tingling warmth inside her sex. But all she said was, 'You're leaving?'

'Of course,' Mel exclaimed. 'I've got things to do. I'm meeting Bella Northrop to learn all about how the committee operates. Then I want to ask some of the other owners about the best workmen to employ. Should I have the patio enlarged first, or should I have a conservatory built? There's a lot to think about when you're an owner.'

'I've heard about your success, Melanie.' Mrs Morgan had entered the shop silently, and was standing behind the counter. 'You've done well.' Jessica thought that Mrs Morgan sounded rather surprised that Mel had managed to recruit a pet on her first attempt. She couldn't have known that Jessica had needed almost no persuasion. 'And you've had the good fortune to obtain a very pretty pet.'

She came from behind the counter and stood in front of Jessica. She was taller than Jessica, and stood closer than Jessica found comfortable. Jessica tried glancing up at her, but was deterred by the steady gaze of her light-blue eyes. And so Jessica was left staring at the front of the shopkeeper's white coat, where it was pushed forward by her large breasts. Once again Jessica formed the impression that the woman was wearing nothing else.

'May I?' Mrs Morgan said.

'Of course,' Mel replied.

Then Jessica stifled a cry of surprise as Mrs Morgan grasped the bottom of her jersey and pulled it up to her neck. Her breasts felt suddenly cold, and jiggled for a moment before coming to rest. To Jessica's shame she felt her nipples hardening.

'Very pretty indeed,' Mrs Morgan said. She cupped Jessica's left breast in her hand and squeezed it. She nodded and murmured her approval. Then she plucked up the hem of Jessica's skirt, at the front and then at the back. 'Very promising,' she said, as if reluctant to be more effusive. 'Still, the pretty ones can be difficult to train.'

'Don't be too hard on her,' Mel pleaded.

'It's all right,' Jessica whispered. 'I don't mind.' But Mel and Mrs Morgan ignored her.

'I'll do what's necessary, Melanie,' Mrs Morgan said. 'I take the view that it's wise to be strict with the pretty ones – as I'm sure you remember. It's important to let them know who's in charge, before they start getting airs.' She looked pointedly at Mel's silk suit.

Mel blushed. 'I'm sure you know best, Mrs Morgan,' she said. She took a deep breath and made for the door. 'After all, your expertise is what we owners pay you for.' She was through the door before Mrs Morgan could reply.

Mrs Morgan chuckled. She went to the door, locked it, and turned round the hanging sign so that it said CLOSED.

'Follow me,' she told Jessica. 'We might as well get started immediately.'

As Jessica followed Mrs Morgan into the corridors beyond the shop, she wondered whether she should pull down her top. Her breasts were still exposed.

'Don't bother,' Mrs Morgan called over her shoulder, as if she had read Jessica's mind. 'You'll not be wearing a stitch for most of today.'

The house behind the shop was as big and labyrinthine as a country mansion. The corridors were panelled with oak and had dark-red carpets laid along their polished wooden floors. Mrs Morgan, looking like a tall, slim, white-clad ghost, glided along them ahead of Jessica, who had almost to run to keep up.

'This is the training room,' Mrs Morgan said, pushing open one of the heavy wooden doors. 'In you go.'

Jessica blinked in the sudden light. She entered a vast room, one side of which consisted of glazed panels through which she could see a veranda, and beyond that a large, walled garden.

'We won't use most of this equipment today,' Mrs Morgan said. 'Some of the owners hire this room for competitions, and so forth, when the weather isn't good enough for outdoor events.'

'Competitions?' Jessica asked.

'You'll find out in due time,' Mrs Morgan replied. 'Now get those clothes off and I'll have a good look at you.'

It didn't take long for Jessica to undo her sandals, pull off her jersey, and unfasten her skirt. She didn't even try to prolong her undressing: Mrs Morgan's commanding attitude was already awakening the physical responses that Jessica experienced when she was with her mentor, and she was looking forward to the delicious humiliation of submitting to being trained. She was nervous, and embarrassed about taking her clothes off, but these feelings only augmented her excitement.

She had time, in any case, to survey her surroundings. The large room's floor of polished wooden tiles was mostly covered with mats and rugs. At one end of the room there was an irregular line of armchairs and occasional tables: this, Jessica assumed, was where the owners would sit when they hired the room. Scattered across the rest of the floor was a remarkable assortment of objects: it looked as though the contents of a furniture store, an obstacle course and a children's playground had been placed at random on the mats and rugs. Jessica tried to imagine what kinds of competitions could be held in such surroundings, and her imaginings made her heart beat faster.

The room reminded her of the gymnasium at the Hillingbury Health and Exercise Club, even though it wasn't really similar, and that alone was enough to arouse her. When she saw, lying on a large desk in the centre of the room, some of the collars, leashes, canes and riding crops that Mrs Morgan sold in her shop, her breath caught in her mouth and she felt her nipples tighten. As she had hoped, it seemed that her training would entail wearing a collar and being punished.

'You'll learn all the pet positions today,' Mrs Morgan said, 'but we'll start with just one of the basic standing positions. Back straight, legs apart, hands on the back of your head. That's it. Now: let's have a look at you.'

Jessica stood still, looking forwards, while Mrs Morgan walked around her. She tried not to flinch or shiver when she felt Mrs Morgan's hand abruptly touching her breasts, her stomach, her hip, her bottom, and then her thighs. But she could do nothing to control the automatic reactions going on inside her, and she knew that she was getting wet.

'I wonder if Mel's a betting woman,' Mrs Morgan said, more to herself than to Jessica. 'You'll do well in the races. You've got the build for it.'

Jessica didn't know whether she should reply. 'Thank you,' she said.

Mrs Morgan laughed. 'I can see that before we proceed I'd better tell you how to address me. You must call me "Mistress". Is that clear?'

'Yes, Mistress,' Jessica said happily. This was getting better and better.

'Good. That's the usual way for a pet to address an owner, and you should use it unless you've been given other instructions. Some owners like their pets to address them in other ways.' It was clear from her tone that Mrs Morgan didn't approve of such deviations from the norm. 'I don't know whether Melanie will require you to use a specific form of address. But until and unless you're told otherwise, all owners are "Mistress" as far as you're concerned.'

'Yes, Mistress.'

'Good. I suspect that you're going to be a fast learner. The next thing, and the most important thing, is to learn the duties of a pet. They are as follows: obedience to your owner; eagerness to please your owner; appearance and behaviour at all times a credit to your owner. Repeat your duties.'

Jessica reiterated the words. It was easy to do, even though she knew that to say such things at all was very strange. And to find herself saying them while she was naked, and posing with her legs apart and her hands clenched behind her neck, was so remarkable that only a few days previously she could not have imagined the scene. Obedience; eagerness; appearance; behaviour. She heard the words coming from her mouth, and she noticed the tremor of desire in her voice.

'Very good,' Mrs Morgan said. 'Don't ever forget those precepts. Everything you do in Hillingbury must be governed by them. I'll test you again, later in the day, to make sure you've memorised them. Now come over to the desk.'

Jessica didn't know whether she should keep her hands behind her head. She decided that she would: appearance was one of the rules, and the position kept her breasts prominent. Their tips jiggled as she followed Mrs Morgan to the centre of the room. She stopped in front of the desk, and found herself looking down at an array of leather articles and implements of punishment.

When she moved her legs apart she felt the lips of her sex open. How many hours would it be before she could go to the club? How long before she could kneel before her mentor and ask for punishment? Her bottom was already tingling in anticipation. She was wet and ready now for anything he might want to do with her.

Mrs Morgan picked up several collars and held them against Jessica's throat. 'This one, I think, will do for now,' she said. She had selected one that was slightly wider than most, in a cream colour. Like all of them it had metal rings set into the circumference. 'If you're to be a pet,' Mrs Morgan went on, 'you must have a collar. Melanie will choose one for you that's to her taste, but this one will do while you're in training. It suits your colouring.' She paused. 'You don't seem surprised.'

'I've seen Mel's collar, Mistress,' Jessica said. 'I mean, my mistress's collar. And I've worn it.' Her voice dropped to a whisper. 'And her lead. And I, you know, I licked her.' She could feel her face burning as she blushed.

Mrs Morgan took Jessica's arms in her hands and lowered them. She studied Jessica's face as she toyed with the tips of Jessica's breasts, making the large, brown nipples stand out hard and proud. 'In that case,' she said, 'you've already learned a lot about being a pet. Some owners don't require much more than kissing and licking from their pets. I imagine you'll spend much of your time with your face between Melanie's legs.'

Jessica thought that she detected disapproval in Mrs Morgan's tone. Or perhaps she wanted to see whether Jessica had any doubts about submitting to such a regime. Jessica was determined not to be put off. 'That's all right,' she said. 'I like it. My mistress tastes nice.'

'Does she, indeed,' Mrs Morgan said. 'Well, it's good to hear that you're eager to please her. Now, I think I'd be more comfortable without this coat. Unbutton it.'

'Yes, Mistress,' Jessica said immediately, although she was daunted by the idea of touching the trainer.

Everything about Mrs Morgan – her imposing height, her short, fashionably styled hair, her piercing blue eyes, her stern countenance, her crisp, brilliantly white coat – seemed to repel intimate contact. With faltering fingers Jessica undid the top button of the coat, revealing more of Mrs Morgan's impressive cleavage.

'Oh!' Jessica exclaimed when she had undone the second button. Mrs Morgan was not, as Jessica had thought, naked under the coat. She was wearing some sort of undergarment. Intrigued and excited, Jessica hurried to unbutton the coat completely.

Mrs Morgan shrugged off the coat to reveal a costume that made Jessica gasp. She was wearing a corset, of black satin, that cinched her waist and emphasised the curves of her bosom and hips. Narrow cups of black lace supported, but did not cover, her large, spherical breasts, and suspenders of the same material held up sheer black stockings. Between the corset and the stocking-tops she was naked: Jessica saw that her light-brown pubic hair had been trimmed to a small V just above the top of the split of her sex.

In the white coat Mrs Morgan had appeared clinical and remote; without it she was simply intimidating. Standing before her Jessica felt very small and nervous – and almost as helplessly excited as when she kneeled before her mentor.

'That's better,' Mrs Morgan said. 'Now we can get down to business. Fasten the collar around your neck.' As she leaned forwards to pull Jessica's long hair aside, the tips of her breasts almost touched Jessica's face.

Jessica drew a deep breath and passed the collar around her neck. Like Mel's, its inside surface was padded, and because Jessica had a long neck the extra width of the collar was not uncomfortable. It fastened with a buckle.

'Some owners like to put the collar on,' Mrs Morgan said, 'while others will expect you to do it. Some owners have their pets wear collars almost all the time, at least during the day while the husbands are away. Others are less stringent. Some add a lock, to ensure that the pet keeps the collar on even when the owner isn't present. My view is that a pet should be collared for as much of the time as is possible. It reminds her of her status and her duties.'

'Yes, Mistress,' Jessica said. 'It does.' The leather encircling her neck made her feel very naughty and submissive, and ready to do anything she was told to do.

'It should be comfortable to wear,' Mrs Morgan went on, 'but sufficiently tight that you can't forget that it's there. This one seems about right,' she added, inserting a finger between the collar and Jessica's neck.

She stood back to look at Jessica. Jessica glanced up at her. She seemed satisfied with what she saw.

'The metal rings, as you already know,' she said, 'are for the attachment of a lead. It can be clipped to the collar at the front, the back or either side. But the rings can also be used, with chains and clips, to restrain a pet, or to secure a pet in a particular position. Some owners buy cuffs, matching the collar, for a pet's wrists and ankles. These also usually have metal rings set round them and, as I'm sure you can imagine, this makes it very easy to secure a pet in a wide variety of positions.'

Jessica could imagine it only too clearly. All her recently remembered fantasies about being tied up came flooding back to her. She vowed to try to get Matt to put her in chains, or at least ropes, next time he punished her.

'To sum up,' Mrs Morgan said, 'every pet has a collar, and must wear it at the very least when first presented to the committee and at other gatherings at which owners bring their pets for display. The extent to which a pet wears cuffs and other restraints is entirely at her owner's discretion. A pet's daytime clothing is also entirely a matter for her owner. Some of the owners devise very fanciful costumes for their pets. And there is an unwritten code for taking a pet outdoors: no underwear, of course, and short skirts. In the winter you'll find that owners allow their pets to wear warm coats while out of doors, but nothing else.

'Now,' Mrs Morgan said, 'I'll take you through the basic pet positions. All pets learn these, but some owners require their pets to learn more. I should mention at this point, I suppose, that it's highly likely that your training will not end with the basic sessions I've arranged with Melanie. If you learn quickly and you're obedient, you'll know enough to pass muster when Melanie presents you to the committee. But most owners have specific requirements for their pets, and I do a busy trade in individual tuition, either here or at the owners' homes. I'm sure I'll be a recurrent feature of your life as a pet.'

Mrs Morgan made her words sound threatening, but Jessica was thrilled. She already suspected that Mel would not prove to be a particularly demanding owner; the prospect of being taught by Mrs Morgan was much more interesting.

'Standing positions first,' Mrs Morgan announced, and Jessica found herself being put through a series of poses. In all of them she had to try to keep her breasts pushed out and her hands behind her back, so that they didn't obstruct her owner's access to her breasts, sex and bottom. There were only four positions, and her favourite was leaning forwards with her legs far apart, her knees slightly bent, her arms folded behind her back, and her head raised. It was a thoroughly undignified position, and quite uncomfortable to maintain for many minutes; it would also, Jessica thought, allow an owner to spank her thoroughly on her bottom, on the insides of her thighs, and on her sex. Just standing like that, with her muscles trembling with the exertion of keeping still, was making her wet. She wondered, with another thrill of shameful pleasure, how long it would be before Mrs Morgan realised that she was utterly aroused.

'On your knees,' Mrs Morgan ordered. 'When kneeling, as when standing, keep your legs apart unless instructed otherwise. Further apart than that, girl. That's better. Now, hands together, palms on the floor, between your knees. Arms straight. Curve your back in, and lower your bottom until it's almost touching the floor. Keep your head up. That's it.'

It was a demeaning position, and one that would be uncomfortable to maintain for very long. Jessica liked it, because she could tell that it made her bottom very prominent and it held her buttocks and her sex wide open, but she was worried that drops of the wetness that had been gathering inside her might begin to drip on to the floor. She knew that Matt would make her show him all the positions that she was learning, and as she kneeled it occurred to her that he might spank her in every position, too. The thought was enough to send a shiver through her body, and she gasped.

'Is there a problem, Jessica?' Mrs Morgan asked.

'Oh, no, Mistress,' Jessica said. 'I'm quite happy.'

'Are you, indeed?' Mrs Morgan said. In one stride she was behind Jessica. 'We'll see.'

Jessica jumped with surprise and cried out. Mrs Morgan's hand was pressed against her sex. Her fingers were pushing inside, and meeting no resistance. Just as quickly, the hand was withdrawn.

'Yes, you are happy, aren't you?' Mrs Morgan said. She stood again in front of Jessica. 'Very happy indeed, I'd say.' Her hand, almost touching Jessica's face, was slick with wetness. Jessica could smell the aroma of her own sex.

'Yes, Mistress,' Jessica said. 'I like being a pet.' She couldn't deny it, any more than she could deny that she had felt a thrill of pleasure when Mrs Morgan had pushed her fingers into her sex. Was it possible, Jessica wondered, that she was a lesbian? She had always believed that she was attracted only to men. But no: even though she enjoyed being the plaything of Mel and Mrs Morgan, it was Matt she wanted.

'Well, it looks as though it's going to be easy to train you,' Mrs Morgan said. 'Some new pets need quite a lot of persuasion. But in your case, I don't think I'll need this at all.'

Jessica looked up. Mrs Morgan had picked up from the desk a long, thin, flexible, wooden dowel. She flicked it through the air, making it sing.

Jessica felt as disappointed as the trainer sounded. If she was going to get the discipline she wanted, she would have to say something, no matter how embarrassing it was to confess to her desires. 'It would be a shame not to use it, Mistress,' she said, 'now that you've gone to the trouble of having it ready for me.'

There was a silence. Jessica felt her heart beating and her face burning. What would the trainer think of her?

'Well, well, well,' Mrs Morgan said slowly. 'You really are quite special, Jessica. I think, under the circumstances, that I might give that pert little bottom of yours the occasional taste of the cane. Just to make sure you're concentrating.'

'Thank you, Mistress,' Jessica said. She was entirely content. Now she was sure that the training session would be an undiluted pleasure. The only things missing were Matt's muscular body and his hard, hot penis. And, if there was time, she would enjoy those later.

'The position you're in,' Mrs Morgan said, 'is the first of the true pet positions. It's the closest that a woman can get to the position a dog or cat adopts when sitting upright: hindquarters on the floor, front paws together. Therefore I call it the sitting position, and you must adopt it whenever you are given the command to sit. You'll find that owners are used to using one-word commands, such as "sit" and "lie", when they want you to use the true pet positions. If you're required to sit in a human fashion, you'll be told to sit down, or to sit on the floor, and so on. But "sit", on its own, means you must immediately sit like a pet.'

'I understand, Mistress.'

'Good. Now we'll do "stand". That means you're to stand like a pet, on all fours. But, because it's difficult and ungainly to stand on your hands and feet, you'll stand on your hands and knees. Remember to keep your bottom pushed out and your legs apart. Ready? Stand!'

It's more like crawling than standing, Jessica thought. All she had to do was move her hands forwards, and her body went from vertical to horizontal. She dipped her back so that her bottom was lifted up. I hope, she thought, that Mrs Morgan realises that in this position I'm ready to be smacked. Her bottom felt very vulnerable. She waggled her hips.

Jessica need not have worried. The cane hissed through the air, and Jessica felt a stinging line across both buttocks. She uttered a sharp cry that became a long sigh of satisfaction. At last! It seemed like an age since she had last been punished. And the anticipation had made the moment even more delicious. She revelled in every moment, from the sound of the cane, to the sharp bite as it landed, to the slowly fading heat. She had been sexually excited all morning, since she had started to wait for Mel to arrive at her door, but one stroke of the cane was enough to lift her on to an even higher plane of arousal.

There were two more strokes, a little harder than the first. They were blissfully painful, and Jessica's bottom and sex began to glow with the fiery heat that only a spanking could kindle.

'Thank you, Mistress,' Jessica said. It was so wonderfully humiliating to be grateful for being punished. What could she do to demean herself even more? She thought of something. But did she dare to say it? She lifted a hand from the floor to sweep her hair off her left shoulder, which she looked over. Mrs Morgan was watching her. 'Excuse me, Mistress,' she said, 'but I ought to tell you that being spanked makes me very excited. Sexually, I mean. I hope you don't mind. It's just that sometimes I get so wet that I drip.'

There. She had said it. She looked at Mrs Morgan and anxiously awaited her response. What would the trainer think of her?

Mrs Morgan merely smiled. 'You're very lucky,' she said. Then a thoughtful expression appeared on her face. 'Are you spanked often?'

Jessica suddenly realised that her excitement had made her careless. She couldn't possibly tell Mrs Morgan about her visits to her mentor at the club. She was sure that the trainer wouldn't approve. And Mel would certainly not be prepared to share her pet. 'Oh, no, Mistress,' she said, trying to sound sad. 'Not often. And not recently. Only in my daydreams.'

'And what do you think of the reality of being smacked?' Mrs Morgan asked, and laid another stripe of fire across Jessica's bottom. 'Does it meet your expectations?' She swung the cane again.

'Oh! Yes!' Jessica gasped. 'Yes, Mistress. Thank you, Mistress.' But it's best of all, she thought, with Matt. He's so tall, and strong, and commanding. And he punishes me so hard.

Mrs Morgan told Jessica how to position herself on the floor when given the command 'lie'. Once again the idea was to copy the way in which a dog or cat would lie on the floor, in a Sphinx-like pose. Jessica's chin rested on her crossed forearms, her knees were drawn up to her sides, her breasts were pressed on to the floor, and her bottom was lifted up and spread obscenely wide. She was sure that by now her wetness was leaking freely from her sex, and Mrs Morgan only heightened

Jessica's arousal by administering another three strokes with the cane.

It was the next position, 'roll over', that gave Mrs Morgan the opportunity to make Jessica's bottom really smart. Jessica had to lie on her back with all four 'paws' in the air, and then she was instructed to use her hands to pull her knees up to her shoulders, so that her legs were doubled up and her bottom and her sex were on display. It was the most humiliating position yet, and one of which Mrs Morgan seemed particularly fond.

'You must learn to hold this position properly,' the trainer said, emphasising her point with strokes of the cane. 'Your owner will never win the pet parade unless you exhibit yourself fully open.' She made Jessica pull her knees higher up her body, and further apart, and closer to the floor, all the time lashing with wristy flicks at Jessica's tightly rounded bottom. She didn't spare the backs of Jessica's thighs, either, and many of the strokes landed across the open leaves of Jessica's sex.

Jessica, holding herself as open as possible and crying out almost continuously as the cane rose and fell, was in a state of ecstasy.

'You do enjoy this, don't you?' Mrs Morgan said. She had stopped whipping Jessica, and was instead trailing the end of the cane along the set channel of Jessica's sex. 'And so do I,' she added, pressing her hand against the front of her pubes. 'I think,' she said conspiratorially, 'that I'd better tell Melanie that you need extra tuition. Now, then: stand!'

Jessica rolled over on to her hands and knees. She swung her hips. Her bottom felt gloriously hot. She wondered whether Mrs Morgan was going to tell her to masturbate. Perhaps she would have to ask for permission to touch herself. She wanted to have an orgasm soon.

She felt the trainer's hand at her collar. Mrs Morgan clipped a lead to the metal ring at Jessica's throat.

'Now,' the trainer said, 'you must learn how to walk properly, at my heel.' Jessica felt a tug on the collar, and she started to move forwards. 'Lift your front paws. Keep your bottom high, and swing it from side to side as you walk. Your owner will want everyone to see what a pretty bottom her pet has. And keep your head up.'

The walk was short. Mrs Morgan stopped in front of a sofa and, still holding the leash, sat on it. She crossed her long, slim, black-stockinged legs, and sat back to look at Jessica. 'Sit!' she ordered. 'Now stand. And now lie. That's very good, Jessica.'

Jessica had remembered all the positions.

'Some of the owners,' Mrs Morgan said, 'are very insistent that their pets should behave like pet animals. They have mittens and boots and headdresses made for them, all of fur. The pets spend most of their time, during the day, on their hands and knees. Such owners call me in, of course, to provide the necessary additional training. Some pets find it very difficult to abandon the human ways of doing things. Other owners are much less particular. I don't imagine that Melanie will want you to be a pussycat or a lapdog. But there is one more pet position I'd like to teach you. It's 'beg'. I'm sure you've seen dogs get up on their hind legs to beg to their mistresses.'

The begging position was almost as demeaning as 'roll over'. Jessica had to squat, with her knees wide apart, and balance on her toes, while holding her hands uplifted and pressed together, as if she was praying.

'That's very good,' Mrs Morgan said. She uncrossed her legs, and very gradually moved them apart. She lifted her feet, and dug the heels of her shoes into the upholstery. The lips of her sex were parted and were glistening with her juice. 'And what are you begging for, Jessica?' she said. 'What do pets love to do for their mistresses?' She tugged on the leash, so that Jessica almost toppled forwards.

Jessica knew what the trainer wanted. 'I'd like to lick you, please, Mistress,' she said. It was true. Jessica would have preferred more spanking, or an orgasm, and she would rather lick Matt's penis than Mrs Morgan's vulva, but the trainer, in her black corset and stockings and shoes, was overpoweringly attractive.

'Come and kneel here, then,' Mrs Morgan said. 'And listen carefully. I'm sure you know that the quickest and easiest way to achieve results is to concentrate on this area, around the clitoris.' She put her hand between her thighs and spread her fingers, making the shining tip of her clitoris emerge from its hood. 'But a pet needs to develop a strong tongue, so I want you to lick inside me, as deeply as you can.' She moved her hand down, and parted her inner lips. 'Right in there. As far as you can reach. And don't stop until I let go of the lead.'

She passed the lead under her right thigh, pulled on it, and kept it taut as Jessica leaned forwards and dipped her head between the trainer's thighs. As her face was drawn up to Mrs Morgan's gaping sex, Jessica stuck out her tongue. The pull on her collar was unrelenting. Her nose was squashed into the sopping folds of skin. She craned her neck upwards. Her mouth filled with Mrs Morgan's wetness. 'Further in!' Mrs Morgan said. 'And lick faster. I can hardly feel that.'

It occurred to Jessica that the trainer was using her as an object: a device for pleasuring herself. The thought made Jessica shiver with happiness. I'm a pet, she said to herself. And I love it.

Mrs Morgan pressed her thighs against the sides of Jessica's head, and Jessica thrilled to the frightening, exciting feeling of imprisonment. She didn't need the insistent pulling on her collar to encourage her to push her face into the trainer's wet sex and thrust her tongue into the warm tunnel of her vagina. Mrs Morgan tasted less sweet than Mel, but no less pleasant, and Jessica would have been happy to lick her for hours.

Mrs Morgan, however, had other plans. She loosened the tension on the lead, and Jessica reluctantly withdrew her tongue.

'Sit!' Mrs Morgan said.

Jessica arranged herself in the correct position. The trainer's wetness cooled on her face.

Mrs Morgan didn't close her legs. Instead, she moved her knees wide apart. Her cheeks were flushed and her eyes were glittering. 'Watch me, Jessica,' she said, and she put her hand, fingers downwards, on her pubes. Once again she spread her fingers on either side of the hood of her clitoris, and she began to slide them gently up and down. She rested her head on the back of the sofa, half closed her eyes, and began to breathe more and more deeply.

It wasn't fair. Jessica had spent all morning becoming increasingly excited, and ever since Mrs Morgan had started to use the cane on her bottom she had been desperate to touch herself. And now she had to sit on her haunches and watch while the trainer brought herself to an orgasm. Jessica wondered whether she could ask for permission to do the same. No: Mrs Morgan was panting now, with her head thrown back, and she wouldn't want to be interrupted. Her fingers, only inches in front of Jessica's face, were moving faster and faster. The tip of her clitoris was standing erect, and when Mrs Morgan moved her fingers together to squeeze it she arched her back and began to cry out. Jessica could only stare in fascination as a climax shook the trainer's body.

'Mmm,' Mrs Morgan said. 'I enjoyed that.' She lifted her head, but remained prone on the sofa with her legs parted. 'I expect you'd like to have an orgasm, wouldn't you, Jessica?'

'Yes, please, Mistress,' Jessica said. Perhaps her unspoken wish was about to be granted.

'Well, you can't,' Mrs Morgan said. 'I'm sorry, Jessica. I know how excited you are, but you must remember that a pet's duty is to attend to her owner's pleasure, not her own. Let this be a lesson for you. Now, I seem to have become rather wet and sticky. Down on all fours between my legs again, Jessica, and lick me clean. Start with the insides of my thighs.'

'Yes, Mistress,' Jessica said. The trouble, she thought as she pressed her lips against the trainer's satin-smooth skin, is that I can't get enough of being ordered to do sexual things. Being told to kneel with my legs apart is sufficient to make me wet. I don't understand it, but I can't deny it. I've always been so independent. Brian leaves all the decisions to me. And here I am, licking the secretions from the private parts of a woman who has just caned my bottom. And I'm more than content: I'm happy and thrilled.

In fact, if there were someone behind me, smacking my bottom again, I'd be in heaven. If that person were Matt, my supercilious mentor, smacking my sex with his hand or his long ruler, I'd probably start to come.

The thought was enough to send little tremors of pleasure through her body. She heard Mrs Morgan chuckle.

'You're going to make an adorable pet, Jessica,' the trainer said. She started to stroke her fingers through Jessica's long, dark hair. 'I think my legs are clean enough now. Put your mouth right down at the bottom, as low as you can. That's it. Here, I'll move forwards a little. Now open your mouth and hold out your tongue. I'll see if I can squeeze out the liquid that's still in my vagina.'

Jessica's jaw was wedged between the seat of the sofa and Mrs Morgan's sex. She could hardly breathe, and it was a strain to keep her mouth open and her tongue extended. She felt the trainer's muscles clench, and a trickle of warm, musky fluid covered her tongue.

'Lap it up, little pet,' Mrs Morgan said. 'Swallow it. That's right, Good girl.' She continued to stroke

Jessica's hair. 'Now lick carefully between my inner lips, and then do each side. Keep going until you can't taste me any more. It may take some time. And go slowly. If you make me come again, you'll have to start all over again from the beginning.'

Is it possible, Jessica wondered as she lapped and licked, to become addicted to the taste of sex? The more she immersed herself in the smell and flavour of Mrs Morgan, the more she wanted. And she found herself hoping that she would lick Mel again soon. Better still, she fantasised about Matt coming in her mouth. His smell was so manly, and he could flood her mouth with his semen so that she felt utterly overwhelmed and helpless.

'I hope you're still concentrating on your pet duties,' Mrs Morgan said. Her voice sounded relaxed rather than threatening. 'Cleanliness is very important. As a pet, you must keep yourself scrupulously clean for your owner. It's partly a matter of maintaining your appearance: a pet with dirty hair or feet reflects badly on her owner. But there are other, more intimate, aspects of a pet's cleanliness. For instance, you should attend carefully to your oral hygiene. And I recommend that you carry with you at all times a little tin of cachous, for freshening your breath. An owner usually likes her pet to display affection, and your kisses should always be sweet. That feels very pleasant, by the way.'

Jessica murmured, to indicate that she had been listening. She had licked clean the folds of the trainer's sex, and her tongue had reached the top of the slit, the site of the urethra and the clitoris. She was licking very carefully and slowly now, not because she wanted to prevent a second orgasm but because the delicious taste was becoming weaker, and she wanted to extend the cleaning for as long as possible.

'I need hardly tell you,' Mrs Morgan went on, 'that you must also keep your private parts completely clean.

Pay particular attention to your anus, and remember that it will open when you adopt most of the pet positions and whenever your owner puts you on display. So clean it often and thoroughly. A pet with a foul bottom brings disgrace on her owner.

'That will do, Jessica,' she said. 'You've licked me clean, I think. Now sit up and listen. It's almost time for us to take a little lunch, and then I have to return you to Melanie. But before we eat I want to be sure that you have learned how to keep yourself clean.

'It's obvious that, however much some owners might regret it, pets can't lick themselves clean in the way that a cat, for instance, can. Therefore you are permitted to use your hands. Your owner will tell you whether you are to use scented or plain soap, and whether you are to wash alone at home, before you go to your owner, or under your owner's supervision. The standard procedure is the same in either case. After your usual bath or shower, and after you've washed and dried your hair and trimmed your nails and put on your make-up and performed any other usual items of your toilet, you must stand in the bath and, using soap lather on your hands, you must wash your breasts, your vulva, and your anus. Be very thorough. Rinse off the suds, and dry yourself. Your owner will let you know what talcum powder or moisturising cream, if any, you are permitted to apply. In a few minutes we'll go to the bathroom and you'll demonstrate the procedure. I think we'd better wash your face, too. It looks wet and sticky.

'Finally, you should bear in mind always that you may also be called on to attend to your owner's toilet. And in such cases you may be expected to use your tongue, as a true pet would. You have just demonstrated your aptitude for licking, so I doubt that you'll encounter any difficulties. I believe that some of the owners rely entirely on their pets for their personal cleanliness. Therefore don't be surprised if you find yourself spending much of your time in Melanie's bathroom. I suspect that she's going to be one of those owners who are very aware of their appearance, and so even if she doesn't have you licking her all day you'll probably have to dress her hair and paint her nails for her.'

Jessica smiled. 'Yes, Mistress,' she said. As long as Mel made her lick her sometimes, and gave her firm orders, and, above all, punished her occasionally, Jessica would be happy.

Mrs Morgan sighed and stood up. 'Stand, Jessica,' she said. 'I'll put you on the lead and walk you to the bathroom. Keep to heel.'

Once Jessica had demonstrated that, squatting in the bath, she could soap and rinse her breasts, sex and bottom to Mrs Morgan's exacting standards, she was taken on the lead to the kitchen.

Lunch was Mrs Morgan's homemade vegetable soup. The trainer sat at the kitchen table; Jessica remained on her hands and knees, and lapped her meal from a bowl on the floor. Although Jessica was hungry she found it difficult to eat like a pet: her long hair kept falling over her face, and she was sure that more of the soup ended up on her face and in her hair than in her mouth.

'You must learn to eat tidily,' Mrs Morgan insisted, holding Jessica's face in the soup bowl with one hand while she spanked her bottom with the other. 'You don't want Melanie to be known as the owner with the messy pet, do you? You've made yourself disgracefully dirty.'

After another session in the bathroom Jessica was declared clean, and she was allowed to dress in her short skirt and her tight jersey top. The collar remained around her neck, and when Mrs Morgan said that they were going to walk to Melanie's house Jessica half hoped and half feared that she would have to make the journey on her hands and knees, with Mrs Morgan holding the lead.

However, the two women simply walked side by side along the tree-lined roads. Neither spoke. Mrs Morgan, with her crisp white coat once more concealing her wickedly black corset, strode forward purposefully. Jessica was grateful for the exercises that Matt had put her through, as she was able to keep up with the long-legged trainer. Jessica was preoccupied with thoughts of her mentor. It was already mid-afternoon, and soon it would be time for her daily appointment at the club. It was inevitable that she would be late. Perhaps, she thought happily, Matt would be particularly severe with her. On the other hand, there was the possibility that he would be seriously displeased. He might even refuse to see her. His inscrutable demeanour excited her, but it prevented her from anticipating his reactions. She wanted him so much, and she didn't know if he even liked her.

Having made herself miserable, Jessica didn't notice that there were other pedestrians on the estate until she almost collided with one: a short, slight young woman with black-rimmed spectacles and a beige raincoat.

'Sorry!' Jessica and the woman said simultaneously as they moved from each other's path. The woman looked at Jessica, in her skimpy clothes and collar, and then at the tall, imposing, medically dressed figure of Mrs Morgan. She lowered her head, and scurried on her way.

'Lives at number forty-two,' Mrs Morgan said. 'Not pet material, apparently. Poor thing.'

Jessica turned to watch the woman hurrying away. That's what I would have been like, she thought, if I hadn't agreed to become a pet. In Hillingbury if you're not an owner or a pet you're nobody: anonymous, lonely, and made even more isolated by the suspicion that there is a society on the estate from which you're excluded.

The next person they met was a tall, slender woman in early middle age. She was wearing a bottle-green coat with a fur collar, and she addressed Mrs Morgan by name, and chatted with her about the weather, before turning to look quizzically at Jessica.

'This is Melanie Overton's new pet,' Mrs Morgan said. 'Her name's Jessica. This is her first day of training, so she still has a lot to learn. But she's made a promising start, I must admit.'

The woman looked down her narrow nose at Jessica. She raised a gloved hand and brushed Jessica's hair from her face. 'Melanie's done well,' she said. 'This is a pretty little thing. Is she proving easy to train?'

'Reasonably,' Mrs Morgan admitted. 'I've had to apply a little discipline.'

The woman's green eyes shone. 'That's all for the best,' she said. 'A pet has to know that her owner is in charge.' She stroked Jessica's cheek. 'Are you going to be an obedient pet?' she asked.

'Yes, Mistress,' Jessica said. 'I'm looking forward to it.'

'That's Olivia Reynolds,' Mrs Morgan told Jessica as they continued their journey. 'She has a reputation for being very strict with her pet, Karen, and any others that come under her jurisdiction.'

There was a cynical tone to the trainer's voice that Jessica couldn't interpret. She made a mental note, however, that Olivia Reynolds was an owner who might prove interesting.

Jessica and Mrs Morgan stood in the porch of Mel's house and waited. Mel's house was, Jessica realised, built to exactly the same pattern as her own, and was therefore one of the smaller houses on the estate. No wonder, she thought, that Mel's first thought on becoming an owner was to extend and augment her property.

Mrs Morgan was about to ring the bell a second time when the door opened. 'Oh, you're here already,' Mel exclaimed. 'I don't know where the hours have gone today. I'm still looking at conservatory designs. I just can't decide. But you'd better come in.'

After this cool reception Jessica was relieved that Mel pulled her into an embrace in the hall. Jessica, mindful of her duty to please her owner, kissed Mel's lips eagerly.

'Enough!' Mel cried, giggling. 'You're ruining my lipstick.' She pulled away from Jessica. 'Has she been good, Mrs Morgan?'

The trainer narrowed her eyes and considered her response. 'All things considered,' she said, 'she's made a reasonable start.'

Mel whispered into Jessica's ear. 'That's high praise indeed, from Mrs Morgan,' she said.

'Before I leave her with you,' Mrs Morgan went on, 'there are a few things I'd like to discuss. Could we go into the sitting room?'

Mel looked at her wristwatch and frowned, but she said, 'Yes, of course. This way.'

Mel noticed Jessica studying the décor of the rooms. 'Lydia was a very kind owner,' she explained. 'She let me choose most of the wallpaper and furniture and so on myself. Of course, I had to be a very good pet.' With a critical frown on her face she considered the carpets and curtains. 'It will all have to be changed now, of course. Keith's going to have to work so hard! But now I'm an owner, the whole house will have to be redecorated and refurnished. I was talking to Bella about it this morning. For goodness' sake don't let me down when you're presented, Jess. I've already ordered rolls and rolls of fabric.'

'I have to talk to you about Jessica's training,' Mrs Morgan said, clearly trying to steer Mel away from her preoccupation with home improvements. 'Jessica, take your clothes off.'

That snagged Mel's attention. 'She's mine!' she exclaimed petulantly, but she didn't countermand the instruction and Jessica, blushing with embarrassment, began to undress. Despite everything that Mrs Morgan had made her do that morning, and all the undignified positions she had been told to adopt, it still felt strange to be naked and wearing a leather collar in her neighbour's sitting room.

'Stand!' Mrs Morgan said, and Jessica dropped to her hands and knees on the carpet. She was becoming used to the position: it felt almost natural. She made sure her legs were parted and her bottom was raised.

'I'm no longer your trainer,' Mrs Morgan said to Mel, 'but if I might offer a word of advice, I suggest that you take a moment to consider this novel situation. The last time I was here, indeed every time that I've been here, until today, I have come at Lydia's request. Many times Lydia and I have stood in this room, and you have knelt between us, as Jessica is kneeling between you and me today.'

'Don't remind me!' Mel exclaimed. 'It's such a relief to be an owner at last.'

Jessica could hear the suppressed impatience in the trainer's voice. 'That may well be,' Mrs Morgan said, 'but nonetheless you will find it useful to remember your life as Lydia's pet. Jessica is becoming aware of her duties to you, but you have responsibilities towards her. If you don't wish to undertake any of her training yourself, you can delegate the entire task to me – I'll allow a discount on my usual rates, as I propose to subject Jessica to a substantial programme of advanced training. I would be pleased to look after that chore for you, and I'm sure that Jessica will benefit from it. However, I cannot be present at all times, and of course you will want to spend many hours alone with your pet so that you can enjoy her.'

'I should think so too,' Mel said. 'Jess is my pet, you know, not yours. What sort of advanced training are you talking about?'

Mrs Morgan sighed. 'Jessica, show Melanie your bottom,' she said.

Jessica felt a tremor of excitement. What would her city friends think if they could see her now – naked, on her hands and knees, between two women who were her owner and her trainer? What would Brian make of it? They would all be astounded, disbelieving, confused. But although Jessica realised how bizarre the situation was, she felt not at all confused. She was content, and sexually aroused, and felt more alive than she had for years. Just the order to display her bottom was enough to make her shiver. With her head bowed low she moved round so that her hindquarters were towards Mel. She lifted her bottom up.

'Now do you see it?' Mrs Morgan asked Mel. 'Jessica is well behaved and learns quickly. The stripes on her backside were not administered as punishment for misdemeanours or slowness. They could rather be considered as a reward. Her state of arousal is visibly obvious.'

'So you're saying . . .' Mel said hesitantly. It was clear that she was still having difficulty understanding the trainer.

'I'm saying that Jessica will perform best as a pet if she is kept under a regime of strict discipline. Therefore I recommend that you send her to me regularly for more training. And I suggest that at all other times you should bear in mind her need for discipline. That's all.'

Jessica's cheeks were aflame. It was wonderfully humiliating to be talked about as if she really were no more than a pet animal, particularly when the conversation concerned the frequency of her punishments.

Mel said nothing for a while. It seemed as though she still found it difficult to accept the meaning of Mrs Morgan's words. 'So you're saying Jess likes being trained?' she asked at last. 'And you want me to smack her and whip her?' She sounded incredulous.

'Of course,' Mrs Morgan said. 'For goodness' sake, Melanie, you must be aware that many of the Hillingbury pets are quite happy with their lot. As long as her owner is firm and fair, a pet with a submissive nature has an enviable existence. Jessica is very obviously submissive, and I am merely pointing out that you will get the best from her if you're aware of her nature and cater for it. Shall I demonstrate?'

'Pets can never have the nice things that owners do,' Mel protested. 'That's not what I call enviable. And what do you mean, demonstrate?'

Jessica knew. She lifted her bottom even higher. Mrs Morgan was going to smack her again. And Mel would be watching, and would see how wet Jessica became.

'I'll show you how to use the looped handle of a leash,' Mrs Morgan said. 'It's an implement you're likely to have with you at all times.'

Jessica heard the leather leash sing in the air, and then with a loud crack a line blazed across her bottom. Three more followed quickly, making her bottom once again sore and hot, just as she liked it. She sighed happily and surrendered to the vibrant pleasure-shocks.

She heard Mel protest, 'That's rather severe!'

'Nonsense,' Mrs Morgan replied. 'You can see how much Jessica's enjoying it. Good, wristy strokes like those are ideal for getting her hot and excited quickly. Here: it's your turn.'

'Me?' Mel squeaked.

'You are her owner,' Mrs Morgan pointed out. 'Fold the leash several times, and leave the loop hanging. Now aim to strike here, in the middle of Jessica's right buttock.'

Jessica wished that Mel would hurry up and use the leash. She was impatient for the next flash of searing, delicious pain.

Slap. The loop of leather landed limply on Jessica's bottom. She moaned with frustration.

'Again, this time on the other cheek,' Mrs Morgan said. 'And you can strike much harder than that, you know. Still, Jessica's your pet, so it's up to you how you discipline her. That's more like it. A few more of those. That's the way. And now aim lower. Lower than that. Try to land the leather along the line at the top of Jessica's thighs. That's right. And now move inwards: get the leash to catch the insides of her thighs, and the innermost lower quadrant of her buttocks. It's more painful there, of course, but I expect Jessica also finds it more gratifying.'

Jessica could only murmur her agreement. She hoped that Mel could remember how to use the leash as a whip when Mrs Morgan wasn't present. She had decided that the curves of her buttocks nearest to her sex were the most erogenous parts of her bottom, at least as far as being smacked was concerned, and Mel, with rhythmic strokes, was successfully making the area pulse fiercely. If anything Mel was becoming too practised: Jessica was so aroused that her sopping-wet sex felt ignored and needy, and she would have welcomed the excruciating sting of a few badly aimed strokes landing there.

'Jessica has an unusually prominent and firm bottom,' Mrs Morgan mused. 'Therefore it's tempting to aim always for the most rounded part, in the centre. And, if your purpose is to colour her bottom, perhaps so that she's got a glowing rear end when you show her to another owner, then that kind of smacking is perfectly adequate. But, as I'm sure you remember, Melanie, from your few training sessions with me, it is always more effective to aim lower. You seem to have mastered the technique, in any case. Pause for a moment, please.'

The smacking stopped. Jessica lifted her head: she knew that she had to appear alert and eager to please, even though what she wanted was more spanking, or Matt's body, or an orgasm, or at the very least to be allowed to curl up and touch her yearning sex.

'I imagine you'll expect Jessica to lick you frequently,' Mrs Morgan said. 'Would you care to try that now?

Jessica's told me that she's already performed for you once. I'm confident that she'll be even better under the leash.'

'How exciting!' Mel said. 'Well, I suppose I don't mind. One thing about being a pet is that you get used to doing things with an audience.' She stood in front of Jessica. 'Jess, pull my skirt up. All the way up to my waist.'

Jessica's hands were shaking with excitement. She was going to be whipped by her trainer while she licked her pretty owner. This was almost as much fun as an afternoon with Matt. She tugged the skirt upwards, revealing lacy stocking-tops, and above them the pale, smooth skin of Mel's thighs, and then the hairless mound and slit. Jessica resisted the temptation to press her face immediately into the enticing, disconcertingly bald V of delicate skin.

She glanced up at Mel. Her cheeks were blushing, but her blue eyes were bright with excitement. 'You can hold on to my hips, Jess,' she said. She parted her thighs and bent her knees, so that her sex was within reach of Jessica's mouth. 'Not yet, Jess,' she said. She stroked a hand over her hairless mound. 'I want you to kiss me here first, and then along this side, and then the other side, before you start licking. Mrs Morgan, don't start smacking her again until I give you the sign. Oh, I say. That was a bit forceful of me, wasn't it? I think I'm getting the hang of being an owner. All right, Jess, you can start kissing me now.'

As Jessica gratefully pressed her lips against her owner's soft, scented skin she heard Mrs Morgan say, 'Yes, I've noticed that even the most timorous of pets can learn to give instructions once she's become an owner.'

Not me, Jessica said to herself. I'm happy as a pet. I think I could hardly be happier. And when Mrs Morgan starts whipping me again, I'll show

Mel how enthusiastically I can lick her. I'll give her such a lovely orgasm.

Field agent's report to the Private House
From: Matt
For the attention of: Mistress Julia

Jessica was late for her appointment with me today. So late that I had assumed she wasn't coming. She arrived in a distracted state, full of apologies, wearing nothing but a short skirt and a clinging top. She had not brought her exercise clothes, and in any case there wasn't enough time for her to carry out her programme in the gym – not if she was going to make her daily report. And it was clear from her excited comments that she had much to tell me. I took her into the mirrored exercise room.

She said she had come directly from the house of her owner, Mel, and once she had obeyed my instruction to undress I could plainly see that she had recently been whipped. She was also in a state of considerable sexual arousal.

She made it clear that she hoped – indeed, expected – that I would punish her, use her for my sexual pleasure, and allow her to masturbate to orgasm. Her desperate enthusiasm for this course of action was touching, and I found it difficult to maintain my façade of icy control. As she kneeled before me, gazing up at me with her big, dark eyes, holding her reddened bottom out for whatever additional punishment I thought fit to administer, I confess that I thought she had never looked prettier, and I had to fight the urge to have her immediately.

But I had to remain in control, and she had to make her report. I decided that she should write an account of her day. This would save me the chore of transcribing my notes of our conversation, and it would provide you with a first-hand, eyewitness testimony of Jessica's first day as a pet. In order to ensure that we received the fullest possible account, I promised her six smacks with the ruler for each page she wrote.

With that incentive she wrote at great length and at a furious speed. I enclose with this report the ten pages that she produced. I hope you can read her handwriting, particularly on the later pages: I think Jessica found that writing down her experiences made her even more excited. She also realised that if she wrote in a larger hand she could cover more pages. All in all, though, I think it is a comprehensive and very interesting report.

I suppose, for the sake of completeness, that I should note that despite the soreness of her bottom she took the full sixty strokes, although I did moderate carefully the force with which I applied them. It's not that it's likely that her husband will see the marks, but she will spend tomorrow with her owner and I'm concerned to ensure that there is no evidence of her association with me.

Despite my care, Jessica's bottom was remarkably red by the time I finished, and I'm sure she will find it difficult to sit this evening. I hope she can sleep comfortably on her side or front. By tomorrow morning I think she will feel only a little residual tenderness.

I was interested – and not a little aroused, I have to say – to note that as I approached the climax of the long, regular spanking Jessica was quite clearly approaching a climax of her own. She seems to be becoming more submissive by the day. Once she is aroused each smack and every curt command makes her tremble visibly. For a mentor such as myself it is very rewarding to have such a student with such reservoirs of natural aptitude.

The fact that Jessica is so very attractive makes my task even more pleasurable, but also more difficult in some ways. I appreciate that a report such as this is not the place to expound on Jessica's charms, but I think it is important that you understand entirely why I believe she would be an invaluable asset to the House. It's not just that she has huge, expressive, deep, dark eyes, and smooth, clear, hay-scented skin that looks as though it's permanently suntanned, and high, round breasts that seem to reach out to you from her slim, lithe body, and slender thighs with an inviting gap below her luscious, full sex, and – well, I'm sure you get the picture. It's not just all that. She's also bright and decisive.

Today, for instance, she was determined that I should use her again. She wanted me to penetrate her, and by pretending to be aloof I was able to make her beg for my penis. She clearly revelled in demeaning herself, and her beseeching became more and more frantic as the time drew near for her to leave the club while I managed to remain resolutely unmoved. At last I relented, and allowed her to please me with her mouth – at which, I should report, she is becoming very skilful. To give you some idea of the height of her sexual arousal by this stage, suffice it to say that the insides of her thighs were wet down to her knees, and even my sternest instructions were not enough to deter her from touching herself. I had to tie her hands behind her back while she fellated me.

I permitted her to masturbate, at last, while I fed to her from my fingers the drops of semen that had sprayed on to her face. I made her play with her anus, and made sure that she knew I was watching her in the mirrors. She came quickly, violently and at great length. As you'll see from her account, she had not been permitted an orgasm all day, and she was clearly desperate for release.

Then it was time for her to leave. She had to arrive home before her husband, so that she could wash herself and change into more respectable clothes. We had time for a brief conversation. It's clear that her duties as a pet will prevent her from visiting me as regularly as I had hoped. We agreed that she should come to me at the club whenever she had a free afternoon, and that her husband will not be suspicious if she visits the club occasionally in the evening.

However, there can be no doubt that I'll see Jessica less often. And, judging by the contents of the report she wrote today, and the marks that were on her bottom when she arrived here, I suspect that being a pet might be enough to satisfy her perverse desires.

It might become difficult for me to retain my influence over her.

I know that your first reaction to this admission will be to recall me to the House and to appoint a female agent to infiltrate the world of the Hillingbury committee. And I know that you'll suspect that my request to be allowed to remain here is coloured by my attachment to Jessica.

All I can say is that at the moment my link with Jessica remains intact, and I believe it would be a mistake to sever it. I hope you agree that we should learn everything we can from Jessica before we change our tactics.

I think she still likes me, wants me and will obey me.

Five

It was almost ten o'clock. Jessica took a final look at her reflection in the wardrobe mirror. Her long, dark hair was loose, and freshly washed and brushed. She considered her make-up: just a little mascara, a touch of eyeshadow, and highlighter above her cheekbones. She was wearing a suspender belt, stockings, and the wide cream collar that was on loan from Mrs Morgan.

She touched her pubic mound. That morning, while she had washed herself according to the method dictated by the trainer, she had shaved not only her legs and under her arms but also the lips of her sex, leaving only a thin line of short hair above the slit of her sex. She hoped Mel would approve.

She decided that, overall, she made a young, attractive and sexy pet. She wanted to look her best for her owner. She turned round and looked over her shoulder. Just seeing the reflection of her bottom made her want another spanking. The marks had faded even more since the last time she had looked. Her buttocks were hardly red at all, and she could barely discern the lines that Mrs Morgan had made with her cane.

Matt had been too gentle with her the previous afternoon. Sixty smacks with the ruler, and nothing to show for it! She had enjoyed the punishment, of course – how could it be otherwise, when he was standing over her, barking commands, watching her with his icy gaze while she displayed her private parts, and stoking the fire inside her with each stroke he applied to her bottom – but she couldn't help worrying that he might be tiring of her. Perhaps he thought that now she was a pet she wouldn't want him any more. But in fact she needed him more than ever. How could she make him understand?

But it was almost time for Mel to arrive. Jessica hurried down the stairs, went to the centre of the hallway, and kneeled on the floor in the 'sit' position. She had given Mel the spare key to the front door. All she had to do was wait.

Mel was late, and as the minutes went by Jessica became more agitated and excited. The position was uncomfortable, but she found that when she rocked back and forth to relieve the tension in her muscles she could make her bottom and her sex brush against the floor between her feet. She was becoming wet already, and she hoped that she wasn't leaving a moist patch on the carpet. On the other hand, if she did then perhaps Mel would punish her.

She heard a key in the lock. The door opened. Mel flew in, her coat unbuttoned. Under it she was wearing a blouse and skirt in matching shades of dark pink. Her lips and nails were painted in the same colour.

'Jess,' she said. 'Good girl.' She stood in front of her pet and pulled up her skirt. She was wearing stockings and pale-pink, lacy knickers. With one finger she pulled aside the front and gusset of the knickers. 'Kiss your owner,' she said.

Jessica needed no encouragement. She adored her owner's neat, pink, hairless sex, and she applied her lips to the top of Mel's mound, kissed it fervently, and then allowed her tongue to lap gently down the slit. She felt Mel's shiver of desire.

'Good girl,' Mel said again, but this time the words were a faint murmur. 'Oh, that's so nice. I know I'm going to enjoy being an owner. But stand up now, Jess,' she said. 'We're going out. Put on your raincoat and those pretty little boots we found yesterday.'

It was raining steadily, and Jessica wore the coat buttoned up to her neck. Although she was more covered than she had been when she had walked with Mel to Mrs Morgan's house, and then with Mrs Morgan to Mel's, she still felt naked and exposed. No one who saw her could possibly suspect that under the coat she was wearing nothing but a collar, a suspender-belt and stockings, but she could feel with every step she took the silky lining material brushing against her bottom and her nipples.

As the two women walked side by side, avoiding puddles, Mel said, 'I've been invited to Martha Smythe's. One of her pets has been misbehaving, and she's called in Mrs Morgan. And Mrs Morgan suggested that I might like to bring you along to see the punishment. It will be a chance for you to meet another owner and her pets. So I want you to be on your best behaviour, Jess. I think Martha will be rather envious of me.'

'Yes, Mistress,' Jessica said. 'Thank you.' She was intrigued, and a little nervous. She had no doubt that she was at least as attractive, in her own way, as any other pet, but she knew that she had had only the most basic training, and she hoped that she would not make any silly mistakes. It would be interesting, in any case, to meet another of the owners, and her pets.

'Mistress,' Jessica said, 'how many pets does Mrs Smythe have?'

'Two,' Mel replied. 'Amy and Jane. They're both quite pretty. I think only Amy will be there today. She's the one who's been naughty.'

Martha Smythe lived in one of the grander houses on the estate. The front garden was surrounded by a wall, which was pierced by two wide gateways. The broad drive was paved with brick, and the porch was large, entirely enclosed with windows that had stained-glass panels, and illuminated on this dark, rainy day by ornate wall-lamps. Mel pointed out all of these features to Jessica while they waited for the door to be opened.

It was Mrs Morgan, in her crisp white uniform, who welcomed them in. She gave Jessica a brief smile, but she frowned at Mel and glanced pointedly at the face of the grandfather clock in the hall.

Although the interior of the house was spacious and gloomy it was warm, for which Jessica was grateful. Once she and Mel had removed their coats, and Jessica had hung them on hooks in the cloakroom, Jessica was as naked as she had been in her own house.

She had butterflies in her tummy, and she couldn't tell whether she was nervous or excited. Mel appeared to be no less timid, and she made no move to lead the way further into the house.

'Let me see your bottom, dear,' Mrs Morgan said to Jessica.

Jessica felt a familiar thrill as she turned, leaned forwards, and presented herself to the trainer. She shivered again as Mrs Morgan's fingers caressed the curves of her buttocks.

'Very good,' Mrs Morgan said, pulling Jessica upright. She lowered her head to whisper in Jessica's ear. 'Hardly a trace. I'll bet you're ready for more already, aren't you?'

Jessica blushed and nodded. There was no point in denying it. The tall, stern trainer excited her in the same way that Matt did – and to a degree that she suspected that Mel, for all that she was pretty and kissable, never would be able to.

'We shouldn't keep Mrs Smythe waiting any longer,' Mrs Morgan said. 'Melanie, are you going to walk Jessica in on the lead?'

'Oh, I suppose I ought to,' Mel said, and she began to search in her handbag.

Mrs Morgan stopped her. 'I've brought one to match her collar,' she said. 'Jessica, stand.'

Jessica dropped to her hands and knees, and the trainer clipped a lead to one of the rings of her collar. Jessica's trepidation increased: even though she was virtually naked, she could have retained a little dignity if she had been permitted to remain standing upright.

Mel stepped forwards. Jessica felt a tug on her collar, and she scurried to keep alongside Mel's patent-leather high-heeled shoes. As she was led from the hall into a reception room she found herself padding across the dark, deep pile of a Persian carpet.

'Melanie!' a woman's voice exclaimed. 'I'm so glad you're here at last.' Jessica saw the speaker's stockinged legs, and her feet encased in decorated satin slippers. There was a sound of a perfunctory kiss. 'And you're looking every inch an owner. What a transformation! I'm so pleased for you, my dear. And this must be your pet.'

'Thank you, Martha,' Mel said, stumbling over her words. 'Do you know, I almost called you "Mistress". Old habits die hard, don't they? I'm so excited about being an owner. I can't wait for the first meeting of the committee. There are so many things I want to do to the house, too.'

'Her name's Jessica,' Mrs Morgan said. 'Sit, Jessica.'

Jessica lowered her haunches between her parted calves and placed her hands together on the carpet between her knees.

'I call her Jess,' Mel said.

Mrs Smythe sat in an armchair. Jessica lifted her head, and was able to see Martha Smythe for the first time. She was a short, shapely woman with a pretty, round face, round-framed spectacles, and a bob of black hair. She was studying Jessica intently, and Jessica, embarrassed by the scrutiny, looked away.

'She's a slim, shapely thing,' Mrs Smythe said. 'And she has very striking looks. She's very definitely a cat-pet, isn't she? She has that feline elegance and mystery. My two are more like puppies, it seems to me: always boisterous and eager to please.'

Jessica formed the opinion that Mrs Smythe liked puppies and disapproved of cats.

'Where's Amy?' Mrs Morgan asked.

'In the kitchen,' Mrs Smythe replied. 'I've sent her to start making up the solution. It will save time.'

Mrs Morgan evidently approved of the decision. 'Good. It's a subtle introduction to her punishment, as well. I'd better go and see how she's getting on with it. Then I'll take her up to the bathroom, unless you want to see her in here.' She picked up a large leather bag from the floor.

'No, I don't think so,' Mrs Smythe said. 'We'll join you upstairs in a moment. I'll take a closer look at Jessica, if I may, Melanie.'

Mrs Morgan strode from the room. Jessica felt the lead being unclipped from her collar. There was a long silence. Jessica knew that she was being watched. From beneath the curtains of her long hair, hanging at the sides of her face, she stole glances at Mrs Smythe and at the heavy furniture and dark fabrics with which Mrs Smythe had furnished her house.

'Roll over,' Mrs Smythe said softly.

Jessica leaned forwards, and then rolled on to her back, turning so that her legs were towards Mrs Smythe. She had remembered that Mrs Morgan had told her that she should always present herself to the owner who was giving her instructions. She held her arms and legs aloft.

Already no part of her body was concealed from Mrs Smythe's owlish gaze. Her breasts rose like two rounded hills from the plateau of her chest; even though her knees were still together, she knew that there was always a gap between the tops of her thighs, and so Mrs Smythe could easily see her newly denuded sex-lips; and, with her legs lifted into the air, her bottom was rounded and her little hole would be visible.

But Jessica knew that she had to expose herself more. She had to pull her knees up to her shoulders, and hold them apart, so that her bottom and her sex were properly on display. As she pulled her legs into the required position, and felt her sex and her bottom lift up and open, Jessica tried to analyse the physical pleasure that flooded through her.

Why on earth, she wondered, do I find it so enjoyable to exhibit myself like this? Partly, she thought, it was because she had abdicated all responsibility for her own sexual pleasure: although she liked to be in control of her life in general, she took a perverse delight in obeying the directions of others in sexual matters. She wondered, as she held herself open for inspection, whether it would be even more arousing if she was tied up in this position. She would be even more aware of her helplessness: she would be unable to prevent Mel and Mrs Smythe doing whatever they liked to her exposed private parts. But there was something more deeply satisfying about putting herself on display. She couldn't pretend that she wasn't an accessory to this act of exhibitionism. She had to face the humiliating fact that she was voluntarily debasing herself.

And humiliation was an important stimulus to her pleasure, she realised. The simple fact that she was on the floor added to her excitement. If she had been on a table, or a stage, her position would have been a little less demeaning, and less stimulating. But she was on the floor, at the lowest possible level, with her owner and Mrs Smythe looking down at her. She knew that she was a clever, confident adult, but when she allowed herself to be Mel's pet, or Matt's pupil, she became a helpless, naughty little girl. A word of command, or a stern look from Matt's eyes, or the sight of a collar or a ruler – each of these slight suggestions, alone, was enough to spark the fire of Jessica's sexuality.

She wished that Matt were there. She would show the two women how she loved to take punishment from him. She would clench her knees to her shoulders for as long as he wanted to smack her bottom and then, when he finally stopped, and her bottom was two hot, pulsating, swollen, smarting spheres, she would beg him to smack her sex and then to put his manhood into it.

Oh, my! That was such a wonderful thought. She hoped that Mrs Smythe wouldn't notice how aroused she had become.

She tried to concentrate on thinking about the causes of her sexual excitement. The final element, she decided, was pride. Perhaps, in fact, it was mere vanity. Now that she had discovered her own submissiveness, she found that those to whom she submitted were minutely interested in her. She was the centre of attention. In the past she had always thought that she had had to deter or avoid the attention she had received because she was attractive; now, under the command of others, she could revel in the fact that her face, her breasts, her bottom and her sex drew people to her, to look and to touch.

'She's willing and obedient,' Mrs Smythe admitted grudgingly. She leaned forwards and ran her fingernails down the back of Jessica's left thigh. 'She can have had only a little training yet.'

'Just one session,' Mel said. 'She's going to be an excellent pet.' She sounded smug.

Mrs Smythe's fingers moved closer to Jessica's sex, making Jessica squirm. 'Do you know,' Mrs Smythe declared, 'I believe she's rather worked up. Yes, look, Melanie,' she said, using her fingers to open Jessica's sex-lips wider, 'she's absolutely sopping. Have you been playing with her? Is that why you were late?'

'Um, no, actually,' Mel said. 'It's just that Jess is very, you know, responsive. I think she likes being told to show off. That's Mrs Morgan's opinion, anyway. You don't mind, do you? I'll have Mrs Morgan give her a whipping if she's displeased you.'

Jessica moaned with frustrated desire. The movements of Mrs Smythe's fingers and the prospect of punishment were sending thrills of pleasure from her sex to her nipples.

'Good heavens, no,' Mrs Smythe said. 'I don't mind at all. It's utterly charming. You're a good girl, aren't you, Jessica?' she crooned, rubbing her knuckles along the slippery cleft between Jessica's sex-lips.

'Yes, she is good,' Mel said. She sounded relieved that Mrs Smythe didn't condemn her pet's wantonness. 'She likes to lick me, too.'

'Then you're very lucky indeed, Melanie,' Mrs Smythe said. 'I had terrible difficulties with Amy. I'd had her for months before she finally accepted that she'd have to lick me. She's come to like it now, of course. You can try her, later, if you like. But little Jessica,' she went on, pinching and squeezing Jessica's labia and making her gasp and writhe, 'you wouldn't object to licking me, would you?'

'No, Mistress,' Jessica said. 'I'd like to. And, please, Mistress, if you want Mrs Morgan to punish me, she could do it while I'm licking you.'

'What a lovely idea!' Mrs Smythe said. 'But I'm afraid there isn't time now. Mrs Morgan and Amy are waiting for us in the bathroom. I'll postpone the pleasure of your tongue. Now: that's enough pet positions, my dear. Stand up, and follow me and your owner upstairs.'

As she climbed the stairs Jessica could feel liquid seeping from her sex. Surreptitiously she pressed her fingers against the top of her shaven slit, and had to stifle a cry as an electric jolt zigzagged through her. She was so close to coming, but she was sure that the owners wouldn't allow her an orgasm. Still, there was pleasure to be had in being kept constantly on the dizzying brink of ecstasy. She felt confused but elated, and her body was full of vibrant warmth. Her breasts felt swollen, and her nipples and her sex were ultra-sensitive. Memories of stinging fire-strips blazing across her bottom flashed continually through her mind.

Mrs Smythe's house had a large bathroom, which seemed only a little crowded with five women in it. The bath, a large, white tub of enamelled metal, extended from the far wall into the centre of the room. Mrs Morgan was standing at the head of the bath, next to the taps and the shower. In the white-tiled room she looked more than ever like a nurse or a doctor. Jessica couldn't see Mrs Smythe's pet at first, and then she saw that Amy, naked but for a collar, was on her hands and knees in the bath. She was facing towards the door, and when she heard footsteps she looked up with tears glittering in her eyes and a forlorn expression on her face.

'Please, Mistress,' she said. 'I'm truly sorry, and I promise I'll always wash myself properly in future. Please don't punish me. Not like this. Not in front of other people.'

Her face was perfectly oval, with hazel eyes and very full lips, and surrounded by auburn curls. If she had been happier, Jessica thought, she would have looked very pretty. Her pale arms and back were freckled, and her pendant breasts were large and heavy. She was, Jessica judged, a few years older than her.

'It's too late for regrets and apologies now, young lady,' Mrs Smythe told her. 'It's not as if this is the first time you've been found out. I insist that my pets are thoroughly clean. It's an absolute rule. It's one of the very first things you learn when you're trained. Isn't that so, Jessica?'

'Oh, yes, Mistress,' Jessica murmured. It was obvious that Amy was dreading her punishment, although Jessica couldn't imagine what form it would take, and

Jessica didn't want to say anything that might make things worse for the young woman.

'Take my advice,' Mrs Smythe said to Mel, 'and examine your pet carefully. First thing in the morning, before you do anything else with her. Not every day; spot checks are better, they keep your pet on her toes.' She stepped back to stand beside Jessica. 'Have you examined Jessica today? No? Jessica, did you wash yourself this morning? Even here?'

One of Mrs Smythe's fingers was suddenly probing the cleft of Jessica's bottom. It pressed into the funnel of delicate skin around her little hole. It was one more reminder for Jessica that she was merely a pet: a plaything for the elite ladies of Hillingbury.

'Yes, Mistress,' she whispered.

'Very good,' Mrs Smythe said. 'I wish Amy was as thoughtful. Her excuse this time is that she had had a bath the previous night, and she didn't think it was necessary to wash again. And, I suspect, she thought I wouldn't notice. It's not just a matter of cleanliness, Amy,' she stated firmly, when Amy began again to apologise, 'it's your duty as my pet to make yourself especially attractive to me. You're going to be punished, and that's all there is to it. And Melanie and her pet are going to watch. It will be instructive for both of them, and I hope that you'll find the experience so humiliating that you'll never transgress again. Please carry on, Mrs Morgan.'

Jessica saw that Mrs Morgan was nursing in her arms a metal cylinder. It resembled a medical syringe, with a plunger at one end and a narrow spout at the other, but it was far larger than any syringe Jessica had previously seen. Holding the spout upwards, Mrs Morgan bent to open the large, leather bag that was at her feet. She extracted from it a length of rubber tubing, one end of which she pushed firmly on to the spout of the syringe. She placed the other end over the edge of the bath, and then she slowly depressed the plunger until a stream of slightly cloudy, colourless liquid issued from the tube and splashed into the bath behind Amy's feet. She held her fingers under the flow and nodded.

'It's cool enough now,' she said.

She rested the syringe on the tiled surface surrounding the head of the bath, and bent to retrieve more items from her bag. As one, Mrs Smythe, Mel and Jessica stepped forwards to see them. The first was, Jessica saw, a rubber nozzle. It was basically cylindrical, but one end was bulbous and tapered to a short, narrow tube. Behind the bulb it was waisted, and then it widened again towards its other end, which consisted of a ridged tube. The second item was a round jar, which Mrs Morgan opened to reveal that it contained a clear unguent.

'Sit, Amy,' Mrs Morgan said. When Amy was kneeling in the correct position, the trainer held out the nozzle and the jar. 'You know where this is going, Amy,' she said. 'Lubricate it, please. Just the bulb and the spout.'

'Please,' Amy whimpered again, but she knew that she could expect no mercy. She sighed, and took the nozzle in one hand and a dollop of cream on the fingers of the other. She spread the lotion over the front half of the nozzle.

Jessica's stomach fluttered with anxiety and, she had to admit, a fascinated excitement. She understood the nature of Amy's punishment. Mrs Morgan was going to administer an enema into the young woman's rectum.

Mrs Morgan, with fastidious fingertips, took the nozzle from Amy. She held out the jar again. 'Take some more,' she said. 'You'd better lubricate yourself, as well.'

Until now Amy's face had shown only tearful trepidation and miserable resignation. With her fingers covered in a thick layer of cream, she seemed to realise at last the full enormity of what was about to be done to her. Jessica understood her feelings. To be given an enema was bad enough, but to have an audience, and to have to collaborate in the penetration and filling of her own bottom – despite her recent practice at imagining humiliating scenarios, Jessica could think of nothing more demeaning.

With her face glowing red, and sniffing back her sobs of shame, Amy lowered her head and put her hand behind her back.

'Push the cream right in, Amy,' Mrs Morgan told her. 'And look at your mistress.'

Amy moaned, and gazed hopelessly at Mrs Smythe.

'Do stop complaining, Amy,' her owner said, and she added cruelly, 'After all, you usually like playing with your back passage.'

Amy uttered a small cry of protest, but continued to massage the lubricating cream around and into her anus. Jessica imagined the emotions and sensations that the young woman must have been feeling, and found herself becoming more and more aroused.

'That will do, I think,' Mrs Morgan said. 'Now turn away, so that you're facing the side of the bath, and beg.'

For a moment Amy seemed confused by these instructions, but with some prompting from the trainer she arranged herself sideways in the bath, facing away from the spectators, squatting, with her hands together in front of her face. Jessica, who was surprised to find herself taking a connoisseur's interest in the female form, admired the young woman's clear, pale complexion, and the curvaceous shape created by her splayed buttocks, trim waist and heavy breasts.

Mrs Morgan pushed the ridged end of the nozzle into the rubber tube, smeared some more lotion on to the exposed remainder, and pressed on the plunger again, very gently, until liquid ran from the nozzle's spout. She took Amy's right wrist, pulled it to her side, and placed in her fingers the lubricated nozzle. 'Put it in, Amy,' she said. 'Keep pushing until all of the bulb is inside, and your little arsehole has closed around the narrow part.'

Jessica started when she heard the trainer say the coarse word. She wasn't used to hearing such language, and she was sure Mrs Morgan rarely spoke it. But then, she had never before seen a woman perform an act as intimate and degrading as the one that Amy was engaged in. The young woman's shoulders shook with little sobs as she held the nozzle in the valley between her widely parted buttocks. She gave a moan of despair, and pushed inwards with her hand. The bulbous head of the nozzle slid easily into her.

'The solution is simply warm water and a very little soap,' Mrs Morgan said. She laughed. 'I'm saving my special ingredients for the next time Amy misbehaves.' She depressed the plunger a little. The rubber tube appeared to move slightly as the solution was forced along it. Amy let out a long, wavering cry as she felt the liquid streaming into her rectum.

'That seems to be working,' Mrs Morgan said. 'We can proceed. Stand up, Amy. But keep your legs apart, and cross your hands behind your back. Jessica, would you go to the other side of the bath and hold Amy? Thank you, dear. Give me your hand; take this, and hold it up, out of the way.'

'This' was the rubber tube. Mrs Morgan explained that Jessica was to hold Amy in an embrace and, holding the tube in one hand, keep it from obstructing the view of Amy's bottom. Amy, murmuring disconsolately, laid her head on Jessica's shoulder, and her large breasts rested on top of Jessica's smaller, firm, high bosom.

Mrs Morgan made Amy stand with her bottom pushed out, and then Jessica understood why she had been told to hold up the tube: the trainer pulled from her bag a short, wide strap of leather on a wooden handle. Amy was going to be smacked.

'It's not comfortable,' Amy murmured into Jessica's ear. 'That thing in my bum's too big. And I can feel the water sloshing about inside me.'

Jessica hadn't the heart to tell her that her tribulations had hardly started. She stroked her fingers through Amy's auburn curls.

'Would you like to use this?' Mrs Morgan said to Mrs Smythe, holding out the strap. 'I need both hands to operate the syringe.'

Mrs Smythe took the strap and looked at it warily. 'This seems rather severe,' she suggested.

Mrs Morgan shrugged. 'Any we give her now will reduce the number she receives later. And it might help to take her mind off the enema.'

'All right,' Mrs Smythe said. A mischievous smile appeared on her round face. 'This is going to be fun, I think. But shouldn't we change sides? I'm right-handed.'

As the two women, intent on causing distress to Amy's proffered bottom, arranged themselves behind the young woman, Jessica looked towards Mel. She had expected to find her owner interested in the proceedings, or perhaps even excited or disgusted by them, but she found Mel stifling a yawn. Jessica felt a spasm of irritation towards her owner: it wasn't polite to be obviously bored by a spectacle to which she had been invited, and – far worse, from Jessica's point of view – Mel's attitude confirmed Jessica's fears that her owner wasn't interested in the details of discipline.

'You start,' Mrs Morgan said, and Mrs Smythe swung the strap with gusto, so that it landed with a surprisingly loud report on Amy's left buttock.

Jessica heard Amy gasp and felt her body stiffen. 'Oh, no,' the young woman exclaimed, and as the second stroke fell she cried out and tried to turn her bottom away.

Jessica tightened her hold on Amy's shoulders, and kept her still. 'Shush,' she whispered, stroking Amy's hair. She knew that struggling would only prolong Amy's ordeal.

Amy cried out again, a long, drawn-out 'Oh!', and Jessica guessed that another pulse of the warm, soapy water had flooded into her.

Mrs Smythe resumed spanking, and regular loud cracks began to echo from the tiled wall as the strap rose and fell. Jessica, peering over Amy's shoulder, saw the young woman's buttocks flatten, spring back, quiver and redden with each stroke. Mrs Morgan's hand remained on the plunger of the syringe, pushing it down slowly but relentlessly, forcing more and more of the liquid along the tube and into Amy.

'It stings so much,' Amy murmured. 'And the water's filling me up. It's so uncomfortable.'

Jessica didn't know what she could say to console Amy. 'They won't hurt you badly,' she whispered. 'They know what they're doing. Relax. Try to enjoy it.'

'Enjoy it?' Amy asked softly, as if she had no idea what Jessica meant.

'I would,' Jessica said simply, and at that moment her gaze met Mrs Morgan's. Had the trainer overheard what she and Amy had said? Mrs Morgan tilted her head and smiled knowingly. Jessica smiled too, and blushed, and averted her eyes.

She and Mrs Morgan understood each other. They both knew that Jessica wanted to be standing in the bath, surrounded by spectators, being smacked hard on her bottom while her insides were filled with warm water.

'That's all of it,' Mrs Morgan announced. The plunger could not be depressed any further. The entire content of the syringe was now filling Amy's bowel and rectum.

'Just a few more, I think,' Mrs Smythe said, swinging the strap with enthusiasm. 'I'd almost forgotten how much I enjoy this.'

Amy, who was by now moaning continuously, punctuated her moans with cries of 'Ow!' each time the strap landed. Jessica winced as Amy's cries became louder and more insistent.

'That's very good,' Mrs Morgan said. She rested her hand on Amy's bottom, and Jessica felt the young woman flinch. 'A very even colouring. She won't need many more. Now, stand up straight, Amy. Jessica, you can return to your owner.'

Jessica went round the bath and stood next to Mel. She took Mel's hand and pressed it against her almost hairless mound as she placed a kiss on Mel's cheek. Mel turned and smiled, and Jessica felt a satisfied glow. She was a good pet.

Amy, standing in the bath, looked a picture of misery. She appeared to be on the point of bursting into tears. Her belly was swollen, and the rubber tube issuing from between her glowing buttocks made her look ridiculous.

'Roll over, Amy,' Mrs Morgan said. 'Lie in the bath, with your bottom towards the taps. Melanie, Jessica, come closer and watch.'

When Jessica came to stand beside the bath she found Amy arranged in a position similar to that which she herself had recently been required to adopt when displaying herself to Amy's owner. Amy, with her eyes squeezed shut so that she couldn't see the circle of faces gazing down at her, was lying on her back with her knees drawn up to her shoulders. Her arms were crossed tightly behind her knees, so that the fronts of her thighs were crushed against the large, soft cushions of her breasts. Her buttocks, Jessica noticed, were already losing some of their redness. And her private parts, from the dark-red curls that fringed her sex to her anus, held open by the nozzle, were obscenely on display.

Jessica suppressed a gasp of surprise. A hand was touching her bottom – caressing it – and it couldn't be Mel's hand, as Mel was standing on the other side of the bath. It could only be Mrs Morgan, touching Jessica secretly while everyone's attention was concentrated on the pitiful figure in the bath.

'Isn't she lovely?' the trainer said, and although it must have seemed to everyone else that she was referring to Amy, Jessica suspected that the location of her hand gave a truer indication of her meaning. 'Sometimes,' Mrs Morgan went on, 'I regret that I don't have a pet of my own. Now, Amy, you know what you have to do next. Take out the nozzle and give it to me.'

'No, please,' Amy whispered. Bright tears welled in the corners of her tightly shut eyes.

Jessica could imagine what would happen when the nozzle was extracted. The liquid inside Amy would begin to leak out of her anus. She could understand why Amy was so reluctant to obey the instruction to remove the rubber plug, but she realised that there was no alternative: the liquid would have to come out, sooner or later.

'Come along, Amy,' Mrs Smythe barked. 'Do you want to be punished for disobedience as well?'

With a despairing cry Amy fumbled for the hose, gripped it, and pulled. She groaned as the bulbous end of the nozzle slid from her anus.

But there was no trickle of liquid. Jessica was perplexed. Mrs Morgan chuckled as she wound up the tubing. 'She's holding it in,' she said. 'Silly girl. It's all got to come out, Amy. Stand back, everyone.'

Jessica, Mel and Mrs Smythe took a step back from the side of the bath.

There was silence, but for Amy's pants and groans as she tried to keep the sphincter of her anus clenched.

Then she let out a cry, and a fountain of liquid jetted from her bottom and splashed against the end of the bath. Spurt after spurt pumped out of her as she tossed her head from side to side. Tears of shame coursed down her face.

'How splendidly disgusting,' Mrs Smythe said. 'Thank you, Mrs Morgan. I think that Amy has learned her lesson now. And we've all seen what a dirty girl she really is.'

'My pleasure, Mrs Smythe,' the trainer said, and once again she caught Jessica's eye.

'It's time for a coffee break,' Mrs Smythe announced. 'Let's all go downstairs. Amy, you will join us once you've cleaned and disinfected the bath and washed yourself. And do it thoroughly, girl.'

Jessica was sent into the kitchen to make the refreshments. As she spooned coffee into a jug and waited for the kettle to boil she had time to reflect on the extraordinary events she had just witnessed. She could hear Mrs Smythe's pet moving about the bathroom above her head.

The most surprising thing, Jessica thought, is that I'm entirely calm. I'm not frightened, or outraged, or angry. And there's no point in denying it: I wanted it to be me being shown off and punished in the bathroom. Quite frankly, Amy didn't put on a very good performance. I'm not surprised her owner isn't pleased with her. I would have done it better. Mel would have been proud of me. And so would Mrs Morgan.

She looked out of the kitchen window. Mrs Smythe's back garden was as densely furnished as her house. There were so many trees and shrubs that there was hardly room on the patches of lawn for all the sundials and bird tables and ornamental wheelbarrows. Blackbirds flew noisily from shrub to shrub. Rain was falling steadily. It looked entirely normal: just like the garden of any suburban house.

But here I am, Jessica thought, as good as completely naked, making coffee for a group of women who can order me to do the most depraved and shameful things. And who certainly will. And it doesn't seem wrong, or particularly strange. As soon as I walk through the door, carrying this tray, they'll all stare at me, and give me instructions. And I know that I'll enjoy it. I just hope that one of them can think of a pretext for punishing me. My poor little bottom hasn't been smacked for ages.

Humming contentedly, Jessica carried the jug, cups, saucers and milk into the reception room. Mrs Smythe, Mel and Mrs Morgan were sitting in armchairs. Amy, still wearing nothing but her collar and looking very dejected, was kneeling in the 'sit' position beside Mrs Smythe's chair.

'Did you find everything, Jessica?' Mrs Smythe asked. 'Oh, yes, I see that you did. Amy, go and help Jessica serve the coffee.'

When each of the three women had been provided with a drink, Amy resumed her position next to her owner, and Jessica kneeled beside Mel. Jessica was slightly worried about her owner: Mel had not seemed to enjoy watching Amy being given an enema, and as a new owner she was clearly not at ease with Mrs Smythe and the pet-trainer. Jessica turned and looked up at her, and smiled, and stroked her legs.

Mel gratefully returned the smile and, encouraged, Jessica nestled her cheek against Mel's knee and began to kiss the soft curve at the top of Mel's calf. Mel put her hand on Jessica's head and played with her hair.

'You've got a very good-natured pet, Melanie,' Mrs Smythe commented. Jessica felt once again the thrill of being noticed and a swelling of pride in her chest.

'Oh,' Mel said. 'Yes, but – you don't mind, do you?'

'Good heavens, no,' Mrs Smythe said. 'On the contrary. You go ahead and enjoy yourself. I often get one of mine to give me an orgasm while I'm sipping my morning coffee. That's one of the reasons I like to have two. One to serve the coffee, and the other on licking duty.'

'Oh,' Mel said. 'Well, I hadn't – but, as long as you don't mind, I admit it would be pleasant. And I've been dying to show you how very obliging Jess is. She's got a wicked little tongue. And you and Mrs Morgan can watch her. I'm sure you've noticed what a pretty bottom she has.'

'Indeed,' was Mrs Morgan's only comment.

Jessica found herself becoming excited all over again. Just as she was beginning to find it natural to be kneeling naked in someone else's house, she was reminded how strange and naughty it was. Now she was going to kneel between Mel's thighs, and lick Mel's sweet, shaved sex, all the while displaying her bottom to the other two women.

As Mel tugged up her skirt and lifted her legs apart, Jessica saw Amy turn towards her owner with a resigned look on her face.

'It's all right, Amy, dear,' Mrs Smythe said. 'I'll defer my pleasure until this afternoon. I'm going to enjoy watching Jessica and Mel. But,' she added, thoughtfully, 'perhaps Mrs Morgan would like to use you. If you're good she might let you off the remainder of your punishment.'

'That's not likely,' Mrs Morgan said. 'But I'll accept your offer, Mrs Smythe. It's a long time since I've had Amy, and I'll enjoy being licked by such a disgracefully filthy pet. I'll make myself comfortable, if I may.'

Mrs Morgan stood up and unbuttoned her white coat. Jessica, who was by now on her hands and knees in front of Mel's chair and kissing the insides of Mel's thighs, caught only glimpses of what else was happening in the room. She saw the glimmering dark blue of Mrs Morgan's corset; she saw Amy's disconsolate face; she saw the trainer pick up her coffee cup and, still standing, start to sip from it as Amy kneeled behind her and reluctantly pressed her face between the slender cheeks of Mrs Morgan's bottom.

For a long time the room was silent, except for the chink of china cups on their saucers and the occasional rustle of clothing. From time to time Mrs Morgan issued a quiet instruction to Amy, but Mel was apparently content to let Jessica proceed in her own way.

Jessica soon became oblivious to everything except the delicious smell and taste of her owner, and the surges of arousal in her own body. Every now and then she remembered that Mrs Smythe and Mrs Morgan could see her bottom and her private parts, and she experienced a more than usually intense thrill.

Soon Jessica noticed that Mel was moving her hips slightly, pushing her sex forwards to meet Jessica's invasive tongue. Jessica lifted her face so that she could concentrate on licking her owner's clitoris. The round tip felt as hard as a gem against Jessica's flickering tongue.

Mel put a hand on Jessica's head. 'Stop, Jess,' she gasped. 'I'm nearly there. It's too soon.'

Jessica pulled her head back and looked up at her owner. Mel's pretty face was flushed, her pink lips were curved in a dreamy smile, and her eyes, under her half-closed lids, were as bright as the sky. Jessica was delighted to see her owner so blissfully happy, and felt proud of her cunnilingual skills. 'I'm very sorry, Mistress,' she said, but with a smile that belied her words. She rested her cheek against the inside of Mel's right thigh, so that she could kiss the delicate skin there and inhale the sharp honey aroma of Mel's wet sex.

Mel returned the smile, and stroked Jessica's hair. 'Oh, Jess,' she whispered. 'I'm so glad you're my pet. I've waited years to have a pet of my own, and now I've got a really good one. All the other owners will want to borrow you, once they see how clever you are with your tongue. But I don't think it would be polite for me to have an orgasm without asking Mrs Smythe first. And she's rather busy at the moment. Look, Jess.'

Reluctantly Jessica turned away from her owner's delectable private parts. She saw that Mrs Morgan had sat in one of the armchairs and, like Mel, had lifted her heels on to the edge of the seat and opened wide her thighs. Amy's pink bottom was very open and prominent, as she was kneeling in front of the chair. The trainer was holding Amy's head firmly with both hands, and pressing Amy's face against her sex. Amy's head was moving up and down at a slow but regular pace. It wasn't clear to Jessica whether the movement was of Amy's volition or was dictated by the trainer's hands.

Mrs Smythe, still fully dressed, was sitting on a footstool beside Amy and was carrying out a thorough inspection of her pet's most intimate parts. The young woman's sex-lips and clitoral prepuce were pulled, pinched, peeled back and held open while Mrs Smythe's fingers probed every crevice. From time to time she stopped and used a handkerchief to wipe Amy's juices from her hand. She pulled the stool closer and, resting her left arm across Amy's back, she used the fingers of her left hand to hold apart Amy's buttocks while with her right hand she carried out a fingertip search of the corrugated skin around Amy's anus.

'She seems clean now,' she announced grudgingly.

'Good,' Mrs Morgan said. 'We must be sure she remembers to stay that way. Now, I think, would be a good time to conclude her punishment. I'm approaching a climax.'

Jessica marvelled at the trainer's self-control. Her voice was as level and stern as ever, and apart from a blush at her throat and high on her cheeks she appeared unmoved.

Mrs Smythe took from the trainer's leather bag a switch of wood. 'Is this the implement you had in mind?' she said. 'I thought you'd want to use it.'

Mrs Morgan hadn't stopped pressing Amy's face into her groin. 'I had planned to,' she said, 'but under the circumstances I'd be grateful if you could administer the final punishment. Hard and fast, Mrs Smythe. This is no time for finesse. Just lay them on hard and fast.'

Mrs Smythe rested the wooden dowel across her pet's bottom, in order to gauge the distance. Amy's buttocks flinched at the touch. Mrs Smythe moved the stool away a little, and resumed her seat. She lifted the switch.

'Martha,' Mel whispered urgently, 'I'm sorry to interrupt. But would you mind very much if I had an orgasm now? I'm afraid Jess's little tongue has worked its usual magic.'

'You go ahead, my dear,' Mrs Smythe said. 'Enjoy yourself. But if you want to delay for a few moments, I'd be happy to give Jessica a taste of the cane after I've finished with Amy.'

'Oh, no, Martha,' Mel said, much to Jessica's disappointment. 'I can't wait. Come along, Jess. Get that tongue of yours working.'

As Jessica kissed, licked and nibbled her owner's sweet little clitoris, making Mel squirm and gasp, she could only think of how unfair it was. She wasn't going to get a spanking of any sort, and with her face pressed into the wet warmth of Mel's sex she could hardly hear, still less see, Mrs Smythe applying the switch to Amy's bottom.

She was aware only of Mel's increasingly abrupt cries and movements and, as a sort of echo, the more distant sounds that Mrs Morgan made as she, like Mel, climbed up towards the precipice of ecstasy.

A few moments later the room was quiet again. Jessica knelt in front of Mel's chair while Mel wiped her pet's damp face with a tissue. Amy, her face wet with her own tears as well as Mrs Morgan's juices, was padding with painful slowness about the room, collecting the coffee cups. Jessica watched her and coveted the bright red stripes that criss-crossed her bottom. Mrs Morgan, still wearing only her corset and stockings, was sitting back with a satisfied smile on her face. Mrs Smythe was watching her pet. The room was full of silence and the smell of female sex.

'That was a very enjoyable coffee break,' Mrs Morgan said. 'I suppose I'd better be on my way. I trust everything was to your satisfaction, Mrs Smythe?' She stood up and pulled on her white coat.

'Perfectly. I don't think Amy's likely to forget to keep herself clean for me, at least not for a while. But it's still pouring down outside. By all means stay a little longer, Mrs Morgan. Perhaps you'd like to see the alterations I've had done upstairs. I've turned the third bedroom into a playroom for my pets.'

'I'd heard you were doing something of the sort,' the trainer said. She went to the window and looked out at the rain. 'Perhaps I'd better wait until this stops. And I would like to see this room of yours.'

'Upstairs, then,' Mrs Smythe cried. 'Come along, Melanie. And bring Jessica. Amy, you lead the way. You can show everyone the stripes you've been given, as we climb the stairs.'

Jessica was at the rear of the column of women that went up the stairs and along the wood-panelled landing, and so she was the last to enter Mrs Smythe's playroom. She was immediately struck by its warmth: she felt comfortable, despite being almost naked, everywhere in the centrally heated house, but this bedroom had two radiators and a fire burning in its fireplace.

'I keep the temperature up,' Mrs Smythe said. 'None of us wear very much when we're up here, and I like to be cosy.'

In Jessica's opinion the room was so cosy that it was almost oppressive. In her choice of décor Mrs Smythe had given full rein to her taste for dark, sumptuous fabrics. The windows were concealed behind curtains of dark-green velvet, and the room was illuminated by lamps on the walls that made pools of yellow light. There were so many swags and garlands of rich material that little of the dark, finely patterned wallpaper could be seen, and the furniture – two large sofas – was thickly upholstered.

The strangest thing about the room, however, was that in the centre, where the bed might have been expected to sit, there was a square corral made of dark, polished wood. Inside it were piles of cushions.

'I've told Tom it's my sewing room,' Mrs Smythe said. 'The poor dear has no idea what sewing entails.'

Mel ran a hand along the polished wood. 'This is for Jane and Amy, isn't it?' she said. 'I remember that you like to watch your pets playing.'

'Quite right, dear,' Mrs Smythe said. 'And this is the playpen I've had made for them. On rainy days such as this the three of us sit up here for hours at a time. And, as I've said before, I can't tell you how useful it is to have two pets. Usually I have one on my lap, to pet and cuddle, while I watch the other playing. And sometimes I just sit and watch them play together. All their toys are in the box in the corner.'

Jessica looked at the wooden chest, which had an upholstered top. It was large enough to contain a considerable number of toys.

'You'd like to show everyone how you play with yourself, wouldn't you, Amy?' Mrs Smythe said.

'Yes, Mistress,' Amy replied without enthusiasm.

'Oh, buck up, Amy,' her owner said. 'Your punishment's over now. You can relax and enjoy yourself in the playpen. Perhaps,' she went on, turning to Mel, 'Jessica would like to join you.'

Mel glanced at Jessica.

'Oh, yes, please,' Jessica said to Mel. 'May I, Mistress?'

'I don't see why not,' Mel said.

Mrs Morgan was at the window. She had lifted a corner of a curtain and was looking out. 'The rain's easing off,' she said. 'I should return to the shop.'

'That's a relief,' Mel said. 'About the rain, I mean,' she added, blushing. 'It's just that it's Bella Northrop's party tomorrow afternoon, and if the weather's fine it will be in her garden. Everyone's going to be there, and I'm going to present Jess.'

'Really?' Mrs Morgan said sharply. 'She's had only one session of training. Do you think she's ready?'

Mel looked defensive but defiant. 'Yes, I do,' she said. 'She's already obedient, and you can see she's always trying to please me. Anyway, I can hardly turn up at the party without her, can I?'

'I would have preferred to have had some more time training her,' Mrs Morgan said. 'But you're probably right. She has very winning ways, and I doubt if the committee will have any reservations.' She smiled at Jessica. 'We can always catch up on her training later.'

'I'm glad you approve,' Mel said tartly.

Mrs Morgan's face resumed its customary expression of stern displeasure. 'If Jessica is to be presented tomorrow,' she said, 'there are a few things to consider. First, you will need a collar and a lead for her. I think cream suits her colouring.'

'I'll come to the shop later today,' Mel said. 'I'll make my own choice, thank you. And I'll return the things we've borrowed.'

Jessica was aware that her nipples had hardened while her owner and the trainer were discussing her. She couldn't help being excited. Mel was going to take her to a party. All the other owners would be there. And all their pets. And they would all want to see her.

'Next,' Mrs Morgan said, 'I strongly advise you, Melanie, to practise the art of discipline.' She held up her hand to forestall the objections she expected. 'I appreciate that Jessica is well behaved. She's obedient and eager, and she enjoys showing off her body.'

Mrs Morgan's icy blue eyes scanned Jessica slowly from top to toe, making her blush. She reached for her owner, took Mel's hand in hers, gave it a squeeze, and placed it on her bottom. She wanted Mel to understand that she didn't mind being punished. In fact, she

152

thought, there wasn't much point in being a pet unless it entailed regular spankings.

'Lydia Henshaw isn't anyone's idea of a martinet,' Mrs Morgan went on, 'and I have my suspicions that virtually the only punishments that you've ever received, Melanie, were those I gave you during your training. So you've little experience at either end of the cane. But every pet needs corporal punishment from time to time, and Jessica is no exception. On the contrary, I've found that she responds well to discipline. To sum up, I think you should give Jessica a spanking, at the very least.'

Jessica rubbed her bottom against Mel's hand. Things were getting better and better. She remembered how she had hated it when, at school, the teachers had towered over her as they discussed the shortcomings of her work. She had felt defenceless and very small. She felt the same now, as she stood naked and collared while other women calmly debated the punishment she should receive. But instead of fear and resentment, now she felt only a mild and rather exciting trepidation – as well as anticipation and an insistent sexual yearning that was, once again, making her damp and hot in her private parts.

'You mean, now?' Mel asked.

'Why not?' Mrs Morgan replied.

'Oh, yes, Melanie,' Mrs Smythe put in. 'Do it now. Mrs Morgan's quite right. You have to be confident that you can keep your pet under control. And it will be lovely to see our pets playing together, and both with red bottoms.'

'Oh, all right, then,' Mel declared. 'I'll give her a spanking. Although she's done nothing to deserve it.'

'I'll help you,' Mrs Smythe said. 'Amy, come here and undress me. Melanie, I think you'd better take some things off, too. It's too warm in here for physical exertion while fully clothed.'

Before Mel had time to ask her, Jessica started to undo the buttons of Mel's clothes. As Jessica removed

Mel's skirt and blouse the two women carried on a whispered conversation. Mel tried to reassure Jessica that she was a good pet, and had done nothing wrong, and that the punishment would be gentle and was intended only as a warning; Jessica tried to reassure Mel that she understood, and that she didn't mind, and she was happy for Mel to spank her as hard as she could.

Once Mel was wearing only her high-heeled patent-leather shoes, her stockings, her suspender belt, and her jewellery, Jessica snuggled up to her and nuzzled the tips of her breasts. Jessica was almost dizzy with excitement. She loved being looked at and humiliated and controlled by these women, but being spanked was best of all.

'Come along,' Mrs Smythe called. She was now wearing only a green basque, which emphasised her curvaceous figure, and stockings, and she was sitting on one of the sofas. 'Sit beside me, Melanie, and we'll have your pet across our laps. Amy, bring me two cushions.'

The cushions went on Mel's lap, under Jessica's belly, to push up her bottom. Mrs Smythe held Jessica's wrists in one hand, and with the other she pressed Jessica's face into her lap. Mrs Smythe smelled of vanilla and talcum powder, and Jessica found that, once she had worked her head into the gap between the woman's spread thighs, her tongue could reach the top of the slit of her sex.

'Oh, I say!' Mrs Smythe exclaimed. 'She is keen, isn't she? She needs a spanking for being presumptuous. Get going, Melanie.'

Mel's first few smacks were no more than the lightest of slaps, but with encouragement from Mrs Morgan and Mrs Smythe she began to use a little force, and Jessica started to enjoy herself. She kept her bottom high, and she moved her legs apart as much as she could, so that Mel could reach the insides of her thighs and her sex. It was only the inaccuracy of Mel's aim, however, that resulted in any of the smacks landing on these sensitive areas, and although Jessica soon found herself gasping and moaning into Mrs Smythe's private parts as she was taken step by step towards the summit of her arousal, in the back of her mind she wished that the punishment was more proficient and, frankly, harder. She wanted Matt, that was the trouble.

Still, her bottom was smarting and throbbing, and each smack produced a resonant sound and a blaze of stinging pain. She was so close to coming that she couldn't keep still, and without a thought for her appearance she thrust her bottom up to meet each slap.

'That's it,' Mel announced. 'My arm's getting tired. Jess's bottom is good and red.'

'And if I know Jessica,' Mrs Morgan said, 'you'll find she's soaking wet, as well. Keep her there for a moment, please.'

Jessica hoped that the trainer was going to finish off the punishment, perhaps with the wooden dowel that had made such attractive stripes on Amy's bottom. But when she turned her head she saw that Mrs Morgan hadn't removed her white uniform and was inspecting the contents of the toy-chest in the corner of the room.

'Could Mel borrow one of these,' Mrs Morgan asked, 'for Jessica? If she's to be presented tomorrow she should be prepared.'

'Of course,' Mrs Smythe replied. 'Take whichever you think best. We'd better hold her still for you.'

Jessica felt Mrs Smythe's hand close more tightly around her wrists, and her head was once more pushed and held between the woman's thighs. Mel, following Mrs Smythe's guidance, grasped the backs of Jessica's knees and held them apart.

Jessica still presumed that Mrs Morgan intended to add to her punishment, and that she had found in the toy-box a suitably devilish implement. She waited impatiently for the first streak of biting pain to flame across her bottom, her thighs or her sex.

Instead, she heard the trainer say, 'That's that. I'd better put some here, too.'

And then she gasped as she felt cool fingers pressing into the valley between her buttocks. Mrs Morgan's fingers weren't merely cool: they felt smooth – almost liquid. Of course: the trainer was lubricating Jessica's anus with the cream she had used for the nozzle of Amy's enema.

Jessica's heart leaped into her throat. Oh, goodness! Was she going to get an enema, too? But no: it couldn't be that. That would have to be done in the bathroom. Before she had time to speculate any more, she felt something cool and hard pressing into the funnel of sensitive skin around her little hole.

'Relax, Jessica,' Mrs Smythe said. 'Let it in.'

Jessica cried out in the darkness between Mrs Smythe's thighs as something opened the sphincter of her anus and was pushed into her.

It was too wide. It was hurting. Would it never stop pushing inwards? She couldn't take it. It was invading her, filling her. And still it hurt. And then the sharp pain was gone, and Jessica was left with a feeling of intrusive fullness and a pulsing ache.

'There,' Mrs Morgan said. 'All inside. I chose a small one, because she's not used to it, and it's got a large base so it can't slip any further in. You should leave it in for at least a few hours, Melanie. I know it seems cruel, but tomorrow Jessica will be grateful that we prepared her.'

'I know,' Mel said. 'I don't think I would have got through my presentation if you hadn't prepared me. Three days with one of those things in my back passage! I hated you for it at the time, you know.'

'You made that very clear,' Mrs Morgan said. 'And now I really must be on my way. Thank you for your hospitality, Mrs Smythe. And, Melanie, don't forget that Jessica's had only the very basic elements of her training. You should book her in for more lessons.'

'I will,' Mel said.

'Thank you, Mrs Morgan, for helping me with my wayward pet,' Mrs Smythe said. 'Amy, go to the door with Mrs Morgan. And say thank you to her before she leaves the house.'

Mel and Mrs Smythe had released their hold on Jessica, but she remained lying across their laps with her bottom in the air. Even the residual ache was diminishing rapidly, leaving her with a feeling of being stretched and filled that she realised was not at all unpleasant. What with that, and the lovely sore tingling of her buttocks, she was unable to ignore her bottom. She wondered what it would feel like to be spanked while she had the thing in her anus, and she decided that she would certainly enjoy it.

'It's time to get off, Jess,' Mel said. 'Stand up.'

'And take off your shoes and stockings,' Mrs Smythe added. You can't wear them in the playpen.'

Jessica felt the weight of the thing inside her as she stood and began to unfasten the clips of her suspender belt. She had deduced that the object must be a bulbous cylinder, like the front end of the nozzle that had been inserted into Amy, with a narrow waist near the bottom, around which her sphincter had contracted, and below that a wide base, which she could feel resting against her buttocks. She was sure that the base would prevent the object from sliding any further into her, but she worried that now she was standing upright it might slip out. It was solid and heavy, and pressed continuously against the inside of her anal ring, widening it until she clenched the muscle and drew the cylinder deeper inside.

As Jessica finished undressing, Amy returned.

'Put the toy-box into the pen, Amy,' Mrs Smythe said. 'And then take Jessica and show her how you play. Doesn't she look lovely with her bottom nicely coloured, and with your black plug in her back passage?'

'Yes, Mistress,' Amy agreed listlessly, and she went to collect the chest from the corner of the room.

Jessica turned to look at her owner, and found that Mel was regarding her with a sympathetic smile.

'It's not too uncomfortable, is it, Jess? And I hope I didn't smack you too hard.'

Jessica simply smiled and shook her head.

'Run along and play with Amy, then,' Mel said. 'Don't worry. I'll be watching you.'

Taking careful steps, and conscious of the slight movements of the cylinder inside her, Jessica joined Amy in the playpen. At last she could see the contents of the chest. It was full of objects that made her imagination reel.

Many of them, made of polished wood or ivory, were long, tapered cylinders, similar in shape, she assumed, to the one inside her anus. They reminded her of Matt's erect penis, and some of them were sculpted to resemble the male member. They varied considerably in size. Some of them had wide bases, and a few of these had narrow waists above their bases; one had a metal ring set into the base, and another a plume of feathers. One of the objects appeared to be made up of two of the cylinders, joined at an acute angle.

There were harnesses made of leather straps; short lengths of chain with screw clips at each end; a set of large beads strung on to a cord; and metal devices that resembled surgical instruments.

Amy picked up several of the phalluses, and thoughtfully selected an artificial penis with a flanged base. 'Choose one of these,' she told Jessica, 'and then we'll get comfortable on the cushions. As long as we're playing quietly the owners won't disturb us.'

Jessica found a phallus that was similar to the one Amy had chosen. She looked towards the sofas and saw that Mel and Mrs Smythe, both unselfconsciously unclothed, were sitting side be side and were deep in conversation. She heard Mel say, 'I've been meaning to ask you, Martha, about where you find all these wonderful fabrics.'

'How are you feeling?' Jessica asked Amy. 'You didn't look as though you were enjoying that enema.' On her hands and knees, she helped Amy to construct a nest of cushions in which the two pets could recline together.

'It was hateful,' Amy said. 'And I could have done without the strap and the cane, too. My bottom's still really sore. Do you think there will be any marks?' She turned away from Jessica and looked over her shoulder.

Amy's broad, round buttocks were now only slightly pink, and Jessica could see only a few faint lines. She ran the tip of a finger along them, and felt Amy shiver. 'There's almost nothing left,' Jessica said. It seemed a shame. Jessica hoped that her own bottom would remain red until she saw Matt, and that he would then give her some marks that would last until bedtime.

'Thank goodness,' Amy said. 'My husband, David, has been away for a few days. He's coming home tonight and I expect he'll want to, you know, make love. He's not very good at it, frankly. I have more fun when Jane puts on her harness and does me with one of these dildoes. But I'd rather not have to disappoint him.'

Amy hadn't altered her position, and Jessica was still stroking her buttocks. She had thought of offering to spank Amy, to restore the fading blush, but she realised that the offer wouldn't be welcome. Instead, as Amy seemed happy to be caressed, she let her fingers slide into the valley between her buttocks, and then towards her sex. Amy sighed, and dipped her back, and edged her knees further apart.

As Jessica began to stroke and pull at the little auburn curls on Amy's sex-lips, she marvelled again at the pleasure she took in women's bodies. It was, she thought, even more surprising than the discovery that she revelled in being controlled and punished. But with her bottom smarting and her anus filled, it was difficult to think about anything but sexual pleasure. She could feel, bubbling inside her like simmering water in a kettle, the desire to be spanked and penetrated. And being naked, with another pet, and being watched by an audience, kept her hot. She glanced towards the sofa.

She found Mrs Smythe looking at her, with her hand in her lap. 'Look, Melanie,' Mrs Smythe said. 'Jessica's started to play with Amy. Don't they look adorable? Please don't be shy about touching yourself, if you'd like to. I always do while I'm watching my pets at play.'

Jessica began to kiss the soft, warm skin of Amy's buttocks. She closed her eyes. Her body was quivering with lust. The sharp smell of female arousal was beginning to permeate through the close, hot air in the room. She pressed the tips of her fingers into the gap between Amy's sex-lips. They encountered no resistance, and slid easily into Amy's open, wet vagina.

Jessica extracted her fingers, drawing a moan of protest from Amy. She crawled alongside Amy and pulled her into the nest of cushions so that they were lying side be side. She put her hand between Amy's thighs and started to press inwards again with her fingers. 'You said you hadn't enjoyed your punishment,' Jessica whispered, with a giggle, 'but you're awfully wet.'

Amy smiled ruefully, and Jessica couldn't resist kissing her plump lips. Amy seemed surprised by this intimacy, but then she smiled again and returned the kiss. Immediately the two pets were face to face with their lips together and their hands exploring each other's breasts and sex.

'I know,' Amy said between kisses, 'it's really galling. I've had enemas before. Martha's obsessive about cleanliness. She always brings that Mrs Morgan woman to do it. I thought I'd seen the last of her when I finished my training. Those cold blue eyes! You know, I think she actually enjoys punishing us pets. Anyway, although I detest the enemas, the embarrassing thing is that afterwards I start to feel ever so excited. I can't explain it.'

It was obvious to Jessica that Amy was very aroused. Her kisses were becoming increasingly passionate; her voluptuous breasts were warm and firm, and their nipples were as hard as walnuts; and Jessica's hand had almost disappeared into the sopping channel between Amy's thighs.

'I'm even prepared to forgive you,' Amy added, squeezing Jessica's left breast.

'Whatever for?' Jessica murmured. She couldn't recall anything she had done to annoy Mrs Smythe's pet.

'I was fourth on the list,' Amy explained as she concentrated on pinching around Jessica's nipples. 'Now I've been knocked down one place.'

'Oh, I see,' Jessica said. 'Oh, that's lovely, Amy. You can do it harder if you like. Look, our owners are watching us. Now that Mel's an owner –'

'Yes, Lydia Henshaw's gone straight to the top of the list, and she'll get the opportunity to recruit the next newcomer.'

Jessica groaned and arched her back. Amy was using both hands now to torment her breasts, kneading, pinching, and pressing her fingernails into the most delicate places around the sides and tips of Jessica's nipples. The uncomfortable weight filling Jessica's rectum seemed to make her breasts feel even more sensitive than usual: it was as if there were chains of nerves connecting her anus to her nipples, and then stretching down to her clitoris. And the little jagged pulses of pain caused by Amy's fingers made the taut chains of nerves vibrate, more and more, until Jessica knew that if she let down her defences a climax would overwhelm her.

'How much longer,' she gasped, trying to concentrate on anything to deflate the orgasmic pressure, 'will you have to wait?'

Amy was now gasping, too. Jessica's fingers were moving deep inside her, and the heel of Jessica's hand was pressing hard against the hood of her clitoris. 'It'll only be, I don't know, perhaps an extra month or two. I'll get my chance before the end of the year, I expect. And,' she added, giving Jessica's nipples a pinch and a twist, 'I hope I get a pet as good as you.'

Suddenly she pulled away. Jessica moaned with frustration.

'We'd better not come yet,' Amy said. 'Our owners will probably notice, and they haven't given us permission. Martha will want to see us using the toys first. Here: lie on your side, like this, with this leg bent. I'll do the same. Now, put your phallus into me, and I'll put this one into you. Feels good, doesn't it? Now we can move these things gently in and out, while we carry on talking and kissing.'

Jessica could find no fault with the arrangement. It was heavenly to lie next to Mrs Smythe's voluptuous pet. She and Amy kissed, and toyed with each other's nipples, and moved the phalluses in and out of each other's vagina.

'When we get bored with this,' Amy said, 'we can put the harnesses on. Martha always likes it when Jane and I take it in turns to pretend to be a man.'

'That sounds wonderful,' Jessica breathed. 'But I don't think I'll ever get bored with this.'

Amy sighed as Jessica's lips closed around her left nipple. 'Sometimes it's not too bad to be a pet,' she said. 'Martha's all right, too. Some of the owners are real tyrants. Try to steer clear of Olivia Reynolds, if you can. She uses a whip. You'll find out which ones to avoid. You've got years of being a pet ahead of you. I'll be an owner soon. On the committee. That's all that matters.'

Jessica wanted to disagree, but her mouth was full of Amy's nipple. She realised that, unlike Mel and Amy, she wasn't really interested in becoming an owner. She was happy as a pet: very, very happy, and at that moment once again getting quite close to coming.

I can easily cope with years of this, she thought. In fact, I don't want it ever to stop. I want to be a pet for ever.

And I hope I meet Olivia Reynolds soon.

By the time Jessica arrived at the Hillingbury Health and Exercise Club it was already late afternoon. Once again there would be no time for her exercise programme: she would have to report to her mentor, tell him everything that she had done during the day, and hope that he had time to punish her and use her.

She had been in a state of arousal for so many hours that she felt disconnected from the world. It seemed as though she had floated, rather than walked, from her house to the club. As the rain had stopped at last, and the sun was out, the raincoat had seemed inappropriate, and she had put on a skirt and a blouse. She was still wearing the stockings and ankle-boots from the morning's outing.

Her breasts, bottom and sex were naked under her summery garments and, of all the sensory stimuli surrounding her as she walked to the club, only the sensations in these erogenous zones managed to hold her attention. In fact she couldn't stop thinking about those sensitive parts of her body, and things that she hoped Matt would do to them. Her bottom, in particular, wouldn't let her forget that it hadn't been spanked since the morning, and then not much. Her skin was tingling with anticipation. And she had become so used to the weight and size of the plug that she had worn in her anus for most of the day that, now it was no longer there, she missed the uncomfortably full feeling.

'You're late again,' Matt said, as soon as they were alone in his office. 'Don't bother to explain, I know you have other commitments now. Undress, please.'

He seemed more austere and remote than ever. It seemed impossible to believe that he cared for her in the slightest. And yet he insisted, each time she left, that she must return. And, as she stood before him, naked but for her stockings, with her hands clasped behind her head, she could see that he desired her.

He walked behind her to lock the door and, instead of returning to the desk, without warning he grasped her wrists in his left hand, bent her over, and delivered six hefty smacks to her buttocks. Jessica hardly had time to breathe, still less to enjoy the painful sensations, and the spanking was over almost as soon as it had begun.

There was no explanation for the punishment. Matt pulled off his T-shirt and his shorts, sat at the desk, and gestured to Jessica to stand at his left side.

'Report,' he said, and positioned a pen in readiness over a blank notepad.

Jessica drew a deep breath. He had hardly looked at her since she had arrived. Did he know, she wondered, how much his disdainful attitude excited her? Was his severe, almost contemptuous manner an act, designed to inflame her perverse desires? Or was it that he truly didn't care?

As she gave a detailed account of her activities during the day, Jessica consoled herself with the thought that Matt must like her, at least a little: he couldn't keep his hand off her. While he wrote copious notes with his right hand, his left was roaming across and between Jessica's blushing buttocks. She talked, falteringly whenever his fingers dipped into the wet channel of her sex, and he wrote without pause, even when she described the events that had taken place in Mrs Smythe's bathroom. He seemed imperturbable.

She couldn't keep her eyes from his manhood, rising like a domed tower between his hard, flat stomach and the front of the desk. She wanted to touch it, and her wish was granted when she began to tell him about the toys in Mrs Smythe's playroom. He stopped writing and pushed his chair back a little.

'You like to have something to play with, do you?' he said. 'Play with that. Continue your report.'

Leaning forwards, with her hand curled round his hot, hard shaft and her right buttock cupped in his left hand, she managed to resume her account. Now that she was holding his erection she felt more disoriented than ever by the strength of her desire. It wasn't enough to have his manhood in her hand: she wanted it in her mouth.

He stopped writing, abruptly, when she told him about the plug that had been inserted into her anus. His hand fell from her bottom.

'Bend over the desk,' he said. 'Legs wide, bottom up.'

He pushed his chair back and stood beside her. He wasn't satisfied with her position. Wordlessly he pulled her arms behind her back and pressed her breasts against the surface of the desk. He slapped her thighs further apart. With the fingers of his right hand he held apart her buttocks. Then, as she had expected, he used his other hand to inspect her little hole. As his fingers pressed and probed a wave of shame swept over her. There was nothing, she realised, that she would not let this man do to her. It didn't matter how much or how little he cared for her, or if he cared at all. Her devotion to him was absolute, unconditional.

She gasped as his finger slid into her. He murmured, as if the ease of entry corroborated her story. A second finger worked its way alongside the first, and Jessica sighed. She realised that she had made another discovery about herself: she loved the feeling of having her anus penetrated. It was so perverse, so intrusive, so satisfyingly filling.

Matt's fingers pushed further in, and Jessica wriggled her bottom.

'You're leaking,' he said. It was true: she could feel the wetness seeping from her sex.

Without extracting his fingers from her, he spanked her again. Another six hard smacks, right in the middle of her bottom, his hand landing on the inside underslopes, his fingers spanking her wet vulva.

Still his fingers remained inside her. His elbow, resting on her back, kept her pressed against the top of the desk. He sat on the desk beside her, with the notepad on his knees and his feet resting on the seat of his chair. 'Continue your report,' he said.

How was she supposed to remember what had happened earlier that day, when all she could think about was what might happen next? Each little movement of his fingers made her think she was about to come. And she didn't want to come yet, even though she had been denied orgasms all day. First she wanted to submit to the harshest punishment he could administer, and then she wanted to lick his penis until the fountain of his semen flooded her mouth. Then, at last, she would masturbate for him, in any position he desired.

With many hesitations and pauses to catch her breath, Jessica completed her daily account.

'Very interesting,' Matt said. He pulled his fingers from her anus. 'You seem to have enjoyed having a toy stuffed up your arse.'

She lifted her head and reached for his erection. 'Yes, I did. And your fingers, too. I expect that's very, very naughty.'

He watched her hand moving up and down his shaft, and then turned his blank gaze on to her. 'You can't get what you want by being nice to me,' he said. 'I'm not susceptible to bribery. After all, you have to obey me. I can have anything I desire from you. If you want something specific, you'll have to ask for it.'

It was true. He knew exactly how and when to remind her of the lowliness of her position. 'Please, Mentor,' she said. 'I just want you to punish me. Very hard, please. I've been thinking about it all day.'

'But of course,' he replied, smiling at last. 'I rather enjoy disciplining you. And I think I can provide something appropriate, even with the limited resources here. Stand up. Go to the middle of the room. Adopt the 'beg' position, as you've described it to me, but with your hands crossed behind your back.'

Jessica liked all the pet positions she had been taught. Every one of them was so indecent. 'Beg' she found particularly humiliating and exciting: once she was squatting, with her knees spread wide apart, it was difficult to move, so she felt very helpless. Putting her hands behind her back, instead of together in front of her, made the position even more difficult to maintain.

Matt advanced towards her. In one hand he was holding a metal cylinder welded to a square base; in the other a disappointingly small cane.

Jessica hoped that Matt would order her to suck his penis: she was at just the right height. But he placed the metal square, with the cylinder rising vertically from it, on the floor behind her.

'This is part of one of the old machines from the gym,' he said. 'I retrieved it, as I suspected it would be useful again. I want you to lift your bottom up a little, move back, and then lower yourself on to the tip of the cylinder. I want it up your arse, of course. Don't worry, the top is round and smooth. And I'll put some of this lubricant on it. You'll have to lean back a little. I'll support you.'

Jessica wasn't worried. From the moment she saw the cylinder she had hoped that she would be required to take it inside her. And Matt was going to hold her! She would have to be careful not to swoon in his arms.

The cylinder was wider than Matt's two fingers; wider than the phallus that had been lodged in her anus for most of the day. But with Matt holding her steady she rested the funnel of her bottom on the tip of the thing, and she felt herself open, and a little of the cylinder was inside her. She couldn't help crying out. It was stretching her, and hurting her. As with the phallus, however, the pain receded, leaving her with the familiar and welcome sensations of being stretched and filled. She was very conscious that her shoulder was resting against the hard muscles of his chest, and that his erect manhood was pressing against her thigh.

'Keep your hands behind your back,' Matt said. He was kneeling beside her, and although he moved away from her a little his strong left arm remained around her shoulders, holding her upright and preventing her from sliding any further on to the cylinder. 'Shoulders back. Chest out,' he said, and he began to whip her breasts with the cane.

For a moment Jessica hardly knew what was happening. The pain was so sharp that she couldn't catch her breath, and so immediate that she wanted to curl into a ball to protect her vulnerable breasts. This wasn't like any punishment she had taken on her bottom: it was crueller, more intimate, and the wristy flicks of the cane were like wasp stings.

But with Matt's arm around her shoulders, and by clenching her hands around her arms behind her back, she succeeded in keeping still. She tossed her head from side to side, and heard herself uttering a succession of gasps and cries. She glimpsed Matt's face beside her: he was frowning with concentration as he flicked the cane as rapidly as he could, giving her no time to recover her breath between the strokes. The tip of the cane caught one breast and then the other. He was aiming for the most sensitive areas, around and just below her nipples. Through the stinging pain she could feel her breasts jiggling and dancing as they were whipped.

There was a pause. Matt tightened his grip around her shoulders, and then allowed her to lean a little further back. Jessica groaned as the cylinder penetrated further into her. Matt's right hand, still holding the cane, cupped her sex, and the tip of the cane nudged into her wide-open vagina. She could feel that she was dripping wet. Her breasts felt hot and swollen, and her nipples hardened suddenly. Her body shook with tremors of desire. She knew that if Matt were to move his hand, only a little, she would start to come.

'You seem to be enjoying this,' he said, and he brought up his hand and resumed caning her breasts.

Now each sharp lash was sheer pleasure. Jessica arched her back, to present her breasts and to push her bottom down on to the cylinder. Jolts of electric energy ran through her body. In a lucid moment she wondered whether it was possible for her to reach a climax this way.

'That's enough,' Matt said. Jessica sighed and moaned as he helped her to stand, and the cylinder slipped from her anus.

She stood with her head bowed and her long hair falling about her face as she recovered her breath. She kept her hands behind her back. She gasped when Matt's fingers touched her breasts, and the surge of pleasure was so intense that her legs almost gave way.

'They'll be sore for a while,' Matt said. 'But I don't think there will be marks. It's getting late, but I suppose I should allow you to have a climax. From your report it sounds as though you've had a frustrating day. So you can masturbate now. Use the cylinder up your arse, if you like. You seem to enjoy it.'

Jessica was so desperate for satisfaction that her hands went straight to her sex before he had finished speaking. It was wonderful to touch the hot, wet, secret places between her legs, with her breasts and her anus still throbbing insistently.

But she wanted more. She wanted Matt. With a sob she took her hands away from her sex. They were wet with her juices. She lifted her head to look at her mentor. 'Please,' she said. She reached out and grasped the shaft of his manhood. 'Please?'

He shrugged. 'Very well,' he said. 'I can't deny that it's pleasant to fuck you.' With effortless strength he took a rolled-up exercise mat from behind the door and threw it on to the floor, where it unrolled. 'Kneel,' he said. 'Then bend over. Head down on the mat, bottom up.'

Jessica was so excited that she thought she might pass out. This, even more than the punishment, was what she had been waiting for all day. She arranged herself in the position he wanted. She placed her knees as far apart as she could, and drew them up to her shoulders, so that her bottom was as rounded and open as she could make it. She pressed her face and her sore breasts against the mat, and shivered with pleasure.

He was going to fuck her again. Even the sound of the coarse word excited her. Not her mouth, this time. Her sex. A proper fucking.

Her hair was spread in a pool all round her head. She could see nothing. She was a vessel, containing nothing but yearning desire, waiting to be filled. She could imagine how she looked, abasing herself on the floor, her bottom and her vulva so prominent that the rest of her might as well not exist. She was nothing but sex; she wanted nothing but sex.

She heard him kneel behind her, between her calves. Then, suddenly, the hot, blunt tip of his erection was pushing between her labia, and then he was inside her, pressing further in, filling her vagina before she had time to recognise the succession of sensations that flooded through her.

He moved back and forth inside her, unhurriedly, and even though he didn't touch her in any other way Jessica was in a state of bliss. If she had been a cat she would have purred. Matt's long, thick member seemed to be growing even bigger and harder.

He withdrew it, until only the tip was nuzzling against her sex-lips. Her vagina felt empty, and she murmured with disappointment.

'I'm sure that was very enjoyable,' Matt said. 'But it isn't what you need. I think we should keep to today's theme.'

Before Jessica could decipher his meaning, she felt the tip of his penis slide from between her labia and up, into the funnel of corrugated skin around her anus.

He was going to use her there.

'I should have whipped you here, as well,' Matt said thoughtfully. 'Never mind. There's no time now.'

For a brief moment Jessica wondered whether she should object, struggle, cry out. Everything was happening too quickly. Before today she had never allowed anyone to put anything into her anus – well, nothing more than the tip of a finger, anyway. Now she was expected to accommodate Matt's rigid, engorged penis.

She relaxed. There was, after all, nothing she wanted more at that moment than Matt's manhood. She felt it test the resilience of the little ring of muscle, and she sighed as the hole opened, and the head of his penis slid into her. I'm losing my virginity all over again, she thought.

She cried out as the pain began, and then her cries became groans of pleasure as the pangs lessened. He was well inside her now, inching into her with little thrusts of his powerful hips. He felt larger than the plug she had worn at Mrs Smythe's; larger even than the metal cylinder she had squatted on while he had caned her breasts. He was like a heated metal bar inside her. Each time he thrust forwards she felt a spasm of pain that melted into the spreading, deepening pool of her blissful delirium.

It's as if I'm being spanked inside my bottom, she thought; it's punishment and pleasure combined. It's humiliating enough to be used this way, but it's utterly degrading to enjoy it. I'm such a naughty girl. Because I certainly am enjoying it. Oh, yes. I hope it feels as wonderful to Matt as it does to me. I want him to use me like this again.

She could no longer think coherently. Her whole body was alive with electric tremors, and she was moaning helplessly in time with the deep pulses of pleasurable ache that spread from her breached bottom. Matt was fully inside her now: the thick base of his erection was stretching open the ring of her anus, and his hairs were scratching her buttocks. His body was bent over hers: she felt the hard pips of his nipples press into her back. He was panting, and uttering little guttural noises. Even as she rode the rising waves of pain and pleasure, Jessica smiled: at last she had succeeded in breaking down the wall of his indifference.

He curled an arm under her stomach. 'Up,' he grunted, pushing her ribcage upwards. 'I want your breasts.'

She did her best to comply. Before the tips of her breasts were clear of the mat, his hand was grasping them. Had he forgotten that they had just been caned, or did he intend to cause her more pain? He wasn't gentle: he grabbed and kneaded the sore flesh, and then, as if regaining his self-control, he began deliberately to pinch and twist the nipples.

More pain; more pleasure. It felt as though a taut wire stretched from her nipples to her rectum: a wire alive with electric shocks. The sensations were too strong, too much, too wonderful to bear. Matt was holding her, he was surrounding her, he was inside her. She was a limp, helpless doll. She was nothing but waves of sensation crashing faster and faster on the shore.

'If you want to come,' Matt said through gritted teeth, 'touch yourself now.'

I'll come anyway, she thought, if you keep on doing the things you're doing. But he was her mentor, and she had to obey. It was difficult: she had to prop herself on one elbow and insert the other arm under her body, reaching back and up until her fingers found the strands of viscous liquid hanging from her sex.

The effort had brought her to the surface of her lake of pleasure. One touch of her fingers on the petals of her sex was enough to send her diving back down into the dark, warm, liquid, pulsing depths.

One touch, and she was starting to come. Her fingers pressed and rubbed frantically, matching the pulses of pleasure-pain, the regular thrusts of Matt's invasive penis, the insistent pinching of his fingers around her sore nipples. The hard, hot bar inside her was suddenly still, and she could feel the cataract of semen forcing its way through the tight ring of her anus as it sped towards its explosive expulsion into her bowels.

An avalanche of emotions swept over her and carried her away. It was as if every pathway in her brain had been thrown open simultaneously. She forgot where she was; she forgot who she was. She just experienced wave after wave of emotion: love, shame, loss, delight, even fear. She realised that her body was shaking and she was uttering loud cries. She felt wetness on her face, and knew she was crying.

She slumped slowly on to her side and lay, curled up, on the mat. She was aware of Matt looking down at her. She felt his hand on her cheek.

'Are you all right?' he whispered. 'I think you lost consciousness for a moment.'

If Jessica had not felt so drained of energy she would have sat up and kissed him. He was concerned about her; he cared for her.

'Mmm,' she murmured, and nodded. 'Yes, thank you, Mentor.'

'Good,' Matt said, standing straight. 'It's bad for business if the members pass out. It's very late. I have work to do, and you have to return home. Whatever that anal plug was supposed to prepare you for, I'd say you're ready for it now.'

He left the office. Jessica dragged herself to her feet. He was right: she had to go home. She was so happy that even the tiredness was wearing off. Her life kept on getting better and better. Suddenly she laughed. What would Brian say, she wondered, if she were to tell him that today she had watched one of her neighbours being given an enema; and then she had spent most of the day naked, playing with the most unusual toys and with the neighbour; and that finally she had had her breasts caned and, for the first time in her life, she had had anal sex. She knew what he would say. He wouldn't believe her.

She laughed again, and with shaking fingers she began to dress.

Field agent's report to the Private House
From: Matt
For the attention of: Mistress Julia

I am aware that the enclosed report is merely a factual, if detailed, account of the activities that Jessica told me about and of the meeting I had with her late in the afternoon. I decided to write this separate note of my observations and opinions.

Thank you, first of all, for responding quickly and positively to my request that I be allowed to remain in Hillingbury and in charge of this operation. I am very sorry that today's events have already demonstrated that your faith in me is not merited.

I have allowed my feelings for Jessica to cloud my judgement. It's true that I have said nothing to her, but after my treatment of her this afternoon I cannot believe that she will want to see me again. I still don't know what possessed me. Jealousy, I suppose. I couldn't bear to hear the happiness in her voice as she told me about the fun and games she's enjoyed as a 'pet'. I was determined to show her that submission entails more than being naked and playing with toys. And she is, Mistress, irresistibly submissive.

Even if she returns to report again, I don't think I can maintain this charade. Every time I write to you I am betraying her confidence. She thinks that I will keep her secrets; instead I send them all to you. What will she think of me when she finds out?

I understand that you must send another agent to complete this assignment. I will remain here until I am relieved of the post, and I will continue to report.

I can't bear to think that I won't see Jessica again.

Six

Jessica didn't bother to dress. As soon as Brian had left the house she ran upstairs, pulled off her dressing gown, and resolved to remain naked until Mel arrived. The previous day's rain had disappeared overnight, and it was a warm, sunny morning: just right for a garden party. And, appropriately for a pet, she thought, she was as excited as a puppy. Today she was to be presented to the entire committee. Her future, and Mel's, depended on her making a good impression. She would have to be on her best behaviour, and looking at her best. Mel was coming early, well before the start of the party, to help her dress.

She couldn't settle. There was no point in doing anything: arranging her hair and putting on her make-up might as well be deferred until Mel was there to supervise her.

Her state of anticipation and trepidation about her presentation was only heightened by the fact that she was still feeling dazed and euphoric from the previous day's events. For the past few days it seemed as though the only time she hadn't been sexually aroused was while she was asleep – and, as she remembered the dreams she had had, she realised that even in sleep her mind could concentrate on only one thing.

She stood before the mirror and forced her hand into the gap at the top of her thighs. Sometimes she liked to pretend that she was resisting unwanted attentions, and she clamped her thighs together. It was no use: her fingers burrowed along the channel of her sex, and pushed upwards. As she expected, she was wet.

You're incorrigible, she told her reflection. Don't just stand there looking smug with your hand in a rude place. You deserve to be punished, young lady.

She shivered at the thought. If only Matt were here, she sighed. Of all the women connected with the HYWAPOC, only Mrs Morgan came close to having the authority and severity that she loved in her mentor. And Mrs Morgan didn't have a big, hot, hard, man-smelling penis. Oh, goodness, but she wanted him. She wanted him inside her. She wanted to feel the semen come boiling out of him, into her.

If she had Matt all to herself for a whole day, she wondered, how many times, and in how many different ways, could he punish her and penetrate her? As long as I'm a pet, she thought, I'm not likely to find out. I seem to have less and less time with my mentor. I must try to see him today. I hope he'll use my little hole again: it feels empty without him. But then, if he uses me that way, I won't be able to take him in my mouth and drink his semen.

She thought about the practicality of buying a little flask that she could keep in her pocket or handbag. But it would have to be a vacuum flask, to keep the semen fresh, so she could have a sip whenever she wanted to remember him. It was no good: how could she explain the flask to Mel?

She stepped up to the mirror and examined her breasts. They seemed larger and even firmer than usual. Was it possible that being permanently aroused was causing a physical change? There were no marks left. Yesterday evening, when she had returned from the club, the tender skin of her breasts had been stippled with scores of angry flecks. Now there was no reminder of what Matt had done to her. Even her little hole hardly smarted any longer.

Wet with the juices from her sex, her fingertip slid easily into the tight ring. She uttered a little 'Oh!' of pleasure, and then giggled when she caught sight of the abandoned expression on her face.

She went to the dressing table and soon found something suitable: a hairbrush with a round handle that tapered to a point at the end, and narrowed again below the bristles. She took the hairbrush and a tub of moisturising lotion to the bed, and then opened the wardrobe door so that she could see her reflection as she kneeled on the counterpane. She coated the handle of the brush with lotion, and then turned so that she was kneeling with her back to the mirror. She moved her knees apart, bent over, and looked over her shoulder.

It gave her a thrill of excitement to show off her bottom and her sex, even though there was no one to watch her. She could understand why Matt and Mrs Morgan liked to see her in this position, and to spank her. Her buttocks were perfectly round, and her hairless sex was plump, and both contrasted prettily with her narrow waist and slim thighs. She could not imagine that a bottom and private parts could look more enticingly vulnerable. It was such a disappointment that Mel wasn't interested in punishing her.

But at least she could rely on Matt. She imagined him standing beside the bed, tall, strong and silent, waiting impatiently for her to begin the next part of her degrading performance. The mere thought of him was enough to make her juices run.

She watched her fingers as they massaged lotion into the funnel of her anus. She scooped more from the tub and slapped it into the valley between her buttocks. It made a squelching sound that was delightfully rude. She pressed her face into the bedclothes, opened her bottom as wide as she could, and smacked her sticky hand between them as hard as she could, over and over again, until her anus was hot and stinging.

As she sank into the welcoming, swirling lake of pleasure, she told herself to stop. It wouldn't do to have an orgasm: she was simply keeping herself amused until Mel arrived. And in any case she wanted to feel the hairbrush handle penetrating her.

She watched herself again as she held the stubby point of the handle against the little hole. She pushed inwards, and the hole opened as the tip of the handle went in. It looked and felt heavenly. She took a deep breath, and resolved to push it in slowly and carefully, resisting the temptation to touch her clitoris and send herself flying towards a climax.

The little hole opened wider. The handle sank into her. It was uncomfortable now – almost painful – and Jessica toyed with the bristle end of the brush, sending tremors deep inside her that amplified the delicious sensations and made her gasp.

Then, as if being sucked in, the remainder of the handle slid into her, and the ring of her sphincter tightened around the narrow waist. Jessica scrambled from the bed, and she discovered that the bristles scratched against the tender skin of the inside slopes of her buttocks. She walked to and fro. The brush handle remained inside her; the bristles touched her with each step she took. It was almost as good as being smacked. The handle of the brush was smaller than Matt's erection, but it was hard and it filled her satisfyingly.

Now, at last, she allowed herself to touch her clitoris: just the lightest pressure, with the tip of one finger, on the prepuce. She shook as a jolt ran through her body. She told herself again that she must not come.

Some time later Jessica was lying on the bed with her eyes closed, stroking the bristles of the hairbrush with one hand and her sex with the other, when she heard the front door open.

She jumped from the bed and ran downstairs, remembering only when the bristles scratched her bottom that the hairbrush was still inside her. There was no time to extract it; anyway, she thought, maybe when Mel sees it she'll punish me for being naughty.

Mel looked resplendent. Her long, blonde hair had been cut and styled into a cataract of waves and curls that framed her pretty face. She was wearing a powder-blue suit. She was breathless, and her blue eyes were bright with excitement. As Jessica ran down the last few steps into the hall she realised that Mel was as nervous as she was.

For a moment the two women looked at each other, wide-eyed, and then they fell into an embrace. During one of the long, calming kisses that ensued Mel's hand discovered the bristly head of the hairbrush protruding from between Jessica's buttocks.

'What's this?' she asked.

The touch of Mel's hand on the brush was making Jessica gasp, but she managed to reply. 'The plug I wore yesterday,' she explained. 'Mrs Morgan said it would prepare me for the presentation today. So I thought I'd help by preparing myself a bit more.'

Mel kissed her again. 'You're such a darling little pet,' she said. 'So eager! But you're quite right: I'm afraid you should have something in your bottom this morning. I've brought the plug for you to wear. I hope you don't mind too much.'

'I don't mind at all, Mistress,' Jessica said. The plug was no longer than the handle of the hairbrush, but it was thicker. 'Will you put it in for me, please?'

'I'm going to do everything for you this morning, Jess. And, first of all, I'm going to give you a bath.'

There were hours to fill before Mel and Jessica had to leave for the party. As a new owner, with a new pet to be presented, Mel was expected to be the last guest to arrive. Jessica was full of questions, about the presentation, and the other owners and their pets, but Mel insisted that she couldn't answer: to coach a pet for her presentation was considered cheating and, as for the other owners and pets, Jessica would see them soon enough. In any case, there wasn't time for gossiping: Mel's pet had to be thoroughly bathed, pampered, groomed, and dressed to impress Mel's neighbours.

Both women found that concentrating on choosing the right perfume, make-up, and hair decorations helped to calm the butterflies in their stomachs. Mel was as good as her word: she did everything for Jessica, from washing her private parts and brushing out her long, dark hair to painting her nails and dabbing perfume on to her pulse points. She shaved and plucked Jessica's sex.

'You're going to be the prettiest pet at the party,' Mel told her, more than once. 'I'm going to be so proud of you.'

At last Jessica was ready to be dressed. It was time for the plug to be removed, but by now Jessica was so full of anticipation that when the plug was gone she almost didn't miss the pleasure of being filled.

Mel explained that it was usual for a new pet to be presented entirely naked. She had seen a few pets presented in stockings, which looked pretty but were ruined when the pet walked on the lead beside her owner. But at least it was easy to choose shoes to go with stockings; if the pet was completely naked, it was difficult to find footwear that was practical and attractive. Mel had brought with her several pairs of stockings, some of which required suspender belts to hold them up. She lined them up on the bed, along with most of Jessica's shoes.

'I don't know,' she said. 'Perhaps we should forget about stockings. It's not as if you need anything to make you look prettier.' She gave Jessica a hug and a kiss. 'It's just that I wanted this to be a special presentation. One that everyone will remember.'

'Me too,' Jessica said. 'I know. I've had an idea. Close your eyes, Mistress, while I get ready. And don't peek.'

Mel turned her back, and Jessica began to open drawers and cupboards in her search for the items she wanted. In a few minutes she was breathless but ready. 'All right,' she said. 'You can look now, Mistress.'

Jessica knew, from Mel's quick intake of breath, that her owner approved of her costume. The two women stood side by side and admired Jessica's reflection in the mirror.

When Jessica had been a little girl she had wanted to be a ballet dancer, and she had continued to take lessons long after it became obvious that she would never become a ballerina. Her feet and her waist hadn't grown since she was a teenager, and she could still wear the tutu and the ballet pumps she had had when she had last danced. Supplemented by a pair of white stockings with elasticated tops, the tiny, stiff skirt and delicate dancing shoes constituted a costume that was simultaneously pretty, innocent and utterly perverse.

The tutu was little more than a ruff of stiff, creamy lace around her waist; it, and the white stockings, framed and emphasised the nakedness of her bottom and pubes.

'Wonderful!' Mel exclaimed.

Jessica twirled. Wearing the pumps again made her want to dance. 'I can go just like this,' she said. 'With a coat, of course, for the walk to Mrs Northrop's. I think the sight of a naked ballerina might cause a bit of a stir, even in Hillingbury.'

Mel and Jessica held hands as they walked to the party. Lunchtime had come and gone, but neither had suggested eating. Jessica was too excited to be hungry, and Mel seemed increasingly nervous.

'Don't worry, Mistress,' Jessica said as they walked side by side along the roads of the estate, into the lanes that had been the first to be developed, where the oldest and grandest houses had been built, 'I'll be very good, I promise.' She squeezed Mel's hand.

It's more difficult for Mel than for me, in a way, Jessica thought. I'm going to be the centre of attention, and I'll be wearing next to nothing, and I'm sure I'll be expected to do some outrageous things. But I'll enjoy it, and at least most of the people will be strangers. But all those people know Mel already, and they've known her for years as nothing but a pet. Now, suddenly, she's an owner, and she has to impress them.

'This is Bella Northrop's house,' Mel said. The two women stood at the garden gate, and looked up at the double-fronted, mock-Tudor façade. The sounds of voices and laughter could be heard, carried on the summer breeze from the garden behind the high wall at the side of the house.

Mel took Jessica in her arms and, with a glance to left and right to make sure there was no one who could see them, she kissed her on the mouth. She unbuttoned Jessica's coat, and then led the way up the path to the imposing porch.

It took a long time for Mel's ring on the doorbell to be answered. The young woman who opened the door was still fastening a scarf around her neck: Jessica guessed that the young woman, who had short, red hair, a freckled face and a wide mouth, was one of Mrs Northrop's pets, and that she had been naked only moments before. She gave a broad smile when she recognised Mel.

'I thought it would be you,' she said. 'Everyone else is here.' She pulled off the scarf, to reveal a red collar, and began removing the clothes she had hurriedly put on. 'Come in, Mel.'

Mel remained in the porch. 'Sarah!' she said firmly.

The red-haired woman blushed and almost dropped the scarf. She lowered her head. 'I'm sorry, Mistress,' she said. 'I forgot.' She looked up imploringly. 'Please don't tell Bella. I'm in enough trouble already. I dropped a plate of sandwiches.'

Mel led Jessica into the hall, which was, Jessica noted, as large as the sitting room of her own house. 'It's all right,' Mel said. 'But be careful, Sarah. I'm not a pet any more. This is Jess, by the way. I'm an owner now, remember that. I'm Jess's owner.'

The two pets looked at each other and nodded in greeting. Sarah, still blushing, slipped off the short dress she had worn to answer the door. Jessica didn't try to hide her interest in the young woman's slight, freckled body. Sarah's eyes widened when Jessica shrugged off her coat to reveal her naked body and the ridiculously brief ballet skirt. 'Oh,' Sarah whispered. 'Oh, Mel, I mean Mistress, congratulations.' She gazed into Jessica's eyes. 'She's lovely.'

'I know,' Mel replied. Jessica was relieved to hear that some confidence had returned to her owner's voice and manner. 'And you can't play with her, Sarah, at least until you learn to address me correctly. Now take Jess's coat, and mine, and then lead us to the garden.'

Mel and Jessica waited indoors while Sarah went to tell her owner that they had arrived. The dining-room was cool and shady; beyond the open French windows the sunlight was harshly bright. Mel stood at the fireplace and checked her make-up in the mirror above the mantelpiece, and then she came and fussed around Jessica, smoothing down her hair, flouncing her tutu, and straightening her stockings. Jessica couldn't take her eyes from the scene framed by the open doorway. The patio and the lawn beyond it were crowded with women. The owners, in expensive summer frocks, were gathered in groups of two or three, sitting on garden furniture or standing in the shade of ornamental trees, sipping glasses of wine or cups of tea. Their pets, who outnumbered them, were almost all naked except for their collars. Several were wearing suspender belts and stockings, which drew attention to the nudity of their private parts, and one was wearing a complicated garment that appeared to be made of black straps. Some were carrying trays of drinks; others were standing, either upright, or in the pet position on hands and knees, beside their owners, many of whom had their pets on leads.

Apart from the nakedness of the majority of the women, the scene was at first sight strangely innocent and mundane. But then Jessica saw two owners, sitting and chatting side by side on a cushioned bench, with a pet lying across their laps. They caressed her naked body as they talked. At the centre of a group of owners and their pets, a pretty blonde pet in the 'sit' position was the subject of the conversation. As Jessica watched, the pet's owner gestured expansively to her friends, leaned forwards to speak to her pet, and then stood back and watched with the other owners while the pet rolled over on to her back and began to masturbate. The owners laughed, and applauded politely.

Jessica counted half a dozen owners and almost twice as many pets, and she couldn't see all of the garden. It was only now that she was on the threshold of the party that she realised how many people would be looking at her when she and Mel made their entrance. But she was more excited than nervous. Mel looked at least as pretty and glamorous as any of the other owners, and Jessica was confident that the new committee member and her naked ballerina pet would turn everyone's head.

'I can't see Mrs Morgan,' Jessica said.

'Of course not,' Mel replied sharply. 'She isn't here. She isn't an owner, Jess. She's just the shopkeeper and trainer.'

Sarah came to the French windows. 'Mrs Northrop is ready to receive you, Mistress,' she said to Mel. She held out her arm. 'Please take your pet to the garden seat on the patio.'

Mel gave Jessica an encouraging smile, and stepped from the shade of the dining-room into the blazing sunlight of the patio. Jessica walked behind her, and found Sarah beside her.

The red-haired young woman rested a hand on the small of Jessica's back. 'It's said,' she whispered, 'that you're good at licking. Everyone's talking about it. They say you like it.'

Jessica blushed and smiled. She was sure that Sarah wasn't supposed to talk to her without permission, and she thought that she shouldn't reply. She looked quickly towards Sarah, and nodded emphatically.

'Good,' Sarah whispered. 'I like it too. I hope we can play together soon.'

Jessica felt Sarah's hand leave her back, and then she shivered as it slid caressingly across her bottom. She glanced over her shoulder and saw that Sarah had stepped back and slowed her pace, so that she was following Mel and Jessica at a distance.

The conversation on the patio, and then throughout the rest of the garden, faded into silence as Mel and Jessica advanced across the paving stones. Jessica kept her eyes lowered, but she knew everyone was looking at her. She heard whispered comments, and she could tell that both the owners and the pets were assessing her appearance. She was very conscious of her nakedness. She felt the warmth of the sun on her shoulders and her breasts. Her sex, too, felt warm and ticklish.

Mel stopped in front of the seat on which Jessica had seen two owners toying with a pet. Now only one owner occupied the seat, sitting straight-backed at its centre. She was tall and lissom, and her face had the cool, ageless beauty of a statue of a classical goddess. Her pale eyes carefully considered Mel and then Jessica. This, Jessica assumed, was Bella Northrop, the most senior member of the owners' committee and the hostess of the party. The pet, whom Jessica had last seen lying wantonly across Mrs Northrop's lap, was now kneeling beside her feet.

'Well, Melanie,' Mrs Northrop said at last. 'You've recruited a pet, it seems. And at your first attempt.' Her gaze returned to Jessica, who shivered. 'She's an attractive thing, too. Unusual looks, but by no means unpleasing. Young, well proportioned, and with a firm bust and hindquarters. I imagine you'll be inundated with requests to borrow her. But is she obedient?'

Mel couldn't keep a note of pride from entering her voice. 'Yes, Bella,' she said. 'Very.'

'We'll see,' Mrs Northrop said. 'Sarah, bring a rug and lay it here, in front of me.'

It seemed to Jessica that in Mrs Northrop's barely concealed opinion Mel had been lucky to obtain a pet and didn't deserve one as desirable as Jessica. She wanted to dislike Mrs Northrop, but couldn't: the tall, calm woman exuded haughty authority, and Jessica couldn't help responding. The patio was crowded now with owners and their pets, and she was sure Mrs Northrop was about to instruct her to do disgraceful things in front of all the spectators. She could hardly wait for the first command.

'You understand, Melanie,' Mrs Northrop stated in a forceful, formal tone, 'that if Jessica fails to demonstrate the required level of obedience, deportment and willingness then she will not be permitted to continue as your pet. And you will resume your duties for Lydia Henshaw.'

The audience murmured, like a congregation at prayer. It seemed to Jessica that the party had been suspended and a ceremony had begun. She stole a glance at Mel, and caught her eye. They exchanged a secretive smile.

'Of course,' Mel replied. 'I have every confidence in Jess.'

Mrs Northrop craned her head forwards and looked closely into Jessica's face. Suddenly she smiled. 'No doubt you have good reason for your confidence,' she said. 'But I must be thorough. Let us begin.'

As Jessica had expected, Mrs Northrop put her through all the pet positions: sit, stand, beg, and roll over. Jessica had no difficulty remembering the attitudes to strike, and she concentrated on presenting her bottom and her private parts as prominently as possible. She was particularly pleased with the costume she had devised: in every position her bottom appeared provocatively from below the ruff of stiff lace, and she overheard several favourable comments as she displayed herself. What with Mrs Northrop's stern voice controlling her, and the sea of faces watching her, Jessica soon found herself becoming very excited. Each position she adopted opened and moistened her sex a little more. By the time she was on her back, with her knees drawn up to her shoulders, presenting her sex and her little hole as widely as possible to Mrs Northrop, she was sure that it was obvious to everyone that she was aroused.

She lay still, with her eyes demurely closed, and felt her cheeks and throat blushing as the warm breeze carried to her the whispered remarks of the owners staring down at her.

'She's adorable, isn't she?'

'How can Bella resist touching her?'

'Or spanking her, in that position.'

'You know, I do believe she's wet. Look, the little hussy's leaking.'

Jessica heard a rustle of clothing, and opened her eyes to find Mrs Northrop kneeling beside her.

'Come closer, everyone,' Mrs Northrop called out. She leaned towards Jessica. 'Can you stay in this position a little longer, Jessica?'

'Yes, Mistress,' Jessica replied. 'As long as you require.'

'Good girl.' Mrs Northrop's fingertips rested on the backs of Jessica's thighs, and began to trail downwards. 'I see that Melanie likes you to be shaved.'

'I like it too, Mistress,' Jessica said. 'It makes me feel more naked.'

Mrs Northrop smiled indulgently. 'Can everybody see?' she asked. 'I'm sure you've all noticed that Melanie's pet has the physique and carriage of a thoroughbred. But look: even her private parts are pretty.'

Jessica was simultaneously so embarrassed and so proud that she could hardly keep still. When Mrs Northrop's fingers came to rest, with their tips lightly touching her sex-lips, she couldn't suppress a gasp and a wriggle. If she kept her eyes open she could look either at Mrs Northrop's studiously calm and classically beautiful face, or at the circle of her neighbours, all of them peering at her most intimate parts. If she closed her eyes she couldn't help concentrating on the sensations buzzing through her body, or on her memories of the things her mentor had done to her: both served only to increase her arousal.

'Her outer labia are delightfully smooth and plump,' Mrs Northrop went on, caressing the parts she was describing. 'And if I just open her a little more, like this ... There you are: her inner lips have such sweet little fronds. And I'm sure you can all see that she's very wet. You like being a pet, don't you, Jessica?'

Jessica nodded. 'Yes, Mistress. Very much.'

'Such a good girl,' Mrs Northrop said, and she began to pat Jessica's sex. 'Would you like a toy to play with?'

Jessica could hardly speak. Mrs Northrop's gentle petting was sending tremors of pleasure into her. She wished that Mrs Northrop would spank her a little harder. Or much harder. 'Yes, please, Mistress,' she said.

'Sarah,' Mrs Northrop said, without ceasing to pat Jessica's sex, 'run and fetch a phallus from the toy-box. Quickly.'

By the time Sarah returned Jessica was gasping and writhing under the ministrations of Mrs Northrop's hand. 'Here we are,' Mrs Northrop said, and her hand stopped patting Jessica. 'Hold out your right hand, Jessica, and take this. Use it to show everyone how you play with yourself.'

Jessica took a moment to recover her breath, and then she tucked her left arm behind both knees, so that her right hand was free and her legs were still pulled up to her chest. She looked at the phallus that Mrs Northrop placed in her hand: it was about the same thickness as the candle in Jessica's bedroom, but it was shaped like an erect penis. Her sex felt more than ready to receive it, and Jessica was becoming almost used to masturbating while being watched – although she had not yet performed for such a large audience.

She held the blunt tip of the phallus against the entrance of her vagina. She wanted to feel it inside her. She wished it was real, though, rather than a toy. She wished it was Matt's. A thought occurred to her: a shameful thought that made her blush again. What should she do? Now that the she had thought of it, she would have to ask, even though saying the words would be mortifying.

'Please, Mistress,' she said, 'which hole would you prefer me to use?' It was, after all, her duty as a pet to please the owners.

'Oh, you little darling!' Mrs Northrop exclaimed. 'How thoughtful. This one,' she said, pushing the tip of the phallus a little way into Jessica's vagina. 'We'll save the other one for a little later.' She stood up, looked down at Jessica for a moment with a smile, and resumed her place on the seat. 'Go on, dear. We're all watching.'

Jessica pushed the base of the phallus, and the tip slid easily into the sopping tunnel of her vagina. Her breath caught in her throat and she began to tremble. She closed her eyes, but she couldn't forget that she was surrounded by the watchful faces of the committee members and their pets – all of them her neighbours. It was even better than looking at herself in the mirror. The veined cylinder went further into her. If only Matt were there, she thought; he wouldn't just watch, or at least not until he had made sure her bottom was striped and sore.

As she moved the phallus in and out she couldn't keep still. The urge to touch her nipples and her clitoris was almost overwhelming. Her breath came in gasps and pants as she felt the warm, swirling waters of an impending climax surge over her. Still, she was dimly aware of the comments and applause of the crowd, and she wondered whether her performance was a usual part of the presentation ceremony.

'Stop now, Jessica,' Mrs Northrop said, and she laid her hand on Jessica's shoulder. 'Relax for a moment, and then sit.'

Jessica heard the polite applause rise to a crescendo as she pulled the phallus from her sex, took several deep breaths, and lowered her legs. She stretched her limbs, and felt the tremors of pleasure subside to a gentle vibration in her loins. She turned over, kneeled facing Mrs Northrop, flounced her tutu into shape, and adopted the 'sit' position. She looked up eagerly. She was more excited than ever, and she was looking forward to whatever test the committee wished to impose next.

Mrs Northrop leaned forwards and stroked Jessica's face. 'Well done,' she said. She raised her voice so that everyone could hear. 'There can be no doubt that Jessica is already a dutiful pet. Not only that, she's pleasing to look at, she's anxious to do her best, and she's sexually responsive. Very responsive, in fact. I've already decided that she's entirely acceptable. Are we all agreed?'

There was a general murmur of approval from the owners. Jessica glanced quickly to her right and her left and found all the women, owners and pets, staring at her. Their faces were friendly, but she was sure she wasn't imagining the hunger in their eyes. They all wanted her.

'In that case,' Mrs Northrop went on, 'we'll proceed with the presentation. Melanie, have you chosen a collar for your pet?'

Mel had already taken the cream leather collar from her handbag. She gave it to Mrs Northrop, who leaned forwards again to fasten it around Jessica's neck.

'Thank you, Mistress,' Jessica said. 'I promise to be a good pet.'

'I'm sure you will be,' Mrs Northrop said. 'And I'm sure it won't be long before you join the ranks of the owners on the committee. Becoming a pet is the first step on the way to being a pillar of Hillingbury society.'

Jessica stifled her urge to protest. She knew that Mrs Northrop meant well, and this wasn't the occasion to make a fuss. But Jessica didn't want to be an owner. She liked being a pet. Apart from being under Matt's instruction, there was nothing she enjoyed more than the feelings of shame, vulnerability, helplessness and arousal that flooded through her when she was displayed and made to perform. She was naked, but for a tiny frill of lace, stockings and her collar, and she was kneeling in a position that obliged her to show off her bottom, surrounded by women who desired her and who had the authority to command her. What more could she want?

'Do you have a lead, too, Melanie?' Mrs Northrop said. 'I think Jessica should be on the leash for the final part of the presentation.'

Mel clipped the lead to Jessica's collar, whispering 'Be brave, Jess,' as she did so, and then she gave the looped handle to Mrs Northrop.

Mrs Northrop tugged experimentally on the lead, and Jessica bent forwards obediently.

'There are already rumours about you, Jessica,' she said. 'I've been told that you enjoy licking your owner. Is that true?'

'Yes, Mistress,' Jessica said. She didn't understand why everyone seemed to find it remarkable. 'She tastes lovely.'

Mrs Northrop leaned back on the cushions that were piled on the seat, and pulled the skirt of her summer dress up to reveal her slim, stockinged thighs. 'That's not really the point, Jessica,' she said. 'It's the duty of a pet to please her owner. The pet's opinion is largely irrelevant. I'll try you. Stand!' She pulled on the lead, and Jessica dropped forwards on to her hands and knees. She felt a familiar thrill of guilty delight as she moved forwards into the shadowy, scented junction of Mrs Northrop's parted thighs.

Jessica's head was shaded from the sun by the hem of Mrs Northrop's skirt, but she could feel the sun beating down on her back and her upraised bottom. The juices in her sex began to run again as she pressed her lips against the soft skin above the stocking-tops. Mrs Northrop's private parts were as nearly hairless as her own, and smelled of arousal and a floral perfume. She nuzzled her mouth and her nose against the slightly parted sex-lips, and felt Mrs Northrop tighten her grip on the lead. Jessica pressed her mouth against the vertical opening, and began to lick.

'That's very good,' Mrs Northrop said, more to the assembly than to Jessica. 'She's keen, isn't she, Mel? Oh, yes. Oh, my goodness. Slow down a little, Jessica. I don't want to reach a climax just yet. I think I can predict, everybody, that Melanie will have a very satisfied smile on her face just about all the time from now on. Now then. There's one more thing we have to do, of course. Do you have the tail, Melanie? Good. It's a little irregular, but I don't want to interrupt Jessica while she's doing such good work, so would you please insert it now?'

Jessica, rubbing her face against Mrs Northrop's sex and adrift in the woman's taste and aroma, hardly heard what was being said. It was only when she felt something touch the lips of her sex that she realised that Mrs Northrop had spoken of inserting a tail. But the object that Mel was sliding into her vagina felt just like the phallus she had been playing with.

She didn't mind, anyway. She was so excited that she would let them do anything, although what she really wanted was a spanking. She couldn't help moving her bottom from side to side a little as she kissed and licked.

The object was withdrawn from her sex, and she made a muffled mew of disappointment. But there it was again – and now it was in the funnel of her little hole, and pressing against the ring of muscle. This was even better. Now Jessica understood why she had been made to wear the plug in her anus: it was to prepare her for this. She pushed her bottom up and back to welcome the intruder, and relaxed the sphincter so that it could enter her easily. Lubricated with the wetness of her vagina, the cylindrical object slid into her, and she gasped into Mrs Northrop's sex as she experienced the stretching, the filling, and the blunt discomfort. She wondered, in a lucid moment, whether she would ever again be satisfied with any other form of penetration.

She licked slowly and deeply as the object was pushed further in. Just like the plug, and the handle of her hairbrush, the object narrowed once most of it was inside her, and she felt her ring tighten around its neck. She clenched the muscles of her buttocks, and this must have produced a visible reaction because she heard shouts, cheers and applause from the audience. She could sense, through her lips and tongue, the tremors that indicated that Mrs Northrop was close to coming. Jessica felt scarcely less close herself.

'That will do, Jessica,' Mrs Northrop said. She loosened her hold on the lead, allowing Jessica to take a step back. Jessica was pleased to note that Mrs Northrop's voice was a little shaky. 'Stand up straight,

Jessica, and walk round the patio. Let everyone see your tail.'

Dizzy with desire and disoriented in the sunlight, Jessica struggled to her feet. Once she was upright the thing in her bottom felt heavy: she wouldn't be able to forget that it was there. It moved inside her with every step that she took. As she paraded around the patio, with Mel holding the end of the lead, she blushed furiously under the pitiless gaze of the assembled owners and pets and she tried to glance over her shoulder to see what the tail looked like.

As far as she could tell the visible part was a short plait of hair, dark brown to match her own, with a cream ribbon tied in a bow at its end. It must have been fixed askew to the part that was lodged inside her, because it rose at a jaunty angle from between her buttocks. It swayed from side to side as she walked, and it was this movement that made the plug part shift inside her.

Once Jessica had made one complete circuit of the patio she felt a tug on her collar, and she turned to see Mel beckoning to her. She went to her waiting owner and stepped into a tight embrace. While Mel kissed her she caressed her back and her bottom, and fondled the plaited tail.

'You were fantastic, Jess,' Mel whispered between kisses. 'You're the best pet in the whole world. And you're mine.'

Jessica responded eagerly to Mel's kisses and caresses, and the circle of owners broke into spontaneous applause and cries of congratulations.

The presentation ceremony was over. When Mel withdrew breathlessly from Jessica's kisses, Jessica saw that some of the owners were dispersing, individually or in pairs, taking their pets with them to other parts of the garden. Other owners, however, were keen to congratulate Mel individually and to welcome her to the committee. And every one of them wanted to pet Jessica.

They complimented Mel on the precocious obedience and willingness of her pet. They admired Jessica's ballerina costume. They stroked her breasts, and tickled her nipples, and toyed with her tail, and made her bend over so that they could see and touch her dripping sex, until Jessica was almost frantic with frustrated desire.

All of them asked Mel, more or less directly, when they could borrow Jessica, and there was much talk of complicated arrangements for pet-swapping parties and for reciprocal loans. To Jessica's disappointment Mel politely refused all such requests: she told each owner that she wanted time to enjoy Jessica by herself, and to become used to owning a pet, before she could even consider lending her to anyone else. Besides, she pointed out, Jessica had had only one session of training, and she would be a more rewarding plaything once she had received more instruction. She promised that she would not forget to swap pets with the other owners, just as soon as she and Jessica were ready. The owners, and Jessica, were happy with these assurances. Jessica was particularly pleased to discover that Mel hadn't forgotten that she needed more training under the stern hand of Mrs Morgan.

At last Mel and Jessica were alone on the patio. They kissed again.

'Mistress, I'm so excited,' Jessica said. 'Will I be allowed to come soon? If I don't I think I'll burst.'

Mel laughed. 'I know how you feel,' she whispered, stroking Jessica's hair. 'I can't wait to feel your tongue and your lips on me. And I suppose I could use you now.' She looked towards the patio seat, where Sarah was now kneeling beneath Mrs Northrop's dress. 'But you can't come yet, Jess,' she said. 'Your duty is to please me and my friends. If you're good, I'll let you come after the party, when we're at home. I might even lick you. Would you like that?'

'Yes, Mistress,' Jessica said. The prospect of ending the afternoon in bed with her owner would make bearable the dizzying frustration of the party.

'Let's take a walk around the garden,' Mel said, 'and we'll see what's going on. I'll introduce you to some of the other owners – just a few of them, because you'll never remember everybody's name.' She beckoned to one of the pets who was serving drinks, and took a glass from the pet's tray. She held the glass to Jessica's lips and allowed Jessica a few mouthfuls. It was white wine and soda, which Jessica found refreshing.

With the glass in one hand and the leash in the other, Mel led Jessica on a tour of the garden.

'Look: there's Martha,' Mel said, and she set off towards a Japanese maple under which Martha Smythe was standing. As Jessica approached she saw that beyond the shade of the tree there was a sunlit, grassy dell, and in it Mrs Smythe's pets, Jane and Amy, were playing.

An owner, with her pet on hands and knees at her side, who was watching the two young women, saw Mel and called out to her. 'You really should come and see Martha's pets, Melanie. They're on good form today.'

Mel acknowledged the advice with a wave. The owner smiled, gave an instruction to her pet, and walked away from the dell with her pet at her heels.

'Hello, Martha,' Mel said as she arrived under the dappled shade of the maple, and once Martha had congratulated Mel on Jessica's presentation, and had toyed with Jessica for a few moments, the two owners fell to chatting about the weather, and the antics of Martha's pets, and whether Martha could possibly lend to Mel the catalogues from which she ordered equipment for the pets' playroom.

Jessica couldn't help staring at the two pets in the dell. She wished she could join in with their games: they were obviously having fun, and seemed oblivious to their audience.

Mrs Smythe's pets were alike only in that both were of medium height and lushly curvaceous. Whereas Amy had pale skin and auburn curls, Jane was as tanned as Jessica and had short, black hair. Both were naked, but for their collars, and they were giggling and kissing as they rolled on the grass. Each was holding an artificial phallus, and they were engaged in mock wrestling. Jane succeeded in grasping both of Amy's wrists in her empty hand, and she sat astride Amy's stomach. Amy, still giggling, pretended to look scared. Jane set down her phallus and took advantage of Amy's helpless position: she leaned forwards and kissed Amy hard on the mouth while she played roughly with Amy's breasts. Jessica thought that Jane's uplifted bottom was perfectly positioned for a spanking, and the thought made her remember yet again how long it had been since anyone had punished her. If she misbehaved she might be chastised, and in front of all the owners, too. But she didn't want to do anything that might harm Mel's reputation as the owner of an obedient pet. In any case, it was Matt she wanted: she could rely on him to punish her thoroughly, so that her bottom stayed hot and painful while he put his erection into her.

Jane stopped mauling Amy's breasts and put her free hand behind her, and tried to push it between Amy's thighs. But Amy resisted, keeping her legs pressed together.

'Let me do you, Amy,' Jane said. 'You've got to surrender.' She brought her hand to the front and slapped Amy's breasts, making her cry out. 'Open your legs, Amy, or I'll smack your titties really hard.'

Amy, laughing between exclamations of pain, withstood a few more slaps before admitting defeat. 'All right!' she cried out. 'You win. You can do me.' She lifted and parted her knees.

Jane used her fingers first, pulling at Amy's sex-lips and prodding into her. 'You're soaking wet,' Jane said accusingly. 'You little slut.'

'So are you,' Amy replied. 'I can feel it. You're making my tummy damp.'

Jane picked up the phallus and held it over Amy's face. 'Do you want it?' she asked.

Amy, her eyes glittering with excitement, bit her lip and shook her head, refusing to answer.

'Beg for it,' Jane told her, 'or I'll smack your titties again.'

'Oh, all right,' Amy said. 'Go on, then. Please, Jane, fuck me with your great big cock.'

'Amy!' Mrs Smythe expostulated. 'You know I won't stand for that kind of language!'

But Amy and Jane were too engrossed in each other even to acknowledge their owner. Jane was staring down into Amy's eyes as she thrust the phallus into Amy's sex.

Jessica wanted desperately to join in. She stroked Mel's arm in the hope that Mel might at least notice her and play with her a little, but Mel was deep in a conversation about the relative merits of velvet and linen as curtain material.

If I had a pet, Jessica thought, I'd make sure her bottom always had punishment marks and I'd give her lots of orgasms, as well as making her give lots to me. And I'd let her play with other pets.

But Jessica knew that she didn't want ever to own a pet. She was happy to be trained, and exhibited, and used to give pleasure to her owner and her owner's friends. She just wished Mel was a stricter owner. She had expected that being a pet would entail more punishment and humiliation than Mel seemed prepared to inflict.

'What's the matter, Jess?' Mel said. 'Are you getting bored?'

'No, Mistress,' she replied. 'Not at all. It's just that, well, Amy and Jane are having so much fun. May I join in?'

Mel looked at Mrs Smythe. 'I don't mind, Martha,' she said. 'What do you think?'

'It's a lovely idea,' Mrs Smythe said. 'But I don't want to monopolise your darling new pet. In any case, I ought to get my two into their harnesses.' She lowered her voice conspiratorially. 'Bella's asked me to equip them with extra large phalluses. She wants them to put on a performance with one of her pets. Suzi, I think. The poor girl's in for quite a surprise: Bella hasn't told her that she's going to perform today.'

'That's all right,' Mel said. 'I should circulate among the other guests. It felt a bit daunting, at first, coming into a party full of owners who have never seen me as anything but a pet. But I think I'm getting the hang of it. And it helps to have such a popular pet.' She put her arm round Jessica's waist and hugged her. 'Come along, Jess. I can hear voices from the other side of that beech hedge. Let's go and see what's going on.'

As soon as she reached the end of the hedge and could see beyond it, Mel stopped in her tracks and said, 'Oh!'

Jessica, following a pace behind and still on the lead, almost walked into her owner. She saw that there was a small group of women – two clothed owners and three naked, collared pets – gathered around a wooden seat.

'That's Olivia Reynolds,' Mel whispered to Jessica. 'Let's leave them. I doubt if they'll want to be disturbed.'

At first Jessica didn't recognise Olivia Reynolds. The owner on the seat looked no older than Mel, and had dark hair arranged in a complicated style that had ringlets falling at the sides of her face. But it was the other who called out to Melanie and invited her to approach. She seemed older, and was tall and blonde. And there was something in her haughty voice – a suggestion that she was not used to being disobeyed – that made Jessica's insides flutter with anticipation. This was Olivia Reynolds, the owner Jessica had met briefly in the lanes of the Hillingbury estate.

'Damn,' Mel muttered. 'I suppose we'll have to see what Olivia's up to. Be careful, Jess: she's cruel and spiteful.' She stepped forward with a smile. 'Olivia!' she called out. 'I can't tell you how pleased I am to be on the committee now.' Her voice fell again so that only Jessica could hear it. 'It means I'll never again fall into your clutches, you vicious bitch,' she added.

The owner on the seat, Jessica found out, was Harriet Benton. She was strikingly pretty, with a glamorous frock of voile and lace and exquisitely perfect make-up. Jessica hoped that Mel would agree to lend her to Mrs Benton as soon as possible. It was no surprise that despite her youth Harriet Benton had recruited a pet on each of her two opportunities. It would be easy, Jessica thought, to fall under such a woman's spell.

One of her pets, Kathy, a serious-looking young woman with a pretty, round face, bobbed dark hair, and a quite spectacularly well-developed bosom, was standing next to the seat. The other, Lisa, a slight young woman with pale skin and dark-red hair, was on her hands and knees in front of her owner. She was moving her hips from side to side and pawing the lawn, as if agitated.

Olivia Reynolds and her pet, Karen, were standing opposite the seat, looking down at Lisa. Mrs Reynolds' gaze was as icy as Jessica remembered it. She was immaculately dressed in a long, cream linen frock, and in her gloved hands she held a long, black, slender, leather-clad whip.

Karen, her pet, was short and wiry, with small breasts and short, dark hair. In her unconventional way she was as strikingly attractive as Mrs Benton, and rather than appearing anxious or eager, as the pet of a whip-wielding owner might be expected to appear, her expression seemed bored and supercilious.

'You're just in time to see Lisa punished,' Mrs Reynolds announced.

'I might have guessed it would be something like that,' Mel replied. 'What has the poor thing done?'

'She simply disappeared,' Mrs Benton said. 'And when I went to look for her, I found her in one of the bathrooms upstairs. She was about to lock the door.'

'You caught her just in time, Harriet,' Mrs Reynolds said.

'I immediately thought of bringing her to you, Olivia. I'm afraid discipline isn't my strong suit.'

Jessica didn't understand why Lisa deserved chastisement, other than for leaving her Mistress's side without permission. 'What's going on?' she whispered to Mel.

Olivia Reynolds overheard Jessica's enquiry. 'Haven't you told your delicious new pet all of Bella's little rules, Melanie? She really should be informed, or she'll misbehave by accident and then she'll require a taste of my whip.'

Yes, please, Jessica thought, but Mel made a grimace of distaste. 'I'll look after the discipline of my own pet, thank you, Olivia,' she said. She turned to Jessica. 'At a garden party, if the weather's fine, pets aren't allowed to use the bathrooms. If you need to pee, you have to ask permission, and I'll find somewhere in the garden for you to do it.'

'Oh,' Jessica said. She realised she was blushing. It would be very embarrassing to have to pee in public, in the open air. Embarrassing and exciting.

'Don't worry,' Mel whispered. 'When the time comes I'll find you somewhere private. Some of the owners aren't at all considerate. They choose very public places for their pets. I think they find it amusing.'

'Lisa's not been a pet for very long,' Mrs Benton said. 'I don't think she can be blamed for forgetting one of the rules. Don't be too hard on her, Olivia.'

'Thank you, Mistress,' Lisa murmured. 'I just forgot the rule, that's all.'

Mrs Reynolds flexed the whip. 'Nonsense, girl. If you forgot, then why did you sneak away from your owner without asking her permission or telling her where you were going? You must have known it was naughty. You set out to deceive. A whipping is what you deserve, and a whipping is what you'll get. But I think we should allow you to relieve yourself first. You must be desperate by now. Beg!'

Jessica watched in fascinated amazement as Lisa, red-faced and apprehensive, struggled into a squatting position, with her legs widely parted and her hands raised in front of her breasts. There could be no doubt about it: the naked young woman was going to be ordered to urinate, here and now, in the middle of a sunny afternoon in a suburban garden, with a little group of her neighbours standing around her and watching her.

'Ask your owner for permission to go,' Mrs Reynolds said.

Jessica was glad that she had had only a few sips to drink since arriving at the party. On the other hand, she reflected, it would be exciting to have to submit to Olivia Reynolds.

'Please, Mistress,' Lisa begged miserably, 'please may I have a pee? I need to, badly,'

'Of course you may,' Mrs Benton said, and she leaned back in the seat and waited for her pet to begin.

Mrs Reynolds tapped the tip of her whip impatiently against her shoe. Her pet, Karen, stared up into the branches of the nearby trees.

Then Lisa uttered a little cry, and a jet of urine issued from her urethra and splashed on to the grass. The two owners clapped their hands in ironic applause, and Lisa sobbed and ducked her head as the fountain continued to stream from her and play on to the lawn. Beads of urine glittered in the sunlight like jewels scattered on the grass.

'Finished?' Mrs Reynolds enquired impatiently.

Lisa nodded.

'Stand up, then,' Mrs Reynolds said. 'Move a few steps back. That will do. Kneel. Legs wide apart, girl. You can't have forgotten your training already. Head down, on the grass. No, not there, you silly girl. Here.'

Mrs Reynolds stepped forwards and grasped a handful of Lisa's dark, copper-coloured curls. She pulled the young woman forward until her head was above the place where her urine had wetted the ground – and then she pushed Lisa's face down into the sodden grass.

'Now stay there!' Mrs Reynolds commanded. 'And get your bottom in the air. Higher than that.' She stepped back and flexed the long, thin whip in her hands, and then swung it experimentally through the air a few times. Lisa's body flinched each time the whip whistled above her head.

'Olivia, don't be too severe,' Mrs Benton said.

Mrs Reynolds stopped swishing the whip and held it out towards Mrs Benton. 'Would you prefer to chastise her yourself, Harriet?'

'Oh, no. You're the expert, Olivia. I'm sure you know best.'

'I do, Harriet. Pets must learn to abide by the rules. And I'll make sure this particular pet won't forget this particular rule again.'

Jessica was desperately envious of Lisa. She knew that if she had been made to pee in front of spectators, and then to position herself for punishment, she would be dripping wet with arousal. Just watching Lisa's ordeal was making her so excited she could hardly keep still. She took hold of Mel's right hand and placed it on her bottom, hoping that her owner would smack her, or play with her little hole, while Mrs Reynolds punished Lisa.

Mel must have assumed that her pet needed comforting, as she caressed Jessica's bottom very gently. It was,

Jessica supposed, better than nothing. 'It would be rude to leave now, Jess,' Mel whispered. 'We'll have to stay. Close your eyes if you don't want to watch.'

Jessica had no intention of shutting her eyes for as much as a second. She wanted to see, and hear, and vicariously enjoy every moment of Lisa's punishment. She imagined that instead of Lisa's slim, pale oval buttocks it was own pert, round, tanned bottom that was waiting, lifted up as if in supplication, for the fall of the whip.

The whip screamed through the air, and landed across the split peach of Lisa's bottom with so much force that Lisa's face was pushed into the urine-soaked grass, muffling her cry of pain.

A line of vivid red appeared on Lisa's creamy skin.

The next strokes were no less powerful, and each followed so fast upon the last that the whip was a barely visible blur, and the whistle it made as it flew back and forth was continuous, and Lisa barely had time to catch her breath in between her increasingly loud and anguished shrieks.

Mrs Reynolds stopped suddenly after the tenth stroke. Lisa's bottom had flushed a deep pink all over, but the lines made by the whip were so red and raw that they stood out, easily visible. Lisa seemed almost unaware that the punishment had ended: she kept her bottom lifted up, and she sobbed helplessly into the wet grass.

No one said anything. Jessica glanced at Mrs Reynolds, and saw her own emotions reflected in Mrs Reynolds' face as she stared at the bottom she had just chastised: desire and excitement. Mrs Reynolds' pet, Karen, was also gazing at Lisa with the same expression.

It must be wonderful, Jessica thought, to be Mrs Reynolds' pet. Karen, she assumed, must receive as many punishments as all the other pets together. And, to judge from the hungry expression on her face as she regarded Lisa's striped buttocks, she was keen for more.

Mel and Mrs Benton wore expressions of fascinated shock. It was only ten strokes, Jessica wanted to shout at them; I'd have wanted lots more than that.

Mrs Benton pulled her pet to her feet and into an embrace. 'Don't cry,' she said. 'Your make-up's already running. It was a nasty whipping, my little darling, but you did deserve it. You'll remember, from now on, won't you, to ask my permission to pee in the garden?'

Lisa sniffed and nodded.

Mrs Benton stroked her pet's hair and addressed Mrs Reynolds. 'Thank you, Olivia. Thank goodness you were here. I'm sure that was just what Lisa needed.' She turned towards Mel. 'What about your little pet, Melanie? She's quite adorable in that tiny skirt. Has she been naughty? Does she need a few strokes of Olivia's whip?'

Jessica gasped as a surge of desire welled up inside her. Yes, please, she wanted to cry out, but Mel was already shaking her head. 'Certainly not,' Mel said. 'Jess is a very good pet. If you're so keen on discipline, Harriet, perhaps you should let Olivia borrow Lisa for a while.'

Jessica saw Lisa's body stiffen, and Mrs Benton's mouth open in an O of outrage.

'There's no need,' Mrs Reynolds said. 'I have Karen to practise with. Come along, Karen. Perhaps it's time that you and I found somewhere private. Punishing Harriet's pet was enjoyable, but not entirely satisfying.' She tucked the whip under her arm and led her pet away.

Jessica was sad to see her go. Mrs Reynolds was the only one of the owners Jessica had so far met who seemed likely to be able to give her the same agonising pleasures that she enjoyed at the hands of her mentor and her trainer. And, to make matters worse, Mrs

Reynolds didn't appear to be at all interested in borrowing other owners' pets. Every owner that had spoken to Mel had asked her when she could have Jessica to play with – every owner except Mrs Reynolds. It was infuriatingly frustrating.

'Mistress,' Jessica said to Mel as they strolled away, leaving Mrs Benton to console her contrite pet, 'perhaps it would be a good idea to lend me to Mrs Reynolds first. I mean, when you decide that it's time to lend me to anyone.'

'Good heavens, Jess. Why Olivia? You saw what she did to poor little Lisa.'

Jessica had her answers prepared. 'Almost all the owners have asked you to lend me to them. And I don't mind, Mistress. It's a compliment to both of us, really. And I just thought that it would be best to go to Mrs Reynolds while I'm still being trained. She's obviously a stickler for the rules, and for pets doing things properly. I'd be happier to get the strictest owner out of the way, sooner rather than later, instead of having her hanging over me as a sort of threat.'

'We'll see,' Mel said. 'I don't want to lend you to anyone just yet. I've hardly had a chance to have fun with you myself.'

Jessica stroked her owner's arm. 'I know, Mistress, and we will have lots of fun together. But I don't think I'll be able to settle down as a pet while I know that at some point in the future I'm going to Mrs Reynolds. I like to deal with problems as they arise.'

'Oh, all right, Jess,' Mel said with a sigh. 'I'll talk to Olivia about it. Look: there's Lydia Henshaw. Let's go and say hello.' She led Jessica towards an open-fronted summer house occupied by two owners and two pets.

Jessica was intrigued to see the woman who had been Mel's owner. Mrs Henshaw was a buxom woman, in her thirties, Jessica thought, with sharp, vivacious features but with an indolent manner and speech. She was wearing a plain knitted suit that Jessica thought too warm for the time of year. The other owner was Helen Travers, who could hardly have looked more different from her companion. She was tall and slim, with very dark eyes, an aquiline nose, and long, straight, dark hair. She was dressed in a long, multicoloured skirt and a halter top, and Jessica thought that there was something rather Bohemian about her appearance.

Both of the pets, Vicki and Tricia, belonged to Mrs Travers, but Vicki was on loan to Mrs Henshaw until she recruited a permanent replacement for Mel. Vicki, a short, slight young woman with her blonde hair in pigtails, was kneeling between Mrs Henshaw's legs, while Tricia, who looked uncannily like her owner except that her hair was light brown and her eyes were hazel, was sitting on Mrs Travers' lap. She was wearing a pale-green corset, and she was the only pet Jessica had seen, apart from herself, who was wearing much more than a collar. The two owners were talking animatedly, and their pets, excluded from the conversation, were amusing themselves by touching each other: Tricia had allowed one of her shoes to fall off and her foot was moving in the gap between Vicki's thighs, while Vicki's hand was pressed into the junction of Tricia's thighs. When they saw Mel and Jessica approaching, the pets stopped playing.

'Melanie!' Mrs Henshaw cried. She waved Vicki away and stood up. 'I know I've already said this, more than once, but I'm so pleased you're on the committee. I knew you could do it. I'm so happy for you. Have you thought about what you're going to do first? You'll be able to redecorate your living room. I know you've always wanted one of the wallpapers that are reserved for committee members.'

'I'm going to have something built in the garden,' Mel said. She and Mrs Henshaw kissed on both cheeks. 'But I haven't decided what yet. Oh!' She laughed and blushed. 'I've just kissed you, Lydia, and it's so very different now that I'm an owner, too. And it's so strange not to address you as Mistress.'

Mrs Henshaw touched Mel's cheek. 'I do miss you, Melanie,' she said. 'I knew I would. You were such an adorable pet, and no trouble at all.'

Mel took Mrs Henshaw's hand in hers. 'And you were a kind and gentle owner,' she said. 'I miss you, too. But,' she added, with a smile, 'I have to admit I don't miss being a pet. It's so much better to be an owner. I feel that I belong in Hillingbury at last.'

'You've got a very promising pet, too.' Mrs Henshaw ran her finger through Jessica's hair and caressed Jessica's left breast. 'Helen's lent me Vicki, of course, and she's a dear little thing, but it's not the same as having a pet of my own. I hope the next newcomer to the estate is as good as Jessica.'

'Have you heard anything yet?' Mel asked.

'There's a rumour that number twenty-three is on the market,' Mrs Henshaw said. 'But no one knows who's going to move in. It's very exciting when someone new arrives. You should have heard the gossip among the owners, Jessica, when you and your husband moved in.'

Jessica blushed. She had had no idea that she had been the object of so much attention. 'Thank you, Mistress,' she said.

There was the unmistakable sound of a hand slapping flesh. Jessica gasped and turned her head to find the source of the sound. She saw that Mrs Travers had given Tricia a smack on the bottom to encourage the pet to leave her lap, and now both owner and pet came to join Mel and Mrs Henshaw.

'I thought I'd take Tricia for a run in the woods,' Mrs Travers said. 'Would you like to come with me, Lydia? Melanie? It's better with a few pets.'

Mel and Mrs Henshaw looked uncertainly at each other. 'The thing is, Helen,' Mrs Henshaw said, 'I know that Melanie's keen to have a chat about her plans for her house. It's too warm for exercise, and I'm not as energetic as you are, my dear. I know: why don't you take Jessica? She hasn't been in the woods yet. Vicki can stay with us, and we'll play with her while we talk.'

'Excellent,' Mrs Travers said. She clipped a lead on to Tricia's collar, and then took Jessica's lead from Mel. She stood with the two pets while Mel and Mrs Henshaw arranged themselves comfortably on the cushions in the summer house, with Vicki lying across their laps. Mrs Henshaw unbuttoned the front of her suit so that Vicki could kiss her large breasts, and Jessica felt a brief pang of jealousy as she saw Mel put her hand between Vicki's thighs.

'Stand!' Mrs Travers said, and Jessica and Tricia dropped to their hands and knees. Mrs Travers led them away from the summer house, towards the end of the garden, where the trees and shrubs were larger and almost concealed the wooden door set into the garden wall.

Jessica had taken a walk in the long tongue of woodland that extended into the heart of the Hillingbury estate, but that had been before she had known anything about the HYWAPOC. It seemed like a lifetime ago. Then she had thought merely that the wood was a pleasant and quiet place for a stroll; now she knew that it was the setting for the kind of games that owners played with their pets. As Mrs Travers unlocked the door she was aware that she was about to leave the private domain of Bella Northrop and her friends, and enter a public place. She was acutely aware that she was naked, but for a tutu and stockings and a tail protruding from her bottom, and on a leash, and walking on all fours. Once she was through the door, anyone walking in the woods might see her. It was utterly thrilling.

'What do we do if someone comes along?' she whispered to Tricia.

'We have to hide in the undergrowth, if we can,' Tricia said. 'But we'll be allowed to stand up and run.'

In fact Mrs Travers told the pets to stand up as soon as they were through the garden door. The ground, covered with twigs and fallen leaves, was still a little damp from the previous day's rain, and Mrs Travers didn't want to ruin Jessica's stockings.

It was dark and chill under the canopy of beeches and oaks, despite the bright sunshine that filtered through the leaves, and Jessica was glad that Mrs Travers set a brisk pace. She and her pet seemed to know where they were going, but as far as Jessica was concerned she was simply being led along fainter and fainter paths into the depths of the woodland.

As Jessica hurried along she couldn't help looking in all directions to see whether there was anyone in sight. Even on a summer's day such as this she would usually wear sensible trousers and shoes for a woodland walk, and the fact that she had to pay unprecedented attention to roots, brambles and whippy, low-growing branches made her acutely aware of her state of undress. And as if her costume of collar and lead, tutu, stockings and dancing pumps was not absurd and inappropriate enough, the anal plug, shifting inside her with every step she took, reminded her continually that she had a tail sticking out of her bottom.

She was breathless with exertion and excitement by the time Mrs Travers came to a halt at the edge of an area where the trees were more thinly spread and the woodland floor undulated in hillocks and dells.

'Here we are,' Mrs Travers said, and she unclipped the leads from the pets' collars. 'It's a bit chilly under the trees, isn't it?' she said. 'Tricia, cuddle up with Jessica while I prepare for the game.'

Jessica was entirely happy to be enfolded in Tricia's arms. The cool breeze was giving her goose pimples, and Tricia's corseted body was warm. And Tricia was pretty, and smelled of a light, floral perfume. Soon the two pets were kissing, and pressing their breasts together, and while Jessica caressed Tricia's bottom Tricia fondled Jessica's plaited tail, making Jessica squirm with pleasure.

Jessica kept an eye on Mrs Travers, however, and she saw that when Tricia's owner stowed the leads in her shoulder bag she took out a brightly coloured ball and a penknife. She used the knife to cut two switches from a hazel bush and then to trim the twigs and shoots from the slender lengths of whippy wood. Jessica knew that the switches could be intended only for use on pets' bottoms, and she became even more excited.

'Now we're ready,' Mrs Travers announced. 'Come along, you two. Here's a stick for each of you. We're going to play a game of fetch. Tricia's played this many times, but I'll explain the rules for you, Jessica. I'll throw the ball, as far as I can, and the two of you will race to fetch it. You must pick it up and carry it in your mouth, of course. The one who brings it back to me is the winner. There will be rewards and punishments, of course, and then we'll play again. You'd better take off those high heels, Tricia, or you'll never outrun Jessica.'

Jessica's heart beat with excitement as she waited for Tricia to remove her shoes. She wondered whether she should simply lose every game: she was sure that the loser would be on the receiving end of a hazel switch.

'Are you both ready? Good. Now, don't start running until I give the word.' Mrs Travers pulled back her arm and threw the ball. Jessica watched it arc a surprising distance under the canopy of green leaves, and fall to the ground somewhere among the humps and hollows. 'Right, girls: go!'

Side by side Tricia and Jessica ran across the carpet of brown and sear leaves. Jessica's breasts jiggled as she ran, but they were not as uncomfortable as the plug in her anus. Tricia was taller and more long-legged than

Jessica, but she was barefoot but for stockings, and Jessica was at least as lithe and fit as she was. Neither could outrun the other, but Tricia gained a slight lead when it came to leaping up and down the leaf-strewn slopes where the ball had landed.

Both pets saw the ball at the same time, lying in the bottom of a steep-sided dell, but Tricia reached it first. The speed of her descent prevented her from stopping next to it, however, and by the time she had turned Jessica was with her in the hollow.

As the two pets faced each other, with the ball between them, it occurred to Jessica that there might have been a reason why Mrs Travers had issued them with the hazel switches. Perhaps they were supposed to use the whippy sticks to fight each other for possession of the ball.

While Jessica was considering whether to use the switch, Tricia threw herself to the ground and tried to bite the ball. Jessica was on her immediately, pushed her aside as she dropped to the ground, and lunged for the ball with her mouth.

Jessica had just about succeeded in grasping the soft ball between her teeth when she felt a stinging lash across her exposed bottom. She opened her mouth to cry out, and dropped the ball. Tricia leaped forwards, grabbed the ball in her free hand, and began to scramble up the side of the dell. As she climbed she placed the ball in her mouth, and turned to look down at Jessica with an expression of triumph on her face.

'Not fair!' Jessica cried. 'You're not supposed to use your hands.' But it was no use complaining: Mrs Travers hadn't seen Tricia's transgression, and all that mattered was which pet brought the ball back in her mouth. Jessica followed Tricia up the slope and began to chase her through the trees.

Tricia didn't take the most direct route back to her owner, and as she ran she glanced over her shoulder to make sure that Jessica was following her. Jessica realised that the chase through the trees was part of the game, and she found that she was laughing with the sheer joy of running naked as she pursued Tricia's slim form. Soon she was close enough to her prey to use the hazel switch, and she aimed for Tricia's bouncing bottom. One lash was enough to spur Tricia on, and put a little distance between herself and her pursuer, and there were only three red lines across her buttocks by the time she arrived, breathless, to kneel at her owner's feet, with Jessica a few paces behind.

Mrs Travers extended her hand and took the ball from Tricia's mouth. When both pets had recovered their breath Mrs Travers declared that Jessica's punishment for losing the game would be to receive twice as many lashes as she had given Tricia during the chase; Tricia's reward for winning was to administer the punishment. Jessica was happy to bend over and take the six strokes of Tricia's hazel switch, and she was delighted to hear Mrs Travers announce that she was ready to throw the ball again.

No one came to disturb the games. It excited Jessica to imagine that there were watchers lurking in the undergrowth, but she suspected that if there were any walkers in the woods that afternoon, they would have avoided the hillocks and dells where she and Tricia were running and shrieking as playfully as puppies.

The more the two pets chased each other, the less the object of the game seemed to be to return the ball to Mrs Travers. Instead they tackled each other, and rolled together in the dry leaves, laughing and giggling and shouting as they fought for possession of the ball. Sometimes they duelled with their hazel switches; sometimes they wrestled; and sometimes they stopped fighting, quite suddenly, and instead began passionately to kiss and fondle each other. They would hear Mrs Travers calling them, and usually they ignored her.

Once she came to look for them, and found them in a hollow: the ball and the switches were lying beside them and, with their mouths pressed together and their hands between each other's thighs, they were oblivious to Mrs Travers until she coughed loudly to announce her presence. They received six strokes apiece, and Mrs Travers threw the ball again for them to fetch.

Jessica felt as carefree as a child – or a puppy. The hazel switches were thin and light, so that the stripes they made faded quickly, but Jessica made sure that Tricia had frequent opportunities to use her switch on Jessica's bottom. Whenever Jessica got the ball she held it tightly between her teeth and refused to surrender it, thus ensuring that she received more than her share of strokes from Tricia's switch.

On two occasions when Jessica had possession of the ball she became so aroused that she thought she might come. The first time was when Tricia wrestled with her and succeeded in pinning her down by sitting astride her and holding her wrists in one hand. When it became clear that Jessica was not going to relinquish her hold on the ball, Tricia became so frustrated that she began playfully to slap Jessica's breasts, and threatened to smack harder and harder until Jessica opened her mouth and released the ball. The weight of Tricia's body was pressing the plug deeply into Jessica's rectum, and the combination of the smacking and the pressure seemed to make Jessica's breasts and anus feel particularly sensitive. She bit down on the soft ball as hard as she could, stifling her cries of pain and gasps of pleasure, and she was sure that she would have reached a climax if Tricia hadn't stopped.

Then, on the one occasion when Jessica was the winner of the game, she refused to surrender the ball to Mrs Travers. As Jessica had hoped, this earned her a punishment. She was ordered to lick Tricia's anus – 'just like a dirty puppy,' as Mrs Travers said – while Mrs

Travers plied Jessica's bottom fiercely with one of the switches. By now Jessica's bottom, although still not much striped, was in all other respects just as Jessica liked to feel it: hot, stinging, swollen, and glowing red. Jessica had reached the point at which every additional stroke, landing as a streak of fire on her buttocks, was sheer bliss. The humiliation of being made to lick another pet's little hole made the punishment even more enjoyable, and Jessica's only regret was that the scene wasn't being played out in Mrs Northrop's garden, with all the owners and pets as witnesses to her degradation.

When the whipping stopped Mrs Travers noticed that Jessica was very aroused. She made several loud, crude and disparaging comments about Jessica's private parts, each of which made Jessica squirm with pleasurable embarrassment, and then she touched Jessica's wet, open sex with the toe of her shoe. Jessica was so ready to be penetrated that she lifted her bottom higher and pushed her sex back against the intrusive leather. Mrs Travers' response was to laugh, and then, very gently at first, to swing her foot back and forth so that with each forward movement the toe of her shoe embedded itself in Jessica's vulva, or nudged the base of her tail, and pushed her face into the valley between Tricia's buttocks. Once again Jessica was soon on the point of ecstasy, but the kicking was neither prolonged nor hard enough to bring her to a climax.

Jessica was sore, weary, thirsty, aroused, frustrated, but very happy, by the time Mrs Travers led the pets back through the wooden door into Mrs Northrop's garden. The party had fragmented into many small groups as the owners, slightly tipsy and feeling warm in the hot afternoon sunlight, had retreated with their pets, or with each other's pets, into shady nooks. Everywhere Jessica looked she saw owners lying singly or in pairs, with their eyes closed and their clothing unbuttoned, each toying with one naked pet while another was kissing and licking between her thighs. There was silence but for the buzzing of insects, the trill of birdsong, and the occasional murmur, gasp or exclamation of pleasure.

Mel and Mrs Henshaw were still sitting in the summer house, and still discussing home improvements, although they were now almost as unclothed as Vicki, who was still lying across the owners' laps. The pet's face was now buried between Mrs Henshaw's open thighs, while Mel had clearly been playing with her private parts: two brightly coloured phalluses were protruding from her sex, and Mel's hand was resting on a third, which was inserted a little way into her bottom.

'Oh, Jess!' Mel exclaimed when she saw Mrs Travers returning with her pet. 'You're all dusty, and there are leaves in your hair. What have you been up to?'

'Don't be too hard on her, Melanie,' Mrs Travers said. 'It's almost impossible to stop pets playing with each other when you let them off the lead in the woods. It's not as if Jessica hasn't had her share of punishments. Turn round and show your owner, Jessica.'

Blushing, Jessica turned and bent forwards, showing off her reddened bottom.

'Oh, my goodness, Jess,' Mel cried. 'Has she been very naughty, Helen? I'm so sorry if she's put you to any trouble. It's not like her to be disobedient.'

'No trouble at all,' Mrs Travers said. 'We've all had a wonderful time in the woods, haven't we, girls?'

It took some time for Mrs Travers and Jessica to convince Mel that Jessica's sore bottom was evidence of enjoyable games, but in the end she had to accept that Mrs Travers had no complaints about Jessica's behaviour.

The party was already drawing to a close: it couldn't extend into the evening, because all of the owners and pets had to return home, wash off the perfume, make-up and other evidence of the day's clandestine activities, and change into plain frocks so that when their husbands arrived home on the evening train they would suspect nothing of what their wives had been doing all day.

'I know it's a bit early to leave the party,' Mel said to Jessica, 'but I want to take you to my house. If we go now we'll have about an hour together before you have to go home. I've been saving myself for you all day, Jess. You're going to lick me all over, and I'm going to have the most wonderful orgasm.'

'Yes, Mistress,' Jessica said. She knew that once she had been taken away from the party, there was little likelihood that she would receive any more punishment; on the other hand, the prospect of an hour alone with her owner was very appealing. 'If I'm very good,' she added, 'will you let me come, too?'

'We'll see,' Mel said with a shrug. 'Perhaps, if there's time.'

Field agent's report to the Private House
From: Matt
For the attention of: Mistress Julia

It's well into the evening now. I might as well face up to it: Jessica's not going to come. I've lost her; I've driven her away.

There's no sign yet, either, of the two agents who have been appointed by the House to take over the project. I imagine it will take several days, at least, to set up an agent as a new householder on the Hillingbury estate. The one who is due to relieve me, however, here at the club, can't arrive quickly enough, as far as I'm concerned.

I know I've made a hash of things here, and I'll be glad to see the back of the place. I'll hold on until my replacement arrives, of course.

For what it's worth, I still believe that Jessica represented our best hope of infiltrating the Hillingbury pet owners' committee. She is completely in tune with the ideals of the Private House, and she would be a valuable addition to our ranks. She has the perfect combination of a strong-willed, independent personality and an utterly submissive sexuality.

And I've ruined everything. I suppose she hates me now, and is even happier than ever playing her lesbian games.

Seven

For the first time in what seemed like an age, Jessica had the whole day to herself. Apparently there was to be a meeting of the committee that afternoon, to which pets would not be taken, and Mel had decided to spend the morning in the city, having her hair done yet again and buying some new clothes so that she would make an impression at her first committee meeting.

Jessica sat at the end of the bed. She didn't know what to do. She had become accustomed to waiting for Mel to arrive. Now she felt the familiar tension inside as her anticipation grew, but there was nothing to anticipate. She could resume her interrupted routine of going to the Health and Exercise Club, but Matt wouldn't expect her until the afternoon. She wasn't even sure that she would find him on duty if she went to the club in the morning.

It was all very frustrating. Jessica had enjoyed the party the previous day, particularly her presentation and the walk in the woods, but wearing the tail in her bottom and having her bottom switched by Mrs Travers had merely whetted her appetite. And, although she had licked Mel assiduously, Mel had enjoyed the experience so much that she had forgotten Jessica's request to be allowed to have an orgasm.

During the night, with Brian snoring gently beside her, Jessica had touched herself, and had almost been tempted to take herself over the brink of a climax. But it was hardly any fun at all without someone watching, and she really wanted to be spanked first. She knew that, if she could only wait until the afternoon, Matt could be relied on to punish her hard, and penetrate her, and watch her come.

During the past couple of days she had not been able to spend much time with her mentor, and she found that she was missing him dreadfully. She vowed that she would make it up to him: she would take his long, hard, hot penis into her mouth and use her lips and tongue until he couldn't hold back from spurting his delicious semen into her throat. It would be wonderful.

But she still had hours to wait. She told herself that she should get dressed in some old clothes and do some of the housework she had been neglecting for days. Not that Brian ever noticed whether the house was clean and tidy. But she wasn't in the mood for housework. Her sex and her nipples felt alive and sensitive. She wasn't in the mood for anything but being spanked and played with.

She could walk to the shop, on the pretext that she needed groceries. She might be able to hint to Mrs Morgan that she'd like a few hours of extra training. She had seen the way that Mrs Morgan looked at her, and she thought it quite likely that the trainer wouldn't be able to resist having Jessica all to herself.

But it wasn't very fair to Mel. Jessica's owner had a right to know when Jessica was being trained. After all, Mel was paying Mrs Morgan's fees.

It then occurred to Jessica that by now Mel would have spoken to Olivia Reynolds. As the committee meeting wasn't until the afternoon, it was likely that Mrs Reynolds would be at home at least until lunchtime. She wouldn't be expecting Jessica to call, but surely Mel must have asked her whether she would like to borrow Jessica?

Jessica's heart fluttered. What was she thinking of? Was she really considering walking up to the front door of one of the owners, and offering herself as a temporary pet?

She recalled the peremptory voice in which Mrs Reynolds issued commands. She pictured the owner's piercing eyes, and the calm deliberation on her face as she wielded the whip. She remembered the high, swishing song of the whip as it slashed through the air.

Yes. Jessica made her decision. She wanted to submit to Mrs Reynolds' discipline. She would go to her house.

She didn't know what to expect when she arrived, but the expedition would take her mind off thoughts of Matt. And at the very least, surely, Mrs Reynolds would give her a spanking for being impertinent.

With trembling fingers she fastened her collar around her neck. She pulled on stockings, and buckled high-heeled shoes on her feet. Her sex was freshly shaved, and even though she had not expected to see her owner she had thoroughly washed her private parts and her breasts, as she had been trained to do. She applied a little perfume to her neck, wrists, breasts and thighs. She put on make-up and, grinning mischievously to her reflection in the mirror, she used lipstick to redden her nipples.

She was ready. She stood before the wardrobe mirror and inspected herself. Her bottom wasn't even the slightest bit red, and the hazel switches had been too light to leave any marks. She touched her sex, and stroked the bare lips before pushing her fingertips between them. She was wet, of course. And walking through the Hillingbury estate, as good as naked, imagining the things that Mrs Reynolds might do to her, would do nothing to lessen her excitement. She hoped that Mrs Reynolds was feeling particularly strict.

She went downstairs to put on a coat, and a scarf to conceal her collar.

By the time she reached Mrs Reynolds' house she was as nervous as she was aroused. But there could be no turning back now. She strode to the front door and rang the bell.

There was no answer for a long time. At last the door was opened by Karen, Mrs Reynolds' pert, dark-haired pet. It hadn't occurred to Jessica that Karen might be there, and the two pets stared at each other with equal surprise. Jessica could only stammer that she had come to see Mrs Reynolds. Karen told her to wait in the porch while she went to inform her owner about the unexpected visitor.

Jessica waited a long time. She was beginning to regret her impulsive decision. Perhaps Mel had forgotten to mention to Mrs Reynolds that she was prepared to lend Jessica to her.

Jessica was on the point of leaving when Karen returned to the door. 'You'd better come in,' she said.

Jessica was so nervous that she hardly noticed the tasteful décor of Mrs Reynolds' home. She couldn't help seeing, however, that when Karen shrugged off the housecoat she had put on to answer the door, she was wearing a remarkable costume. It was made entirely of black leather, which went well with her dark hair and eyes. Her collar had, as well as the usual rings, conical spikes of metal. Her boots had high heels and platform soles, and were so long that their tops almost reached her sex, which was as hairless as Jessica's. Her torso was contained within a harness of leather straps and metal fastenings that left her small breasts exposed. Her muscular buttocks, Jessica noted as she followed her into the house, were pale and unmarked.

Jessica, too, had removed her coat, and was very conscious that she was walking naked into another woman's home.

Mrs Reynolds was waiting for them in her sitting room. Jessica was surprised to find that instead of being cool and haughty, the tall blonde was red-faced and flustered, and appeared to have dressed in a hurry. She was sitting restlessly on a large sofa. Jessica could only assume that she had interrupted the owner while she was playing with her pet. The timing of her visit, Jessica thought, could hardly have been worse.

'Jessica,' Mrs Reynolds said. 'This is a surprise. What can I do for you?' The owner gazed at Jessica's naked body with puzzled interest rather than with the desire that Jessica had hoped to inspire.

Jessica didn't know how to begin to explain. 'Mel didn't talk to you,' she asked, 'about borrowing me?'

Mrs Reynolds looked thoughtful, but then shook her head. 'I don't think so,' she said. 'But I didn't ask to borrow you, Jessica.'

The situation was becoming more and more embarrassing. 'I know,' Jessica said. 'But I suggested – I mean, I thought it would be a good idea. But if Mel hasn't mentioned it . . .' It occurred to Jessica that the longer she stayed, and the more she said, the less well Mel would look to her fellow owners. It was clear that the committee disapproved of owners who failed to control their pets. 'I think I'd better go,' she said. 'I'm sorry to have troubled you. And this was all my idea, not my mistress's, I assure you.'

She turned to leave, but neither Karen nor Mrs Reynolds made any move to show her to the door. Instead they were looking at each other with inscrutable expressions on their faces.

'What was your idea, Jessica?' Mrs Reynolds said. 'What precisely did you come here for?'

Jessica wanted only to leave. She certainly didn't want to explain any further. But she couldn't ignore such direct questions. She took a deep breath and ordered her thoughts. 'At the garden party, Mistress,' she said, 'nearly all the owners asked Mel when they could borrow me. My mistress managed to avoid making any definite commitments, but it's clear that before long I'll be lent to all the other owners, or swapped with their pets. So I suggested to Mel that I should come to you first.'

'Why?' It was Karen who asked the question.

'Well, Mistress,' Jessica replied to Mrs Reynolds, and she felt her face blushing as she spoke, 'you have a reputation, I'm told, for being a strict disciplinarian, and I thought it would be a good idea to come to you first, while I'm still being trained, and so I can find out about being disciplined properly.'

The two women stared at her. 'Well, that's a first,' Mrs Reynolds said lightly. 'No pet has volunteered to come here before.' She looked concerned. 'Have you done something wrong, my dear? Or are you unhappy with Melanie?'

I knew it, Jessica thought. The more I explain, the worse it gets. She closed her eyes and tried to decide what to do or say. And when she spoke, in a rush, even she was surprised at what she said.

'I like it,' she said. Her face felt burning hot, and she couldn't look at Mrs Reynolds. 'I saw what you did to Lisa yesterday. And I – Well, I wanted it to be me.' She took a deep breath. 'I like being spanked, Mistress.'

Mrs Reynolds and Karen burst out laughing. Jessica was bewildered.

'I'm so sorry, Jessica,' Mrs Reynolds said. 'We're not laughing at you, dear. It's just that this is a very strange and ironic situation. Sit here, next to me, and tell me everything. You're among friends here. Karen, be an angel and make us all a cup of coffee.'

'OK,' Karen said, and gave her owner and Jessica a broad grin before disappearing into the kitchen.

It seemed to Jessica that the atmosphere in the house had changed, suddenly and utterly. Karen, who always seemed so bored and petulant, was friendly; Mrs Reynolds was no longer aloof, but warm and chatty.

And so Jessica found herself telling Mrs Reynolds everything: her old fantasies about being captured and tied up by pirates, and her sense of coming home when she was recruited by Mel as a pet. She even talked a little about Matt, and the things he had done with her, but she didn't name him and she made it sound as though she had known him some time ago. During her account Karen returned with coffee cups, but Mrs Reynolds was listening so attentively that Jessica hardly noticed.

'Well, well,' Mrs Reynolds said when Jessica's story drew to a close. She put her arm round Jessica's shoulders and kissed her cheek. 'You're a very brave pet, my dear. It takes a lot of courage to admit one's perverse desires. If only I had had the nerve –'

She was interrupted by Karen's discreet cough. The owner and her pet exchanged another long, mysterious look.

'Let's see if she's wet,' Karen said abruptly. She came to stand over the sofa on which Mrs Reynolds and Jessica were sitting. 'I'm sorry, Jessica, but you must understand that we can't take a tale such as yours at face value. The only way to be sure is to see what you respond to.'

'All right,' Jessica said. Things were beginning to look up. She didn't understand what was going on, but she was pleased to have an opportunity to display herself. She turned and kneeled on the seat of the sofa, with her arms crossed on the back, her legs apart, and her bottom sticking out. She knew that she was wet already, from the embarrassment and excitement of telling her story, and putting her private parts on show would make her even more aroused.

It was Karen who inspected her. The pet's fingers, warm and firm, roamed briefly over Jessica's thighs and buttocks before parting her sex-lips and probing inside. Jessica uttered a little murmur of pleasure, and then a cry of mortification as she heard the moist, sucking sound that Karen's fingers made as they withdrew.

No one spoke. Jessica assumed that Mrs Reynolds and her pet were again communicating wordlessly. Jessica remained still: she liked showing off, and she hoped that Mrs Reynolds would inspect her next, and might even give her a spanking immediately.

'Shall we tell her?' Mrs Reynolds said.

'No one knows about us,' Karen replied. 'We haven't told a soul.'

'We've never met anyone like Jessica,' Mrs Reynolds said. 'Let's tell her, Karen, please. I've been so lonely, you know.'

'All right,' Karen said. 'You're the owner, after all. Let's take her to the schoolroom, and show her what we do.'

Mrs Reynolds helped Jessica to stand, and Karen led them towards the back of the house. She stopped before a closed door, and turned to Mrs Reynolds, who gave her a key. Karen unlocked the door, threw open the door, and ushered Jessica through it.

The room beyond was furnished, at first sight, like a school classroom. There were bookshelves, and desks, and a blackboard on an easel. Jessica soon noticed, however, that much of the furniture was not what it first appeared to be. The easel was made of struts of wood that were far sturdier than was required to support the blackboard, and it had metal rings screwed into its feet and uprights. Each desk had a seat attached to it, but both the seat and the surface of the desk were padded and upholstered in leather, and there were stirrups attached to both sides of the seat. Everything in the room, from the vaulting horse in the corner to the heavy light-fittings suspended from the ceiling-beams, had been designed or altered so that it could be used for restraint and punishment. Jessica went from one piece of equipment to the next, touching the varnished wood and the worn leather, and feeling her sex tingle with arousal. Matt, she thought, would love this room. And so do I.

This was quite obviously the place where Mrs Reynolds played with her pet. A teacher's traditional gown was hanging from one corner of the blackboard, and a long, thin cane was dangling by its crooked handle from the other. A gymslip was lying across one of the desks, and next to it was a red leather collar. It seemed as though Jessica was correct in her assumption that she had interrupted a game.

Karen was standing by the blackboard. Mrs Reynolds stood in the centre of the room. Jessica waited for Mrs Reynolds to say something, but it was Karen who spoke first. 'You'd better just show her,' Karen said.

Mrs Reynolds blushed, closed her eyes, and began to unbutton her dress. Jessica turned to look questioningly at Karen, but the pet was staring at her owner with an unreadable expression on her face.

Mrs Reynolds shrugged off the dress and dropped it on a desk. She was now wearing nothing except for a pair of stockings. Her tall, slender body looked lithe and supple, and would have been envied by most women half her age. Her teardrop-shaped breasts were full, but appeared hardly less firm than Jessica's. They were blushing as pink as her cheeks, and their tips were erect. Below her narrow waist and flat belly her hips were generously rounded and her pubic hair had been shaved off.

She looked at Jessica. 'This is how it is,' she said. She picked up the red collar and buckled it around her neck. Then she took a deep breath, turned round, and bent down across the padded top of a desk.

Mrs Reynolds' bottom was pale and firm. Like Jessica's, it looked particularly full because her waist and thighs were slim. The lips of her sex were glistening with wetness. The flanged base of a phallus, lodged in her anus, protruded from between her buttocks, which were bright red and marked with six horizontal lines.

The room was silent while Jessica tried to understand what she was seeing.

'Olivia's always such a naughty girl,' Karen said. Jessica turned to see that the pet had pulled on the teacher's gown and had picked up the cane. 'I can never get through a lesson without having to punish her at least once. She's been particularly badly behaved this morning. What have you been punished for today, Olivia?'

Mrs Reynolds stood up, turned round, and faced Karen with her eyes downcast and her hands behind her back. 'Playing with myself in class, Miss,' she said meekly. 'I got a spanking and the plug in my bottom for that. Then fidgeting. That was ten strokes of the strap. Then not paying attention. That was six with the cane.' She glanced up quickly, caught Jessica's eye, and gave her a mischievous little smile.

Jessica was dumbfounded. The previous day, at the garden party, Mrs Reynolds had seemed haughty, aloof, and the epitome of a disciplinarian owner. And Mel was clearly in awe of her reputation for severity. Now she was acting just like a naughty schoolgirl, and was obviously enjoying being punished by her pet. That, at least, Jessica could understand. Karen, in her black leather costume and black gown, looked thoroughly intimidating, and Jessica wanted more than anything to have a chance to play at being a pupil in Karen's class.

'And?' Karen asked.

Mrs Reynolds blushed again. 'And making wet marks on the furniture,' she whispered. 'But I couldn't help it, Miss, honestly.'

'I made her lick it up,' Karen told Jessica. 'And I was just about to give her another six with the cane when you rang the doorbell.'

'I'm very sorry, Miss,' Jessica said, and she saw Karen's eyes widen with interest. 'I really shouldn't have been so inconsiderate.'

Karen sighed with pretended exasperation. 'So now I have two naughty girls to deal with,' she said. 'Bend over your desks, both of you.'

Mrs Reynolds received six strokes, and Jessica twelve – to even things up, as Karen put up. The pet was clearly delighted to have two attractive bottoms presented to her, and she made Jessica and Mrs Reynolds stay in position for a long time, with pauses between the cane-strokes during which she inspected and played roughly with their sexes. The schoolroom setting, the cruel sting of the cane, and the physical and verbal humiliations inflicted by Karen, all combined to make Jessica so aroused that her sex was dripping wet long before her punishment was over. She was blissfully happy, and her only regret was that she didn't have a phallus in her little hole.

Back in the sitting room, Karen lounged on the sofa while Mrs Reynolds kneeled in front of her and kissed the insides of her thighs. Karen took Jessica across her lap and spanked her and played with her sex until Jessica came. Then, while Jessica sucked on Karen's small breasts, Mrs Reynolds licked her pet to a climax. Karen and Jessica remained on the sofa in a post-climactic embrace, toying with each other's nipples, and Karen gave Mrs Reynolds permission to touch herself with one hand while she extracted the phallus from her anus with the other. The two pets watched Mrs Reynolds as she used her fingers and the phallus to bring herself to a shuddering orgasm.

'So that's my secret,' Olivia said to Jessica a little later, as the two women lay together on the sofa and smoothed ointment into each other's sore, striped bottoms. 'I'm like you. When it comes to sex, I like to be controlled and punished by someone strict. When Bella Northrop recruited me as one of her pets, I thought I was in heaven. It was wonderful to have an owner to tell me what to do. But I soon realised that it couldn't last. As my name crept further and further up the list, I knew that I would be expected to recruit a pet of my own. I was dreading it.'

'What happened?' Jessica asked. The gentle ministrations of Olivia's fingers were making her shiver with pleasure, but she concentrated on listening to Olivia's story. It had already occurred to her that one day she would have to seduce a newcomer.

'I didn't even try,' Olivia admitted. 'Afterwards I told Bella that the new girl was revolted by the idea of being a pet, but the truth is that I didn't even mention it to her. I didn't want to become an owner. I thought that as long as I didn't try to do so, I could remain a pet.'

Jessica sat up. Olivia's account was beginning to worry her. 'Why couldn't you?' she asked. 'What happened?'

Olivia sighed. 'Oh, I let myself be persuaded, I suppose. Or bullied. Bella made it very plain that she was disappointed in me. I hardly saw her for weeks. And a pet becomes rather dependent on her owner, you know. Once you're aware that all these houses are full of owners and pets having fun with each other, you feel terribly isolated if your owner doesn't want to play with you. The other owners were almost as bad. I'm a little older than most of the pets, and it was made very clear to me that everyone expected me to become an owner as soon as I could.'

'I suppose you couldn't admit that you just wanted to be a pet.'

'I don't know. I used to think about it all the time. I'd prepare speeches, and rehearse them in my mind, and try to imagine how Bella would react.' Olivia sighed again. 'I honestly think that if I'd said anything of the sort I would have been ostracised. The one thing that all the pets talk about is becoming an owner and getting on the committee. It's the only way to become part of Hillingbury society. The committee decides everything. I decided I couldn't take the risk. I'd become used to socialising with everyone here. A part of me wanted to be on the committee, I suppose. It's very difficult to oppose an opinion that's held unanimously by everyone else you know. Anyway, I didn't have the courage to speak out when I had my first chance to recruit a pet. And then I wasn't given time to think about it.'

'Why? What happened? Your name must have gone to the bottom of the list again. You must have had another few years as Bella's pet.'

Olivia shook her head sadly. 'That's what I expected. But Bella was so sure that I'd make a good owner that she decided to bend the rules for me. I had to pretend to be grateful. The committee agreed to give me another chance. I was allowed to recruit the next newcomer. And I steeled myself to do it.'

'And the next newcomer was Karen!' Jessica exclaimed. 'Olivia, you were so lucky.'

'I know. It was easy to persuade Karen to become my pet, once she knew that it was the only way to become an owner. That's all she was interested in, of course. She was prepared to put up with a few years of being a pet, in return for a subsequent career as an owner. She was very excited at the idea of owning pets. It was when she told me how much she would enjoy disciplining them that I thought of a way to keep both of us happy.' She touched the collar at her throat.

'In public you're the owner and Karen's the pet,' Jessica said. 'And in private –'

'In private she's terribly strict,' Olivia said. Her eyes were sparkling. 'It's rather like my first few weeks as a pet, when I was being trained by Mrs Morgan. But it's even better because we can spend day after day together. Sometimes, when my husband goes away on business for weeks at a time, I have Karen here to stay. My poor bottom gets no respite at all.'

'How wonderful!' Jessica said. 'It sounds perfect.'

'It is,' Olivia said. Her face fell. 'There's just one problem. Karen is getting near the top of the list. When her turn comes she'll have to try to recruit a pet of her own. The committee will expect it: they all think that Karen has been suffering for years as the pet of the infamously severe Olivia Reynolds. And anyway, Karen wants a pet. I would, too, if I had Karen's predilections.'

'So your paradise is going to come to an end,' Jessica said.

'It's worse than that,' Olivia replied. 'When I lose Karen I'll have to borrow a pet from one of the other owners, until I recruit a new one. And then I think my secret will be discovered. I can pretend to be strict for a while. I just imagine that I'm the one on the receiving end of the punishment I'm dishing out, and I can manage to chastise a pet rather effectively. But I know that it's only temporary, and that when I come home with Karen she'll humiliate me and punish me, and everything will be all right again. I don't think I can pretend to be a strict owner for ever. I don't know what I'll do. Perhaps I'll have to move away from Hillingbury.' The brightness of her eyes was now the glittering of tears.

As Jessica ate a light lunch at her kitchen table she considered everything that had happened at Mrs Reynolds' house. She was pleased and excited to have found an owner and a pet who understood about discipline, and she was looking forward to visiting Olivia and Karen again – now that Olivia had shared her secret with Jessica she had promised to ask Mel to lend Jessica to her as soon as possible.

But the more Jessica thought about Olivia and Karen, the more frustrated and angry she became. It was unfair that neither of them could admit to their true nature. Jessica had been a pet for only a few days, and already she was impatient with the inflexible rules of the committee. Most of the owners, she realised, were interested only in competing with each other: which of them had the prettiest, most willing pet; which had the most up-to-date wallpaper pattern. Not one of them, it seemed, was truly interested in exploring and expanding the dark areas of desire, whether her own or her pet's.

At least I've got a mentor, Jessica thought. Perhaps I should introduce Olivia to Matt, when she loses Karen. But I don't really want to share him.

As usual, Jessica found that once she had thought of Matt she couldn't help imagining what he might do to her on her next visit to the Health and Exercise Club. She had been caned and spanked, and had had an orgasm, but it wasn't enough. Her bottom wasn't even sore any more: it was just a bit tingly and sensitive, so that it was continually reminding her that she wanted to be punished again. And she wanted Matt's big penis, too, inside her.

She hadn't dressed since arriving home, and so it was easy to sit at the kitchen table with her hands in her lap, teasing the lips of her sex while she conjured in her mind images of herself being subjected to Matt's harsh discipline. She lifted her bottom from the chair so that she could put one hand behind her and play with her little hole. It was soft and open, and wet with lubrication that had seeped from her sex. She wanted Matt's penis in there, of course, but not until he'd smacked her thoroughly. But did she want to be smacked on her bottom, or her breasts, or her sex? With his hand, or with a strap, or with a cane? She couldn't decide. She wanted everything. It seemed that when she was aroused there was almost no limit to the amount of spanking she desired.

Perhaps he would tie her up. She was looking forward to being punished very hard while tied up tight and completely unable to move. He might have to put a gag in her mouth to stop her crying out. Then he would remove the gag and use her mouth for his pleasure, while she was still tied up and helpless. That would be wonderful. She would feel his hard cock begin to pulse, and then he'd pull it out and shower his semen all over her face.

And then – Oh, goodness, this was such a dirty, degrading, exciting idea. Jessica's fingers rubbed furiously along her slick sex-channel. Then he would untie just one of her hands, and he would watch her play with herself, and he would allow her to have an orgasm as he washed his semen from her face by peeing on her.

She pulled her hand from her lap and took several deep breaths. She had been very close to coming.

It was no good. She couldn't wait another minute. She had to go to the club, even though Matt wouldn't be expecting her yet. If she told him about her fantasy, he would certainly punish her. And perhaps he would let her come while she writhed and spluttered under a stream of his hot, acrid urine.

A few minutes later, with her teeth and hair brushed, her sex washed, and her body perfumed, she slid her coat over her naked body and set off for the club.

Matt wasn't at his usual post at the desk inside the entrance. Another member of the club staff greeted Jessica, but she barely noticed the young man. Matt wasn't by the pool, either, or in the gym. In the end Jessica had to return to the desk to ask for him. And she was told that Matt had left the club, and was going away.

At first Jessica couldn't understand the words she heard. Then, when she became almost distraught, the young man hurriedly suggested that she could look for him in his room. He might still be there, the young man said. There were few trains during the afternoon. He gave her directions to the accommodation above the club.

Jessica ran: along the corridor, through the door marked PRIVATE, and up the stairs.

She burst into Matt's room to find him folding clothes. A suitcase was open and half-filled on the bed.

'Jessica,' he said. He stared at her, and then shook his head. 'I didn't expect to see you again.' He looked embarrassed, and defensive.

Jessica didn't know what to say. He was leaving. That was obvious. And he hadn't told her. 'Mentor?' she said. She blinked. She was determined not to cry. 'Matt? What are you doing?' She pointed to the suitcase, and couldn't stop a tear welling in her eye.

'I thought –' Matt began, and then was lost for words. He tried to speak again. 'I thought it would be best to leave. I thought you weren't coming back. Now that you're a pet, with an owner, and a trainer, and lots of new friends on the estate. I thought I wouldn't see you again.'

Oh, goodness: he was going to cry, too. 'You idiot,' she yelled at him, and she didn't know whether to laugh or to cry, whether to be angry with him for thinking of leaving or delirious with joy because he cared about her. 'You can't go. I need you. I want you. No one understands me the way you do.'

He flinched, as if her words were unwelcome. He didn't step towards her. He shut his eyes for a moment, and when they opened again they were cool and emotionless. 'It's not as simple as that,' he said. 'You've told me everything about yourself: your desires, your fantasies, your experiences, your induction into the secret world of the committee. I haven't been honest with you. I've kept things from you. I've misled you. I've used you. I have, at least, realised that I can't do it any longer. And so I'd better go.'

'No,' Jessica said. 'It's not for you to decide whether you've deceived me, and how much I care about it. That's up to me. Tell me everything you haven't told me, and I'll decide what I think.'

Matt took a deep breath. 'Very well,' he said. 'The Private House doesn't seek publicity, but we're not a secret organisation. You'd better sit down. This will take a little while.'

Jessica listened attentively while Matt told her a tale that was so remarkable that it almost defied belief. He told her about the Private House: a way of life, a regime of obedience and sexuality, a rambling manor in the heart of the countryside, an association of dedicated sensualists and perverts, an international organisation with control of vast corporations all over the globe – the Private House, it seemed, was all this and more.

He explained that his mission was to discover everything he could about the committee and, if possible and appropriate, to subvert it so that the most suitable members could be recruited to join the House. Jessica was to have been the tool with which he hoped to pierce the veil of secrecy around the committee. She had already provided a considerable amount of useful information, all of which he had conveyed to his superiors in written reports.

'I see,' Jessica said. She looked at the floor. She felt sick. She had trusted him. She had told him everything, just because he had a handsome face and a muscular body. He had known exactly how to exploit her unusual desires. He had deceived her, and as a result she had betrayed the committee.

'I'm sorry,' he said. He was sitting on the bed, his great shoulders hunched, staring at her. She was sitting in the room's only chair, facing him, staring at him. Even now, she realised with a shudder of revulsion, she was attracted to him. She remembered that she was naked beneath her coat, and she pulled it tightly around her.

'So why did you stop?' she asked belligerently. 'Have I ceased to be useful to you? Have you learned everything you can from me? Is that why you're going?'

He squeezed shut his eyes. He uttered a bitter laugh. 'No,' he said. 'You don't understand. I can't do it any more. I'm a failure. Field agents aren't supposed to become involved with the, er, the subjects of missions.'

'Involved,' Jessica said. 'That's your expression for fucking me up the arse, is it?'

He flinched again. 'No, no. I don't mean that. I mean emotionally involved. I was getting too close to you. Too concerned. I couldn't get you out of my mind, Jessica. I still can't.'

Oh, goodness. What was he saying? Could it be true? Did he care for her, after all? Or was this just another of his deceptions?

No: it couldn't be. He couldn't have known that she would come to see him. He really had been packing to leave.

'But what do you care, anyway?' he said, suddenly angry. 'You dropped me just as soon as you had alternative entertainments arranged. You made no attempt to disguise the fun you were having with your pretty owner, and your strict trainer. You'd found your way into Hillingbury society, and you didn't need me any more. I've hardly seen you for the last two days.'

She could see the pain in his face. 'I couldn't get away, Mentor,' she said softly. 'I told you that once I was a pet it would be more difficult for us to meet. But I've wanted to come to you. I've been missing you terribly. You must believe me.'

They looked at each other and, gradually, simultaneously, they began to smile.

'I think we've both been jumping to conclusions,' Jessica said. 'But how could I have known that you were really interested in me? You've always been so cold and distant.'

Matt shrugged, and smiled awkwardly. 'I sort of had to remain aloof,' he said. 'It was part of the game we played. I mean, you wouldn't have enjoyed it if I'd been chatty and gushing.'

'Very true,' Jessica admitted. 'I hope you haven't forgotten how to be severe. Can you guess what I'm wearing underneath this coat?' She undid the top button.

His eyes widened, and he leaned forwards. Then he slumped again. 'But, Jessica,' he said, 'I can't simply forget that I've been deceiving you. Every detail of everything you've done with me, and of everything you've told me about being a pet, has been reported to the Private House. How can you possibly forgive me?'

Jessica giggled. 'I have to confess, Mentor,' she said, 'that there is something rather exciting about the thought of all my misdeeds being written down and read by complete strangers. So I'll have to forgive you like this.'

She stood up and wriggled her shoulders, and the coat slid to the floor. The hungry look on his face as he saw her naked body made her catch her breath.

'Lie down,' she said. 'I'm going to undress you. And then I want you to spank me and fuck me as hard as you can.'

It took only a few seconds to pull off his T-shirt and his shorts. He was as ready as she was: his penis seemed bigger even than she remembered it, and when she straddled his hips and impaled on it her hot, wet sex she let out a sigh of pleasure as it filled her.

She rested her head on his shoulder, and he put his left arm across her back. His head and shoulders were propped against pillows at the head of the bed, so with his right hand he could easily reach behind her. She tried to remain completely still while he spanked her. She didn't want to make him come until her bottom was radiant with heat and exquisitely sore. And in any case, as the warmth and shame of the punishment flooded through her body she wasn't sure that she would be able to postpone her own climax if she were to feel his manhood moving inside her.

As always, he seemed to know just what she wanted, and he interrupted the spanking from time to time, and played roughly with her nipples and her little hole while she kissed his mouth, so that each time he resumed smacking her the slaps were more painful and she was even more aroused.

At last she was so excited that she couldn't help lifting her bottom to meet the smack of his hand, and she could tell by his gasping breaths that the movements of her hips were about to bring him to a climax. She was almost at the same point herself. She was now uttering a breathy 'Oh!' of delight and pain each time that his hand crashed against her bottom, but between her gasps she found herself whispering, again and again, 'I love my Mentor. Spank me harder, please.'

And then his body was suddenly rigid, and he groaned, and she felt his penis grow even larger within her, and she felt its spasms as he came. 'I love you, Jessica,' he breathed, as his shudders subsided.

Jessica would have been disappointed if he had allowed her to come at the same time as he did. These days she preferred the humiliation of being instructed and watched.

He didn't disappoint her. When he had recovered his breath he told her to dismount from him, and to fetch him a glass of water and a belt. He sat up straighter against the pillows, and had her curl herself beside him, with her knees drawn up to her chest and her head resting on his hard thigh. She licked clean his softening penis while he sipped water, played with her sore bottom, and pushed his fingers into her little hole.

Each touch, whether gentle or cruel, threatened to tip Jessica over the brink of her climax. The taste of Matt's semen mingled with her own juices filled her mouth and her senses. When he told her to hold her legs apart, and then spanked her sex with the tail of the belt, the intensity of the pain nearly made her forget her self-control. Her cries filled the small room. And though her eyes were wet with tears, she saw whenever she glimpsed his face that as he aimed the belt with deliberate severity at her most sensitive parts there was nothing in his expression but devotion to her.

He pulled her into an embrace and held her against his chest. Watching her face the whole time he pushed two fingers into her little hole, as far as they would go. 'Is that enough spanking and fucking?' he whispered.

She shook her head. She was so aroused she could hardly think. Her entire body consisted of pain and pleasure. 'More, please,' she said. 'I love you so much, Matt. I don't think I'll ever have enough.'

'That's enough for now,' he told her. 'I want to see you come now. You can touch yourself.'

He thrust his fingers in and out of her anus while she masturbated. They gazed into each other's eyes. There was no need for words, and in any case Jessica was unable to compose a coherent thought. She had never felt happier, and her orgasm came slowly, in long, deep tremors that shook her body like earthquakes but which felt like the lapping of warm water.

Jessica sat cradled in Matt's lap, luxuriating in the warm afterglow of orgasm and in the strength of his arms. Slowly, with many interruptions for long kisses, she told him about Olivia Reynolds and Karen.

'All in all,' she concluded, 'I'm beginning to have serious misgivings about the Hillingbury Young Wives' Association Pet Owners' Committee. Most of the owners are interested only in scoring points against each other by having the newest curtains and the best-dressed pet. And most of the pets just want to be owners. It's not about having fun at all. It's been set up so that the most senior owners can keep all the power and influence in Hillingbury.'

'I agree,' Matt said. 'The Private House thrives on letting each member discover and explore his or her own particular drives and desires. The committee sounded similar, at first, but it's actually completely different. I mean, look at poor Olivia. She's bound to lose Karen, and soon, and it's very unlikely that her next pet will be interested in playing the kind of game that Olivia likes. It's a ridiculous situation.'

'It's tragic, Mentor,' Jessica said. She caressed the few blond hairs on his chest. 'And it will happen to me, too, eventually. I wonder how many more of us there are: pets who want to stay as pets, and reluctant owners.'

'You don't have to worry about becoming an owner for a long time,' Matt pointed out. He teased her nipples. 'And you've still got me. I think I'll unpack my suitcase and stay. You need someone to make sure you get your daily spankings.'

'Mmm,' Jessica said. 'Oh, that feels good. But do stop a moment, Matt. I've had an idea.'

Field agent's report to the Private House
From: Matt
For the attention of: Mistress Julia

... Jessica is, as I have said before, formidably organised and persuasive. As she explained her plan, and then set about marshalling our allies, it was hard to believe that only a little while earlier she had been the naughty girl who was my submissive plaything.

And it was Jessica, of course, who led us along the sylvan lanes of the Hillingbury estate, towards the house of Bella Northrop.

The door was opened by a petite, pretty, red-haired, freckle-faced young woman whom I now know is named Sarah.

'Jessica!' she said, looking in consternation over Jessica's shoulder at the rest of us. 'What are you doing here? There's a meeting of the committee in progress. Pets aren't allowed. Even Suzi, Claire and I can't go in.'

'I know,' Jessica replied. 'But this is rather important. I'm sure Bella and the others will want to hear what I have to say. Are you going to let us in?' She pointed with her thumb over her shoulder, hinting that if Sarah didn't let us through then we had the manpower to force our way in. 'No one will blame you for admitting us.'

Once inside the house, Jessica asked us to wait outside the meeting room until she called for us. And she told Sarah to announce only that Jessica had come to address the meeting of the committee.

Jessica stood in the doorway of the sitting room. Over her shoulder I could see the owners, smartly dressed, attractive, polite and respectable women, no more than ten of them, sitting on the armchairs and sofas.

I could hear everything that was said. I recognised Bella Northrop from Jessica's description: she did indeed have the flawless beauty of a classical goddess. Her voice was as cold as an icicle as she demanded to know why Jessica was interrupting the meeting.

I heard the laughter in Jessica's voice. 'I'm hear to announce the takeover of the Hillingbury Young Wives' Association Pet Owners' Committee,' she declared. In the astonished silence that ensued she went on, 'The management structure has become moribund. It is redundant, and no longer serves the interests of the owners, and still less those of their pets. The new management is based at the Hillingbury Health and Exercise Club. I'd like you all to meet Matt, James and Miranda.'

I led my colleagues into the room. For a few moments there was pandemonium as all the owners began to protest at the intrusion into their meeting. Jessica shouted them down, and made them listen while I explained that James, Miranda and I were agents sent from the Private House, which had recently acquired the club. As I told the women about the aims, methods and organisation of the House, they listened more attentively. At least some of them, I think, were beginning to realise that their committee was a minnow that had come to the attention of a shark.

'That's all very interesting,' Bella Northrop said when I finished. 'But it is of no concern to us. The pet owners' committee has been in existence for more than ten years, and it has no need of outside assistance. You may leave us, Jessica, if you wish, although you must understand that no one in Hillingbury will speak to you again. Set up your own little club if you want to. It will have a membership of just one.'

'Two,' said a voice from behind me. Karen entered the room and stood beside Jessica. The committee members muttered angrily.

Karen scanned the room until she found her owner. She smiled, and beckoned. Blushing, Olivia Reynolds rose to her feet. 'Three,' she said, and stepped forward to join Jessica and Karen.

'Mel?' Jessica said.

Melanie Overton stood up. 'I don't know,' she said. 'I like being an owner, Jess. I'm sorry.' Looking confused, she sat down again.

'I'll join you,' another of the women said. She was short and curvaceous, with a round face made more owlish by her spectacles and her bobbed hair.

'Martha,' Jessica said. 'I'm so glad. And I expect Amy and Jane will come with you. They'll have a wonderful time.'

There were now seven owners still seated around the room; standing with Jessica were two owners, one pet and three strangers from the Private House. Things were beginning to look a little more equal.

When Mrs Morgan, wearing a brilliantly white coat and carrying a riding crop, walked into the room and joined Jessica's group, the committee members began to look worried.

Bella Northrop remained defiant, however, and told us all to leave.

Instead of leaving, Jessica called in Lucy. She was wearing her uniform, so there could be no doubt what she represented.

'Good afternoon,' she said. 'I'm Chief Inspector Lucy Larson. Normally I'm in plain clothes, but the uniform impresses people, I find. I'm not from the local force, but I have some influence in most police districts. And I'm attached, shall we say, to the Private House. I'm here to inform you that while the Hillingbury Health and Exercise Club will, I'm sure, remain of no interest to the local police, the same will not hold true for your committee. Your activities have already come to the attention of certain parties at local headquarters. I guarantee that if you are so unwise as to continue with those activities, you will find that the police will take a very particular interest. I cannot guarantee that police monitoring will stop short of arrests.'

'This is outrageous!' Bella Northrop exclaimed. 'Are you suggesting that your Private House organisation can tell the police to harass respectable citizens? It's simply not credible.'

'You'd better believe it,' Lucy said.

At this point Jessica intervened again. Lucy, in her official uniform, had been the stick; now Jessica produced the carrot.

'Under the auspices of the Health and Exercise Club the activities of owners and pets can continue very much as they have always done,' she said. 'In a few minutes I'm going to ask you to vote on the proposition that your committee should join the Private House. If you vote against, the committee will be split: some owners and pets will no doubt remain in a truncated version of the arrangement you have now, for as long as the police allow it; others will join our club. If you vote in favour, then the society of Hillingbury owners and pets will remain intact and undivided, and we will all continue to enjoy each other.'

'So we'll keep our pets?' one of the women asked. 'We'll still be owners?'

'As you've heard,' I put in, 'the rules of behaviour in the Private House are almost the same as those of your committee. We are dedicated to the pursuit of sexual pleasure through obedience and discipline. The only significant difference is that all individuals in the Private House are free to choose the roles they wish to play. From now on, therefore, whether you're an owner or a pet will depend entirely on your own preference. And in the constitution of the Health and Exercise Club, all members, regardless of their role in the games we play, will have an equal voice in club matters.'

'I've never heard such nonsense,' Bella Northrop said. 'Who would volunteer to be a pet?'

'I would,' Jessica and Olivia said together.

'From nine in the morning until six in the evening the club will be closed to ordinary members,' I said, pressing on as persuasively as I could. 'Only those affiliated to the Private House will be permitted to enter. If you vote in favour of joining us, then all of you and all your pets will have the entire club at your disposal. I know that many of you visit the club, and make use of the pool and the Turkish baths. And therefore you know that the place is perfectly suited to the games that you like to play. The premises are large, and there are rooms that we will convert into themed areas. The gardens and courtyards are entirely private. There are many advantages to joining a large organisation, such as the Private House, that has the resources to provide all the facilities you could wish for.'

The committee was almost won over. 'What do you want in return?' Bella Northrop said. She was belligerent and suspicious, but her question revealed that she was on the point of conceding the argument.

'The Private House wants you,' I said. 'It thrives because it chooses its members. And it chooses to invite only those who are in sympathy with its aims, and who are desirable and uninhibited, and who have some influence in the world outside the House. All of you have husbands who work in the city; your menfolk are, or will be, powerful and influential in their various fields of endeavour.'

'You're not going to invite our husbands to join?' one of the women cried. She sounded aghast.

'By no means,' I replied. 'They're all far too busy, and most of them wouldn't even be interested, if I know anything at all about the ways of the majority of men. But I'm sure that all of you know how to persuade your husbands to do whatever you want them to. Once you're in the Private House, we'll expect you, from time to time, to use your powers of persuasion in the interests of the House. A loan agreed here, a planning application granted there. You'll find it easy.'

Of course the committee voted to disband itself. Bella Northrop and two other longstanding residents voted against the motion: they realised that their position at the apex of Hillingbury society depended on the continued existence of the committee. But some of the other six, such as Martha Smythe, were tempted by the idea of having the club as their new, luxuriously appointed play-area; others, I think, were like Olivia, and had never been entirely comfortable in the role of owner; and a few could see that the committee's rules were unfair and inflexible.

The Hillingbury Young Wives' Association Pet Owners' Committee is no more. And the Private House has twenty-six new members: nine ex-owners, sixteen ex-pets, and Mrs Morgan. The trainer is, I must say, as attractive as she is implacable in her application of discipline, and she will prove to be a considerable asset to the House. I suggest that we invite her to the House as soon as possible. The other twenty-five should also be inducted at the House, of course, but I think we should leave them for a while to enjoy the spacious, discreet and luxurious facilities of the club. Besides, I want some time to enjoy Jessica.

Eight

Jessica and Matt walked hand in hand along the gallery that overlooked the pool. The Hillingbury Health and Exercise Club was so capacious that Jessica thought it could never seem crowded, but it was certainly busier than she had ever seen it.

'Look,' she said. 'Amy and Jane are playing in the jacuzzi. Martha's giving them instructions from her sunlounger.'

She was standing with her tummy pressed against the handrail, and she gave a sigh of contentment as she felt Matt's hand come to rest on her right buttock. He was standing at her shoulder, and she took her hand from the rail and placed it against the front of his shorts. She felt his erection pulse as she touched it through the thin cotton. Although none of the women in the club was wearing more than a towel, Jessica was still deliciously aware of her nakedness, and a thrill ran through her whenever Matt touched her.

'I'm surprised that Amy, at least, elected to stay a pet,' Matt said, running the tips of his fingers down the cleft of Jessica's bottom. 'Considering your description of her reaction to the enema.'

'I think she really likes playing with Jane,' Jessica said, holding on to Matt's manhood for support as his fingers pinched the sensitive skin around her little hole. 'And they both enjoy pleasing Martha. Look at what Amy's doing to Jane with that enormous phallus!'

Jane, resting her arms on the side of the small pool and with her hips lifted just out of the bubbling water, heard Jessica's voice and looked up at the gallery. She grinned as Amy pressed the tip of the flexible cylinder against her anus. The other end of the curving phallus was in her vagina.

'I'm going to race them in the pool once they've both got their holes stoppered!' Martha Smythe shouted.

Jessica waved. She felt Matt's hand sweep her long, dark hair from her shoulders. He touched her collar.

'I thought you'd told Mel that you weren't going to be her pet any more,' he said.

Jessica turned. She looked up at him. Was it possible that he still didn't understand how much she wanted him? 'I did tell her,' she said. She pressed the tips of her breasts against his chest, and placed both hands against the hard column of his erection. 'I'm not her pet any more. But I'm still yours, Mentor. I'm wearing the collar for you. I'm afraid I need lots of punishment, but I can be very obedient. You'll see.'

'I'm glad to hear it,' Matt said. He leaned forwards to kiss her, and pinched her nipple until she was gasping with pain into his mouth. 'I intend you to give a performance at the party, and afterwards I'm going to make you available for the use of all the guests. But we can't hold the party until all the rooms have been finished, and that won't be for several days. So I have something else for you to do today.'

'What kind of performance?' Jessica asked excitedly. This was the first time that Matt had revealed anything of his plans for the party.

'I haven't worked out all the details,' Matt said, caressing her breasts as he spoke. 'But I think there will be swabbing the decks with your bottom in the air, and perhaps with the Jolly Roger flying from your anus. Dancing the hornpipe. I still haven't entirely decided what that will entail. The cat o' nine tails, of course. And then walking the plank, into the pool.'

'My pirate fantasy!' Jessica exclaimed.

'Did you think I'd forget?' His smile was as gentle as his fingers were cruel. Jessica loved his smile: whenever she saw it she felt like a besotted teenager. 'We'll have to rehearse the various scenes over the next few days,' he added. 'But not today. Today I have something else in mind. Sit, Jessica.'

She kneeled on the cold tiles, and placed her hands together between her parted knees. When she looked up at Matt her face was almost touching the front of his shorts.

He stroked her hair while he looked down from the gallery. He seemed to be searching for someone. 'Now beg,' he said.

She pushed herself up into a squatting position and, when she was balanced on the balls of her feet, she brought her hands together in front of her face. She imagined that she could almost feel the heat of his erection, which she was almost touching. The thought of his hardness against her fingers and her lips made her sex tingle with anticipation. He hadn't yet punished or penetrated her today, and she was becoming desperate for him to do both.

'Put your hands down,' Matt said. 'One in front and one behind. Play with your sex and your anus. I don't want you to come, but I want you to arouse yourself.'

'Yes, Mentor,' she said. She looked up at him and smiled. 'I'm already very aroused.' It was true. The begging position opened wide her bottom and her sex, and even before her fingers encountered her labia she could tell that the delicate membranes were slick with wetness. 'I'm as wet as a swimming-pool down there,' she added, blushing, as the fingers of both hands paddled at the entrance of her vagina.

She slid the fingers of her right hand up from her vagina to the hood of skin above the tip of her clitoris. She pressed gently, and gasped at the thrill of pleasure.

When the wet tip of the first finger of her left hand slid easily into the ring of her little hole, her entire body trembled. It would be difficult to suppress an orgasm, even though she hadn't been spanked.

'Good little pet,' Matt said. He continued to stroke her hair for a moment, and then he walked away.

It was only as Jessica watched him stroll along the gallery, away from her, towards the stairs, that she became aware of how exposed she was. The gallery consisted of only a walkway with thin safety rails on both sides. Her bottom, open wide and pushed out, would, she realised, be visible to everyone in and around the pool below her. Everyone there would be able to see her caressing her sex, and her finger as it moved in and out of her little hole. She tried to glance over her shoulder, but the curtain of her long, dark hair prevented her from seeing the pool. She tried to overhear the fragments of conversation that floated up from the poolside: had anyone noticed her?

And then she heard a voice say, loudly and distinctly, 'Oh, look, everyone. There's Jessica!'

She felt her face flame. Her nipples became painfully hard. Even though she couldn't see them, she knew that everyone around the pool was now looking up at her splayed bottom. She was performing the most intimate acts of self-pleasuring, and she had an audience. And although she knew she should be appalled, the responses of her body told her that she was a naughty, depraved girl who enjoyed showing off her private parts and her private pleasures. She deserved and needed painful correction. Her craving for a spanking became almost insupportable, and in her imagination the gazing eyes of the women by the pool were replaced by the sensations of Matt's fingers on her nipples and the flat of his hand landing on her bottom.

She would have started to come if she had not heard footsteps approaching. Gasping for breath, she made her hands remain still while she opened her eyes, turned her head, and focused her eyes on her mentor. He was walking towards her along the gallery, and he was deep in conversation with Mrs Morgan, who had taken off her white coat and looked supremely assertive in a wine-red corset and high-heeled shoes. Even the careful steps that she had to take to avoid slipping on the tiled floor seemed to make her appear more poised. She was carrying a riding crop and a leather leash.

'I see you've gathered some spectators,' Matt said. 'But don't stop touching yourself. Carry on for a little longer.'

'Yes, Mentor,' she said. She pressed with her fingers, front and back, as tenderly as possible. Did he have any idea how close she was to an orgasm? she wondered, briefly, before the sensations overwhelmed her again.

Matt and Mrs Morgan were standing in front of her. She could see their shoes and legs. They watched her in silence for a few moments.

'As you were saying,' the trainer said, 'Jessica is utterly submissive and utterly adorable. I'd be more than happy to look after her whenever you're away.'

'I'm delighted to hear it,' Matt said. 'And I'll lend her to you from time to time, anyway. I understand she hasn't finished her training.'

Mrs Morgan laughed. 'Frankly, Matt, Jessica has such natural aptitude, and is so eager to please, that I can hardly teach her to be more obedient than she already is. And she learns very quickly.'

'But you mustn't treat her leniently, Elfrida,' Matt said. He sounded worried. 'She needs a considerable amount of corporal punishment, and frequently.'

'You hardly need to advise me how to train pets,' Mrs Morgan replied. 'I have experience of all sorts, including the submissive ones. I trained Olivia Reynolds, after all. I think you'll find that I have several ideas that will help you to test Jessica's limits. I suspect that I'll be less easy on her than you are, Matt. Men, I find, tend to let their romantic feelings interfere with the application of a professional level of discipline.'

'You may be right,' Matt agreed. He brushed aside Jessica's hair so that he could see her face. 'I love to see her like this.'

'Yes,' the trainer said. 'And then you're tempted to use her for your pleasure, and after that you don't feel strict at all. You feel satisfied, and you let her have an orgasm too, and that's it for the day. Men have so little staying power. We women are more resilient. When I'm training Jessica I'll have her pleasure me whenever I become so aroused that it interferes with the training, but I certainly won't let her reach a climax and I'll continue to instruct and chastise her. Jessica, stop!'

With a gasping cry Jessica slumped forwards on to her knees.

'She was just about to have an orgasm,' Mrs Morgan said. She grasped a handful of Jessica's hair and pulled back her head. 'I assume you had forbidden her to do so?'

'I couldn't help it, Mentor,' Jessica moaned. 'You were talking about punishing me.'

'Has your owner used you for his pleasure?' Mrs Morgan asked Jessica fiercely. 'Has he administered all the punishments he deems necessary? Has he given you permission to reach a climax?'

Jessica tried to shake her head, but the trainer's grip was too tight. 'No,' she whispered.

'You're a spoiled little pet,' Mrs Morgan said, and released her hold on Jessica's hair. 'She needs more training than I thought,' she added, to Matt. 'She has to be taught, until it becomes almost instinctive, that her sole duty is to obedient to her owner, and that her own pleasure is entirely at her owner's discretion. There are self-control techniques that I'll teach her, and I have a number of training devices that will help.'

'That all sounds excellent,' Matt said. 'I'll arrange to leave Jessica with you soon. I hope that within a week or so we'll be able to have Jessica at our disposal for longer periods. Sit up, Jessica, and listen. I haven't told you about this yet.'

Jessica adopted the sitting position, and rested her head against her mentor's thigh as he spoke. She had almost recovered from being pulled back from the edge of an orgasm, but her body still felt shivery and sensitive.

'The Private House,' Matt went on, 'has agreed to my request, and has arranged for Jessica's husband to be given a substantial promotion. He'll be a senior partner, which will entail working more hours, of course, and to make that easier his company will provide an apartment in the city. He'll stay there during the week, and so Jessica will be available to me on weekday evenings as well as during the day.'

Jessica looked up gratefully at her mentor. He was so thoughtful.

'I'll be able to have her overnight for intensive training,' Mrs Morgan said. She swished her riding crop through the air in front of Jessica. 'And I'll be able to use this,' she added. 'I find it the most subtle and effective implement, but I haven't been able to use it on most of the pets I've trained because the marks tend to linger.'

'For the same reason,' Matt said, 'I've so far been able to use only the very lightest of canes on her breasts.' He reached down and handled Jessica's taut globes. 'There are a number of new punishments that she'll be able to enjoy. I'm looking forward to being able to spend the night with her. I'll be able to make sure that she's punished last thing in the evening and first thing in the morning.'

'You can supervise her toilet training, too,' Mrs Morgan said. 'Being punished, or being required to give pleasure, while desperate for the toilet is very good for a pet's self-discipline.'

'Being able to urinate on command is a useful technique for submissives who like to be put on display,' Matt said, 'and Jessica certainly likes to show off. The most important benefit from having her available for longer, though, is that I'll be able to take her to the House. The Supreme Mistress has asked to see her. I'm sure that before long Jessica will be asked to carry out missions of her own for the House. After all, this is entirely her achievement.' He spread his arms to indicate the entire club, full of owners and pets.

Jessica was so proud, embarrassed and aroused, all at the same time, that her body felt electrically charged. She had perceived the incorporation of the pet owners' committee into the Private House merely as the solution to a particular problem; now she realised that it also opened the door to a world of new punishments, pleasures, and opportunities.

Best of all, she would be able to sleep with her mentor. They could spend entire nights together. And in the morning, she imagined, he would stand over her while she sat on the toilet, wriggling and waiting for his permission to pee. And he might choose to make her wait. He might cane her breasts, to test her obedience. And then, because he would be naked, having only just risen from the bed they had shared, it might seem to him convenient to have her kiss and lick his erect penis while he played with her sore, striped breasts. Perhaps he would let her pee, at last, while he spurted his delicious semen into her mouth, or on to her face. The release of pressure on her bladder would feel almost as good as an orgasm. She vowed to suggest it to him, the first time they had a whole night to themselves.

'Thanks for this,' Matt said to Mrs Morgan, and interrupted Jessica's daydream by clipping a lead to her collar.

'Keep it,' the trainer said. 'I don't suppose,' she added, 'that you'd allow me to watch?'

'Not this time, I'm afraid,' Matt said. 'But I intend to put her on display towards the end of the afternoon. I'll tie her up for a spanking, and let everyone take a turn. Most will want to show their gratitude to her with a few smacks, and those few who still feel annoyed with her can take out their resentment on her bottom. Jessica will enjoy it either way, I'm sure.'

'An excellent idea,' Mrs Morgan declared. 'Well, you'd better run along and enjoy her now. Don't hold back just because you know she's going to be punished later!'

'Don't worry,' Matt replied with a laugh. 'I'm as addicted to chastising her as she is to being chastised. She's soon going to have a very sore bottom.'

It couldn't be soon enough, as far as Jessica was concerned, but her mentor made her wait. She padded beside him on her hands and knees as he led her through the club. He stopped for a chat every time he met someone, and as the club was crowded he stopped often. Each time, he revealed his plan to let everyone help him give Jessica a spanking later in the day. He made Jessica sit, and then beg, and ask politely to be spanked, and then he made her turn round and push her bottom up so that her wet state of arousal could be seen.

Jessica was beside herself with shame and excitement by the time he led her to a closed door at the back of the club.

Olivia and Karen were waiting for them in the room beyond the door. It was a room Jessica hadn't previously visited, although it resembled the exercise room in which Matt had punished her in that its walls were clad with mirrors. This room was smaller, however, and more softly lit. At its centre were two exercise machines, side by side. There was also a wooden frame which, to judge from the leather straps attached to its corners, was designed to hold a person bound and helpless. There was also a large, cushion-strewn couch, and a cupboard with its doors open to reveal a jumble of ropes, straps, canes, and phalluses.

Olivia was naked, and was tied to one of the machines. It resembled the exercise bicycles that Jessica had used in the gym, but it had no saddle. Olivia's feet were strapped into stirrups that were attached, like the pedals of a bicycle, to a wheel. Her wrists were tied to handlebars that she had had to stretch forwards to reach. A padded bar across the small of her back kept her spine arched downwards, and another in front of her hips ensured that her bottom was kept pushed back. Her breasts, pendant, pink-tipped cones, swung gently below her.

Karen was wearing her harness of black leather, and was impatiently flexing a thin cane. 'At last!' she said. 'We were just about to start without you. My pet's getting wet just thinking about getting this cane across her bottom.'

'Not as wet as mine, I'm sure,' Matt said. He unclipped the lead from Jessica's collar and helped her to stand. 'You must learn the virtue of patience, Karen. Pets like to be made to wait.'

'Yes, but I don't,' Karen said, laughing. 'Anyway, let's get on with it now. I'll help you tie Jessica on to the bike.'

'It's a straightforward race,' Matt explained to Jessica as he and Karen bound Jessica's ankles and wrists to the apparatus. Jessica and Olivia mouthed a hello to each other, and exchanged mischievous smiles. 'You and Olivia will pedal for ten minutes. The machines will register how far you both travel, notionally. The winner will be the one who has pedalled further, obviously. Karen will encourage Olivia, and I'll encourage you. We'll both have these long canes to help with the encouragement. Oh, and you'll both have phalluses in you. Two each.'

'It sounds lovely,' Jessica said. 'Will there be a prize for the winner? After all that caning I'll be ever so ready for an orgasm.'

'The winner,' Matt said, 'will be allowed to join Karen and I on the couch. The loser will be tied to the wooden frame and will be able only to watch what the rest of us are doing.'

Jessica was determined that she would win. She was already so aroused that her sex, her lips and her little hole were prickling with the anticipation of being used. Pedalling on the machine, with Matt flicking the tip of the cane against her buttocks and her filled sex, would make her yearning desperate. She would have to win.

'Mentor,' she said, 'I suppose we're going to be able to play games like this every day from now on.'

'Every day,' Matt said. He ducked under the handlebars to kiss her lips and tease her hanging nipples. 'I promise. Except when you're being trained by Mrs Morgan, or when you're at the Private House.'

'It's going to be perfect,' she whispered to him. 'Cane me hard, please. I want to win.'

Nexus

NEXUS NEW BOOKS

To be published in December

VELVET SKIN
Aishling Morgan
£5.99

Henry Truscott, hero of *The Rake* and *Purity*, returns in *Velvet Skin* to continue his habits of indulgence and dissipation. There are ample opportunities in eighteenth-century Devon for an imaginative aristocrat to pursue his perversions. Even so, Henry manages to find himself in trouble – like being caught pony-carting by the local vicar, for example. But the fiendish, rapacious Lewis Stukely, a neighbouring landowner, makes Truscott look like a monk – and Stukely has designs on Suki, Truscott's beguiling servant-girl.

ISBN 0 352 33660 9

THE BLACK FLAME
Lisette Ashton
£5.99

For private investigator Jo Valentine it is a surveillance operation unlike any other: a coven of witches practising orgiastic pagan ritual; a sadistic preacher intent on extracting penance from every nubile young sinner who falls beneath his cane; and an ongoing feud with her submissive partner. Caught in the midst of this volatile situation, alone, bound and helpless, Jo is subjected to a dark revelation in the pleasures of pain. Tied, teased and tormented, she is immersed in so many sexual excesses that it borders on being a religious experience. The next volume in Lisette Ashton's series of bestselling erotica.

ISBN 0 352 33668 4

Nexus

NEXUS BACKLIST

This information is correct at time of printing. For up-to-date information, please visit our website at www.nexus-books.co.uk

All books are priced at £5.99 unless another price is given.

Nexus books with a contemporary setting

ACCIDENTS WILL HAPPEN	Lucy Golden ISBN 0 352 33596 3	☐
ANGEL	Lindsay Gordon ISBN 0 352 33590 4	☐
THE BLACK MASQUE	Lisette Ashton ISBN 0 352 33372 3	☐
THE BLACK WIDOW	Lisette Ashton ISBN 0 352 33338 3	☐
THE BOND	Lindsay Gordon ISBN 0 352 33480 0	☐
BROUGHT TO HEEL	Arabella Knight ISBN 0 352 33508 4	☐
CANDY IN CAPTIVITY	Arabella Knight ISBN 0 352 33495 9	☐
CAPTIVES OF THE PRIVATE HOUSE	Esme Ombreux ISBN 0 352 33619 6	☐
DANCE OF SUBMISSION	Lisette Ashton ISBN 0 352 33450 9	☐
DARK DELIGHTS	Maria del Rey ISBN 0 352 33276 X	☐
DARK DESIRES	Maria del Rey ISBN 0 352 33072 4	☐
DISCIPLES OF SHAME	Stephanie Calvin ISBN 0 352 33343 X	☐
DISCIPLINE OF THE PRIVATE HOUSE	Esme Ombreux ISBN 0 352 33459 2	☐

DISCIPLINED SKIN	Wendy Swanscombe ISBN 0 352 33541 6	☐
DISPLAYS OF EXPERIENCE	Lucy Golden ISBN 0 352 33505 X	☐
AN EDUCATION IN THE PRIVATE HOUSE	Esme Ombreux ISBN 0 352 33525 4	☐
EMMA'S SECRET DOMINATION	Hilary James ISBN 0 352 33226 3	☐
GISELLE	Jean Aveline ISBN 0 352 33440 1	☐
GROOMING LUCY	Yvonne Marshall ISBN 0 352 33529 7	☐
HEART OF DESIRE	Maria del Rey ISBN 0 352 32900 9	☐
HIS MISTRESS'S VOICE	G. C. Scott ISBN 0 352 33425 8	☐
HOUSE RULES	G. C. Scott ISBN 0 352 33441 X	☐
IN FOR A PENNY	Penny Birch ISBN 0 352 33449 5	☐
LESSONS IN OBEDIENCE	Lucy Golden ISBN 0 352 33550 5	☐
NURSES ENSLAVED	Yolanda Celbridge ISBN 0 352 33601 3	☐
ONE WEEK IN THE PRIVATE HOUSE	Esme Ombreux ISBN 0 352 32788 X	☐
THE ORDER	Nadine Somers ISBN 0 352 33460 6	☐
THE PALACE OF EROS	Delver Maddingley ISBN 0 352 32921 1	☐
PEEPING AT PAMELA	Yolanda Celbridge ISBN 0 352 33538 6	☐
PLAYTHING	Penny Birch ISBN 0 352 33493 2	☐
THE PLEASURE CHAMBER	Brigitte Markham ISBN 0 352 33371 5	☐
POLICE LADIES	Yolanda Celbridge ISBN 0 352 33489 4	☐
SANDRA'S NEW SCHOOL	Yolanda Celbridge ISBN 0 352 33454 1	☐

SKIN SLAVE	Yolanda Celbridge ISBN 0 352 33507 6	☐
THE SLAVE AUCTION	Lisette Ashton ISBN 0 352 33481 9	☐
SLAVE EXODUS	Jennifer Jane Pope ISBN 0 352 33551 3	☐
SLAVE GENESIS	Jennifer Jane Pope ISBN 0 352 33503 3	☐
SLAVE SENTENCE	Lisette Ashton ISBN 0 352 33494 0	☐
SOLDIER GIRLS	Yolanda Celbridge ISBN 0 352 33586 6	☐
THE SUBMISSION GALLERY	Lindsay Gordon ISBN 0 352 33370 7	☐
SURRENDER	Laura Bowen ISBN 0 352 33524 6	☐
TAKING PAINS TO PLEASE	Arabella Knight ISBN 0 352 33369 3	☐
TIE AND TEASE	Penny Birch ISBN 0 352 33591 2	☐
TIGHT WHITE COTTON	Penny Birch ISBN 0 352 33537 8	☐
THE TORTURE CHAMBER	Lisette Ashton ISBN 0 352 33530 0	☐
THE TRAINING OF FALLEN ANGELS	Kendal Grahame ISBN 0 352 33224 7	☐
THE YOUNG WIFE	Stephanie Calvin ISBN 0 352 33502 5	☐
WHIPPING BOY	G. C. Scott ISBN 0 352 33595 5	☐

Nexus books with Ancient and Fantasy settings

CAPTIVE	Aishling Morgan ISBN 0 352 33585 8	☐
THE CASTLE OF MALDONA	Yolanda Celbridge ISBN 0 352 33149 6	☐
DEEP BLUE	Aishling Morgan ISBN 0 352 33600 5	☐
THE FOREST OF BONDAGE	Aran Ashe ISBN 0 352 32803 7	☐

MAIDEN	Aishling Morgan ISBN 0 352 33466 5	☐
NYMPHS OF DIONYSUS £4.99	Susan Tinoff ISBN 0 352 33150 X	☐
THE SLAVE OF LIDIR	Aran Ashe ISBN 0 352 33504 1	☐
TIGER, TIGER	Aishling Morgan ISBN 0 352 33455 X	☐
THE WARRIOR QUEEN	Kendal Grahame ISBN 0 352 33294 8	☐

Edwardian, Victorian and older erotica

BEATRICE	Anonymous ISBN 0 352 31326 9	☐
CONFESSION OF AN ENGLISH SLAVE	Yolanda Celbridge ISBN 0 352 33433 9	☐
DEVON CREAM	Aishling Morgan ISBN 0 352 33488 6	☐
THE GOVERNESS AT ST AGATHA'S	Yolanda Celbridge ISBN 0 352 32986 6	☐
PURITY	Aishling Morgan ISBN 0 352 33510 6	☐
THE TRAINING OF AN ENGLISH GENTLEMAN	Yolanda Celbridge ISBN 0 352 33348 0	☐

Samplers and collections

NEW EROTICA 4	Various ISBN 0 352 33290 5	☐
NEW EROTICA 5	Various ISBN 0 352 33540 8	☐
EROTICON 1	Various ISBN 0 352 33593 9	☐
EROTICON 2	Various ISBN 0 352 33594 7	☐
EROTICON 3	Various ISBN 0 352 33597 1	☐
EROTICON 4	Various ISBN 0 352 33602 1	☐

Nexus Classics
A new imprint dedicated to putting the finest works of erotic fiction back in print.

AGONY AUNT	G.C. Scott ISBN 0 352 33353 7	☐
BOUND TO SERVE	Amanda Ware ISBN 0 352 33457 6	☐
BOUND TO SUBMIT	Amanda Ware ISBN 0 352 33451 7	☐
CHOOSING LOVERS FOR JUSTINE	Aran Ashe ISBN 0 352 33351 0	☐
DIFFERENT STROKES	Sarah Veitch ISBN 0 352 33531 9	☐
EDEN UNVEILED	Maria del Rey ISBN 0 352 33542 4	☐
THE HANDMAIDENS	Aran Ashe ISBN 0 352 33282 4	☐
HIS MISTRESS'S VOICE	G. C. Scott ISBN 0 352 33425 8	☐
THE IMAGE	Jean de Berg ISBN 0 352 33350 2	☐
THE INSTITUTE	Maria del Rey ISBN 0 352 33352 9	☐
LINGERING LESSONS	Sarah Veitch ISBN 0 352 33539 4	☐
A MATTER OF POSSESSION	G. C. Scott ISBN 0 352 33468 1	☐
OBSESSION	Maria del Rey ISBN 0 352 33375 8	☐
THE PLEASURE PRINCIPLE	Maria del Rey ISBN 0 352 33482 7	☐
SERVING TIME	Sarah Veitch ISBN 0 352 33509 2	☐
SISTERHOOD OF THE INSTITUTE	Maria del Rey ISBN 0 352 33456 8	☐
THE TRAINING GROUNDS	Sarah Veitch ISBN 0 352 33526 2	☐
UNDERWORLD	Maria del Rey ISBN 0 352 33552 1	☐

------ ✂ ------------------------------

Please send me the books I have ticked above.

Name ....

Address ....

....

....

.... Post code ....

Send to: Cash Sales, Nexus Books, Thames Wharf Studios, Rainville Road, London W6 9HA

US customers: for prices and details of how to order books for delivery by mail, call 1-800-805-1083.

Please enclose a cheque or postal order, made payable to **Nexus Books Ltd**, to the value of the books you have ordered plus postage and packing costs as follows:
  UK and BFPO – £1.00 for the first book, 50p for each subsequent book.
  Overseas (including Republic of Ireland) – £2.00 for the first book, £1.00 for each subsequent book.

If you would prefer to pay by VISA, ACCESS/MASTERCARD, AMEX, DINERS CLUB or SWITCH, please write your card number and expiry date here:

....

Please allow up to 28 days for delivery.

Signature ....

------ ✂ ------------------------------